SINISTER PROMISE

A DARK MAFIA ARRANGED MARRIAGE ROMANCE

IVANOV CRIME FAMILY
BOOK SIX

ZOE BLAKE

CONTENTS

Blake, Zoe
Sinister Promise
Cover Design by Dark City Designs
Photographer Emma Jane
Model Robbie McMahon

Welcome to the deep end.
You've been warned.

Zoe B.

CHAPTER 1

ALINA

I flattened my back against the wall, shrinking into the shadows.

He was here.

Pavel Ivanov.

His very name a threat.

He was the kind of man whispered about in the back rooms of bars but never spoken about above a hush. As if saying his name too loudly would summon the devil himself.

Dangerous. Unhinged. Mafia.

The kind of man women craved for a forbidden one-night stand, an encounter that would haunt their fantasies forever...assuming they survived...but would run screaming from when it came to boyfriend material.

When he first arrived from Russia, he was all my coworkers would gossip about.

They would relate stories about passing him in a hallway, or being trapped in an elevator with him, as if they had survived a brush with death.

I'd kept my mouth shut about my own run-in with him.

It'd happened the first week he arrived.

I was supposed to be alone on that office floor. Just me, my vacuum, the fake lemon scent of furniture polish, and the rhythmic hum of music through my headphones to keep me company through another night of cleaning the lower offices and meeting spaces in the boutique hotel.

After I'd accidentally knocked over a trash can with the cord of my vacuum cleaner, I'd been on my hands and knees picking up the thin strips of shredded paper that had tumbled out, sneezing from all the kicked-up paper dust, when a low male rumble said, "*Bud' zdorova.*"

I froze.

It was *him*. I knew it without even looking.

I held my breath, keeping my head down, hoping— praying—he would just walk away.

He didn't.

The excruciating silence warred with the panicked screeches in my mind.

When I couldn't take the tension a moment longer, I dared to look.

Slowly, my gaze traveled from the tips of his black combat boots up over his dark denim jeans to his fitted black T-shirt, which showcased his full sleeve-tattooed arms.

The man was nothing but raw brutality wrapped in sinister ink.

The tattoos crept up his neck in intricate patterns and were even etched across his face. Everyone knew that anyone with face tattoos was someone to be feared and avoided at all costs. It was the ultimate zero-fucks-given power move.

Pavel Ivanov stood over me, his intense, gunmetal stare holding the cold calculation of a man who had earned his reputation for seizing what he wanted without hesitation or remorse.

When I'd heard my coworkers' stories about him, I'd honestly thought it was just Russian. Nope. His intimidating presence alone was a warning, without him even having to speak.

Of course, the terrifying-Russian-thing didn't hurt.

I knew too well what men like him were capable of.

Learning the harsh lesson from the time I was a child: that money and power didn't make a man civilized.

The only trace of warmth about Pavel was his amused grin as he leaned a shoulder against the doorjamb, his arms crossed over his chest. There was no way to tell how long he had been there.

I'd known better than to look. To see. *To know.*

When I was hired, my boss had been very clear about the rules.

See nothing.

Say nothing.

Hear nothing.

The man had actually pointed to one of those silly monkey sculptures on his desk to reinforce what he was saying.

Judging by the criminal clientele in the building, what my boss had really meant to convey was…

See no evil.

Say no evil.

Hear no evil.

Literally…

It was why this job paid twice as much as similar positions everywhere else.

Crime paid.

They paid for discretion. For blind silence.

My job, as part of the overnight crew, wasn't just to clean.

It was to keep my head down and my mouth shut.

Usually that wasn't a problem.

Until that moment.

Not knowing what to do, I'd squeaked out a weak "thank you" before turning on my knees to shove the fistfuls of paper I was still clutching into my trash bag so I could get the hell out of there.

I'd realized my mistake when the silence in the room was pierced by the sharp intake of breath through his teeth.

There wasn't a doubt in my mind he was enjoying the view of my bent-over ass in yoga pants.

I closed my eyes as embarrassed agony warmed my cheeks.

Scrambling to my feet, I latched onto my cleaning cart and lowered my head, determined to slip past him.

No such luck.

He'd stretched his arm across the door, barring my escape. Then his free hand had caught my chin, forcing my face up to meet his. "What is your name, little one?"

The thick Russian accent had made his question sound more like the growl of a black bear despite the highly inappropriate endearment. His touch had burned against my skin, unwanted heat spreading through me even as fear tightened within me.

I'd swallowed hard as my hands grew slick against the plastic handle of my cart. Clearing my throat, I told him, "Mary."

A lie.

Before he could respond, I'd shoved the cart forward and ducked under his arm, breaking the spell of his touch. The cleaning cart clattered as I'd sprinted down the hall, praying with every fiber of my being that he wouldn't follow.

That had happened weeks ago and just the memory of it still rattled me to my core.

Ever since then I'd been excruciatingly careful to make sure our paths did not cross again.

And it had worked...until now.

I rubbed my knuckles against my sternum to fight the panic threatening to take hold.

Although it was a risk, I leaned my head forward and hazarded a peek down the marble corridor.

Several men surrounded a man tied to a chair.

The man was blubbering. "He'll kill me if I tell you."

I strained to hear Pavel's response over the rush of blood in my ears.

"Why do I keep hearing those words? Every time I bring in some asshole working for Solovyov, I always hear 'oh, but he'll kill me if I tell you.' Motherfucker, I'm going to kill you anyway. The only thing you get to decide is how much I'm going to make you suffer first."

Kill him anyway?

5

Oh God. This was so fucking bad.

The men weren't even trying to speak in lowered voices.

They assumed they weren't being watched—or worse, they didn't care.

Either way, I was in serious danger just by standing here.

I was a witness.

Anyone who watched crime shows knew the only good witness was a dead witness.

My vision blurred and I teetered against the door frame, lightheaded from my rapid breathing.

I needed to get the hell out of here.

I was far down the hallway in the shadows, but that didn't mean I was safe from detection.

Just then, Pavel's head swung sharply in my direction.

My blood froze in my veins.

His expression was unreadable, his face cut from ice as his stare penetrated the darkness between us, seeming to claim me even from this distance.

Oh shit. Could he see me?

Only after he turned his attention back to the man in the chair did I dare to breathe again.

Pavel shoved his boot between the man's legs, then leaned over his bent knee as he flicked open a switchblade. "Tell us where Solovyov is, and I will give you a clean death. Don't, and I call the man who haunts your fucking nightmares, and I tell him about the new toy just waiting to play."

"I don't know," the man cried out in desperation.

In response, Pavel flipped the knife to grip the handle

before driving the sharp point into the man's hand. A bloodcurdling scream tore from the man as he writhed in agony, twisting his wrists against his binds.

My eyes widened as Pavel took a step back and pulled a gun from inside his jacket.

Oh no. No. No. No.

He aimed it at the man's head.

Holy hell. He isn't going to—

A gunshot.

Loud.

Deafening.

The sharp crack echoed off the walls, reverberating through my bones.

The victim's head snapped back, a bloom of red exploding across the pristine white floor and the wall behind him. The heavy copper stench filled the air instantly, reaching me even from where I stood.

Horrified shock overrode all sense of self-preservation.

A scream ripped from my lungs.

I stared at the body slumping sideways in the chair, the man's sightless eyes seeming to stare straight at me as a pool of blood formed around him.

In that moment only one thought crossed my mind... fucking RUN!

CHAPTER 2

ALINA

I spun on my heel and bolted down the hallway. The slick soles of my worn sneakers squeaked against the polished marble floor, but I didn't care.

I just ran harder, pushing my legs as fast as they could carry me, ignoring the burn in my lungs.

I darted around a corner into the nearest hiding spot— a cramped janitor's closet.

I slammed the door shut, my fingers fumbling to try and lock it, but the stupid lock was tiny and my sweat-slicked fingers couldn't grasp it.

Giving up, I pressed my palms and an ear to the door, desperately trying to hear something, anything, to tell me whether he was out there.

Darkness swallowed me as my heartbeat raced so loudly, it felt like it would give me away.

The air was thick with the acrid stench of bleach and old mop water, the cramped space pressing against me like a coffin.

There was no relief in being hidden, only terror knowing he was hunting me.

It was just a matter of time before he found me.

Tears fell to my shirt as I sucked in deep breaths.

I tried to slow my heart; it was beating too fast, too loud, a bass drum in my ears screaming that he was coming for me.

I pressed a trembling hand over my mouth, forcing myself to stay silent despite the sobs wracking my body.

If he caught me, he would kill me.

If it was just me, I wouldn't care.

I might have even welcomed the release of death, but my poor grandmother depended on me. I was all she had left in the world.

Seconds stretched into eternity.

Then footsteps broke the silence.

Slow. Measured.

A cold sweat broke over my skin.

I stared down at the dim gleam of the silver knob, waiting for it to turn.

Had he followed me?

Of course, he followed me.

He should've opened the door by now.

The knob didn't jiggle.

Maybe I was safe.

Maybe he would keep moving down the hall.

Or maybe he'd give up looking for me.

And maybe a flying unicorn would suddenly appear and carry me away.

I forced myself to wait.

One second.

Two.

Three.

Then…the scrape of a shoe.

A shift in the shaft of light under the door.

My breath came in ragged, uneven pants in my fight against the rising panic clawing at my throat as I stepped back from the door.

The doorknob slowly turned before the door swung open with a violent bang.

Pavel's steel eyes, cold and unreadable, stared into mine.

The sick stench of blood that clung to him filled my nose; my stomach rolled with the bile rising in my throat.

There was no way to pretend I hadn't seen him execute that man.

There was no way he didn't see me as a threat.

Pavel took a single unhurried step toward me. The gun was at his side, his finger still on the trigger.

"Fuck." His whisper was soft and low, his hard glare focused on my mouth.

I shivered as the possibility of him doing…other things…to me before he killed me became a very real threat. My gaze became fixated on the strong, tattooed hand gripping the gun, imagining it wrapped around my throat while he forced my thighs open.

Fuck.

My hands trembled as I kept backing away, feeling for the wall behind me. "Please…"

He took another step toward me. "You know who I am. And now I know who you are."

My fingers brushed the cool cinder block as I slid along the wall, away from him.

My eyes darted to the open door slightly to the side and behind him.

There was only one chance for me to get out of here alive, and it wasn't even a good one.

Still, I had to take it.

Before I could second-guess myself, I bolted past him.

I didn't get far.

A dark laugh sounded behind me right before his gun fired.

The wall in front of me exploded in a cloud of dust and plaster fragments.

I screeched and jumped a mile.

Was he playing with me, or did he actually miss?

There wasn't any time to stop, to think.

Every instinct I had demanded I run.

My lungs burned, my legs ached, but it was this or death.

I turned the corner and ran harder, knowing he was right behind me.

I swore I could feel his heat on the back of my neck.

My stomach dropped as I hurtled around another corner so fast my shoes slipped on the tile floor, and I barely kept my balance.

A door loomed twenty feet ahead of me. I ducked inside and this time I was able to lock it behind me.

I wasn't stupid enough to think that I had won, or that I had gotten away.

But I had bought myself at least a few minutes.

The room was almost pitch-black, swallowed in darkness. The only light came from a small window where the faintest amount of moonlight pierced through the cracked-open blinds, casting thin, faded lines down the walls and onto the floor.

It wasn't enough to see clearly, but I had vacuumed this room hundreds of times and emptied every garbage can in here. I knew my way around well enough that the dim light was all I needed.

I was in an office space, a bullpen of sorts.

There were dozens of cubicles in tight little rows, each with their own desk, chair, and basic computer setup.

Silently dropping to my knees, I crawled through the aisles until I was somewhere in the middle of the room. Then I huddled under a desk and pulled my knees to my chest, curling into the smallest ball possible. It was the one thing I was truly good at…making myself invisible.

Sucking in a deep breath, I tried to calm my frayed nerves, but it was pointless.

Instead, I listened. Straining my ears for something that could tell me how close he was, how many men he had brought in to help hunt me down.

For a moment, there was nothing.

Just deafening silence.

No people shouting or footsteps echoing down the hallway right outside the door.

Not even a door handle jiggling.

Hope blossomed in my chest.

Maybe I lost him at the last corner?

How many turns did I take?

Could he have passed the door and continued down the hallway?

I prayed it was true as I tucked myself deeper under the desk.

Even if I did escape this building alive, where did I go from here?

I would have to move now. Get a new job.

Where was I going to work that paid this much?

Maybe I would just stay hidden until morning.

If there were other people around to witness it, surely he wouldn't be able to shoot me.

Just as I pulled the desk chair in to block me off from the rest of the room, all my hopes of escape were dashed.

Wood splintered as the door was kicked open, shattering the grim silence. Light flickered in from the hallway for a brief moment before the room was thrust back into darkness as that same door was slammed shut.

I wasn't alone anymore.

He was here.

On the prowl.

Pavel's footsteps were slow and even as he walked down each aisle, back and forth, methodically searching for me.

My chest rose and fell with ragged gasps as I bit down on my lip, hard enough to draw blood in my effort to stifle the scream trying to claw its way out of my throat.

Shoving my fist against my mouth, I muffled my desperate breathing, the need for silence as he drew closer battling against the sob that wracked through my shaking body.

"Come on out, little kitten."

Why did death sound so seductive?

I squeezed my eyes shut, my body trembling so hard I

was afraid the desk would shake with me, betraying my hiding place.

He prowled closer.

Slowly.

Purposefully.

"Come out, come out, wherever you are," he purred.

He was enjoying this.

Of course he was.

Predators loved the chase.

They got off on it, and I was stupid enough to have put myself in his crosshairs.

I knew better.

I knew I should never have taken this damn job.

I'd been seduced by the money. Paid to ignore the danger, to look the other way.

"There is no place you can hide, Mary. Or should I say Alina?"

My body jolted.

He knew my real name.

Worse than that, he knew I'd lied to him before.

He paused, and the air shifted to something less playful and far more sinister. "Come out. Now. Before you make me angry."

There was no escape.

There was never an escape.

Even if I had gotten out of the building, he would have found me.

Trapped, I was as good as dead.

CHAPTER 3

PAVEL

*I*t looked like more than one person was going to die tonight.

I'd given explicit orders.

This office building was supposed to be empty.

Not a single soul inside.

No external security, no late-night meetings or ambitious new hires burning the midnight oil to prove themselves.

And no cleaners.

That was why I had scheduled this meeting for midnight.

It was the dead of night, shrouded in complete darkness, away from prying eyes.

It had taken me weeks to get everything set up.

There were supposed to be no interruptions, no mistakes.

Everything was riding on this one night. And since neither Gregor nor Artem had any idea what the fuck I was doing, it had to be flawless.

Yet here she was, the sweet kitten who had been avoiding me for weeks.

Putting everything, including her life, in danger.

She thought I hadn't noticed her all this time. But I had. Oh, I definitely had.

The first time I saw her, down on her hands and knees, still haunted my dreams.

Did she not know the way her pants hugged her ass made every man want to bend her over and fuck her?

For weeks, I'd watched her from the shadows as she cleaned, gliding through the offices like a ghost, quiet and efficient. Always so careful not to disturb anything, not to be seen.

The woman practically dripped sex appeal.

From the way she bit her lip in concentration, to how she moved with a silent grace, unaware of the attention she drew.

Three weeks ago, I'd caught one of the night guards watching her. His eyes had followed her as she bent to empty a trash can, his tongue darting out to wet his lips. The next night, he came to work with a broken arm. No one asked questions. No one ever did.

Only I was allowed to watch her.

To savor the innocent way her gaze would stay on the floor.

A natural submissive.

Every time I saw her, I wanted her.

To take her, ruin her, corrupt her.

Every cell in my body screamed that she was mine. A possession no one else would ever touch.

Last Friday, I'd watched her from my darkened office

as she cleaned the conference room across the hall. Some drunken accountant had stayed late, cornering her by the doorway. I made sure he "resigned" the next day.

She never knew I was the reason he disappeared.

Never knew that she already belonged to me, because I'd been forced to rein in my lust.

Gregor made it very clear—the staff were off-limits.

Initially I'd had no intention of going against his wishes, at least until after Solovyov was dead.

After that, he and Artem would be too busy with their power struggle to notice where I stuck my cock.

But all bets were off now.

She was here, where she wasn't supposed to be.

My men assured me she had left.

I caught her scent before I even opened the closet door a few minutes ago. The same floral fragrance I'd memorized from the nights I'd followed just behind her, her hips swaying to whatever music she was listening to on her headphones. My movements shrouded in the dim, after-hours lighting.

Now she was running through the building like a frightened rabbit.

The warning shot I'd fired was my gift to her—a chance to play the game I'd been dying to initiate for weeks.

Unfortunately, she wasn't a temptation anymore.

She was a problem.

My sweet little kitten had seen things not meant for her eyes.

That had turned her into a liability.

We did not suffer liabilities.

Of all the things she could've seen, a stone-cold murder was the worst.

A clean, efficient bullet to the head of the last of Solovyov's men.

Once I made a call to my cousin, Roman, we'd finally take out Solovyov himself.

And then the threat to the Ivanovs would be over.

No loose ends, no weaknesses.

At least there wouldn't have been, if she hadn't seen everything.

It wasn't even the type of killing she could have been persuaded to believe was self-defense.

It was an execution, and she witnessed every second.

She shouldn't have fucking been here.

My jaw tightened as I considered the options.

I'd killed men for far less than what she'd witnessed.

Part of me wanted to keep her alive just to watch her break under my control. The other part knew that breaking the rules for this woman might cost me everything I'd built.

Last month, when I noticed she was working late by herself, I'd stationed two of my most trusted men nearby. Not that she knew. But I'd made sure she got to her car safely, watching from the window as she drove away. I told myself it was just to protect a company asset.

I was lying to myself even then.

Finding it hard to concentrate.

And now, the way she tried to run from me made my cock hard.

She'd made herself prey.

Fuck, I loved prey.

I tracked her to one of the office spaces, a large room filled with cubicles. The lock on the door was no barrier —one solid kick and it splintered open.

There had always been something so appealing about the chase; the adrenaline, the power, the raw intensity was just so appetizing.

This little kitten was begging to be chased down, to be hunted.

"You can't hide from me," I called out, my voice slicing through the darkness. "I've been watching you for weeks. I know your every move."

I advanced slowly, my footsteps deliberate.

Each aisle a new hunting ground in my methodical search for her.

"Did you think I didn't notice you?" I continued. "The way you avoid the east wing after ten. How you always double-check that the executive bathroom is empty before cleaning it? The little sandwiches you sneak from the cafeteria when you think no one's looking?"

The desks weren't that deep. I spotted her almost immediately, her fair skin caught in a shaft of moonlight angling across the floor to where she sat huddled in a cute little ball.

I could've gone straight to her, but where was the fun in that? I wanted to savor this.

"I've known your real name for weeks, Alina," I called as I walked down her aisle, catching the way her body trembled harder with each step I took. "Did you think that silly fake name would protect you? Nothing protects you from me."

For the second time tonight, her perfume would have

given her away as I neared her hiding spot even if I hadn't already seen her. A light and fresh fragrance, but tainted now with the sharp, almost salty scent of fear. It was intoxicating.

Finally I stopped in front of the desk she was under, dropped to my haunches, and leveled my gaze on her. "Either come out willingly or be dragged out. The choice is yours."

I gave her a moment to realize how fucked she really was.

Literally.

There was no escape. No place to run or hide.

I could practically see her thoughts racing, calculating odds, searching for options.

It was fascinating, the way hope drained from her eyes when she realized there was only one way this night would end. With her surrender.

She hesitated, then uncurled herself and got onto her hands and knees.

"That's it," I encouraged, my voice dropping lower as I rose. "Come to me."

Christ. I shifted my hips as my cock lengthened inside my jeans.

When she crawled toward me, I caught sight of the soft curve of her breast beneath her shirt. A single glimpse, and I wanted to tear the fabric from her body, to mark every inch of her pale skin as territory I'd claimed.

I didn't take a step back, forcing her to look up at me.

I inhaled sharply.

Fuck.

Making her crawl to me was a mistake.

She was so small, so delicate.

Her wide brown eyes shone with terror, her soft lips trembling as she whispered, "I didn't see anything."

A lie. A cute lie, but a lie all the same.

I cupped her chin and forced her head back. "Remember two weeks ago when that security guard cornered you in the stairwell? Did you wonder why he suddenly requested a transfer?"

Her expression shifted to confusion.

"Or that supervisor who kept finding reasons to 'check your work' after hours?"

The tears tracking down her cheeks should have evoked mercy.

Instead, they tempted me to taste them, to consume every drop of her terror before replacing it with a far more addictive emotion.

My lips curled into something between amusement and warning. "You saw me kill that man, didn't you, *moy kotyonochek?*"

My sweet little kitten.

Such a fitting name for such an enticing little creature caught in my trap.

Finally, I took a step back, letting her rise to her feet.

"I swear, I won't tell anyone, I won't say—" She swiped at the wetness trailing down her face, her brown eyes glistening as she stared up at me.

"Tsk. Tsk. Tsk. I don't believe you." I traced the barrel of my gun along her jawline.

She sucked in a soft hiss through her teeth at the contact, her gaze breaking away from mine and darting left, then right.

She was looking for an escape.

She wouldn't find one.

"Don't even think about running again," I warned. "I've memorized every route you take through this building. I know where you'd go."

Part of me wanted to let her run, just so I could chase her again.

Maybe if we'd been truly alone, I would have let her.

Let her tire herself out running down the halls, finding new places to hide that I could discover.

Each time I found her, I'd remove a piece of her clothing as my reward.

It was tempting, but my men were still in the building.

And I was going to be the only one who played this game with her.

"Please," she begged. "I'll do anything. Just let me go."

"Anything?" I raised an eyebrow. "That's a dangerous offer to make to a man like me. A man who just blew someone's brains across the marble."

Her body started at my cold-blooded admission.

Slow and steady, I moved forward, herding her to exactly where I wanted her.

Forcing her back until she hit the wall and opened her lips to let slip a little squeak of terror.

I lifted my hand, brushing a stray curl that had fallen out of her cute ponytail from her face, not with my fingers, but with the still-warm barrel of my gun.

Her breath hitched, and she flinched away.

"You should be afraid," I murmured. "But you should also know that for weeks I've made sure no one else laid a hand on you. I've been watching over you, Alina.

Protecting you. So you can understand how angry I would be, now that you have put us both in a very…difficult…position."

"I promise, I won't tell a soul about what I saw."

I raised an eyebrow. "You promise? Well that changes everything as long as you promise."

Perhaps it was cruel to taunt her, but then again, I was a cruel man.

I tilted my head, studying her.

Her pulse hammered violently against the delicate column of her throat.

Even terrified, she was beautiful.

But there was something else beneath the fear.

She enjoyed being hunted by the big bad wolf, whether she realized it or not.

By dawn, she'd know exactly what belonged to me.

Her fear.

Her body.

Her obedience.

I'd carve my name into her soul until she couldn't remember a time before she was mine.

I smirked. This was going to be so much fun.

"The question, *moy kotyonochek*, is what am I going to do with you now?"

CHAPTER 4

ALINA

*P*avel trailed his gun along my ear as a scream caught in my throat.

I wanted to cry, to beg, to fight—to do anything but whimper at his touch.

Fight or flight should have kicked in.

All those true crime podcasts I'd binged while working, the ones I thought would save me if I ever faced a killer.

All those times I'd rolled my eyes at victims and smugly thought, *I'd survive.*

I'd grab a weapon, find the perfect hiding spot, maybe even pull some Jackie Chan shit.

And now? When death was literally staring me in the face?

I had nothing.

Not a single coherent thought. Just white-hot panic flooding every synapse until even breathing felt impossible.

"Look at me," he commanded, pressing the barrel

harder against my skin. "Your pretty eyes tell me everything I need to know."

"Please…" I gasped, trying to flatten myself against the wall. "You gain nothing by killing me."

He moved closer, invading my space with his imposing frame. "Who said anything about killing you? Not yet, anyway."

The pistol caressed my skin, still warm from being fired. My stomach recoiled at the thought of that man's blood being smeared across my cheek.

"This shouldn't be happening," I whispered, more to myself than to him.

His eyebrow arched. "And what exactly should be happening to a girl lurking where she doesn't belong?"

"I was just doing my job," I managed, struggling to keep my breathing steady.

"Your job?" He laughed, cold and sharp. "Your job was to clean. Not witness executions." His fingers traced where his gun had been. "Tell me why you're really working here. A girl with your education, mopping floors in a building full of criminals?"

I blinked in surprise. "How did you—"

"I know everything about you, Alina. Everything." He circled me slowly. "Georgetown scholarship. Bright future. Then suddenly, you're working a dangerous job for shit pay. Why?"

Shit pay. Maybe to him. My monthly salary was probably pocket change he'd find between the cushions of his sofa. *FML.*

My mind raced. How could he possibly know these things?

"Answer me," he demanded, suddenly behind me, his breath hot against my neck.

"My father," I admitted, the words bitter on my tongue. "His gambling debts."

Pavel chuckled. "Ah, the sins of the father. Always so entertaining."

I turned to face him, finding a fraction of courage. "Not to those paying for them."

"Tell me more," he demanded, backing me against the wall again. "Tell me why a smart, beautiful girl sacrifices everything."

Beautiful? The word caught me off guard, sending an unwelcome warmth through my chest even as danger surrounded me. I pushed the feeling away, disgusted with myself for noticing anything beyond the threat he posed.

"My grandmother raised me after my mother died." The words tumbled out as his gun slid along my collarbone. "When they came collecting, my father gave them my name and disappeared. I had to protect her."

"So noble," he mocked, but something flickered in his eyes. "And now you clean blood from floors to pay debts that aren't yours."

I swallowed hard. "What choice did I have?"

"Choice?" He laughed again. "There's always a choice, *moy kotyonochek*. Sometimes just between bad and worse."

The foreign words rolled off his tongue, somehow both threatening and intimate.

"What does that mean? Moy ka-tyoh-nuh-chek?" I dared to ask, sounding out the foreign phrase.

"My little kitten," he translated, tracing my jaw with

29

one finger. "Small, skittish, trying so hard to hide in the shadows."

I flinched away, but there was nowhere to go.

"Your father," Pavel said, his tone shifting. "Do you know where he is now?"

The question surprised me.

Why would he care about my pathetic excuse for a father? Unless...

A chill ran through me as I realized what Pavel might be asking.

Was he planning to hunt my father down?

To make him pay for his debts—or for transferring them to me?

I should be horrified at the thought.

I should warn my father, protect him despite everything.

But the hot flash of vindictive satisfaction that surged through me was immediate and overwhelming. Would I mourn if this man put a bullet in my father's head? The honest answer disturbed me more than Pavel's gun against my skin.

"No," I finally answered, my voice steadier than expected. "He disappeared three years ago. Haven't heard a word from him since he threw me to the wolves."

"Tell me about these men who hold your father's debt," he demanded, suddenly intense. "Names. Amounts. Everything."

"Why would you care?" I challenged, instantly regretting my boldness.

His eyes narrowed. "Because I don't share what's mine."

Mine.

The word hit me like ice water.

I wasn't his.

I wasn't anyone's.

Yet something about the raw possession in his tone made my breath catch.

No one had ever wanted to claim me before—they'd only wanted to use me.

The difference shouldn't matter.

It shouldn't send that forbidden rush through my veins. But it did.

The gun pressed between my breasts. "Did you know, when someone lies, their heart races. Unless something else is making your heart pound."

I gasped, panic clawing at me. I squeezed my eyes shut, begging whoever might be listening to make this stop. To let me wake in my bed, for this all to be just another nightmare.

"Open your eyes. Look at me," he demanded.

I obeyed.

Because that was what good girls did.

That was what I'd always done—followed the rules, kept my head down, worked hard.

It was supposed to keep me safe, not standing here facing death.

"*If* I let you go," he murmured, "how do I know you won't run to the police?"

"I—" Terror choked me. "Please, I won't—I promise. I know they can't protect me from men like you."

"Men like me," he repeated, his mouth twisting into a cruel smile. "And what do you know about men like me?"

31

"Enough to be afraid," I whispered.

He leaned in with deliberate slowness, his breath warming my skin. His lips barely brushed my neck before trailing along my jaw.

"Your father's debt," he murmured against my skin. "How much remains?"

"Seventy thousand," I answered, my voice breaking. "Three years of payments and I've barely touched the principal."

He pulled back, studying me. "Three years of sacrifice." His eyes darkened. "All for an old woman who would rather die than see you enslaved this way."

A chill ran down my spine.

How could he know what my grandmother repeatedly said to me?

"I had a grandmother too," he said, as if reading my thoughts. Shocking me with this unexpected personal detail. "She would have cut off her own hands before letting me suffer for her."

"Please—just let me go," I pleaded, my eyes welling up.

"No," he replied, the single word crushing my last hope.

"What do you want from me?"

A slow smirk crossed his sharp features.

"This."

His mouth crashed down on mine, claiming me in a punishingly possessive kiss.

CHAPTER 5

PAVEL

*H*er lips had the faintest hint of obedience.

At first, she leaned away, attempting to melt into the wall behind her.

After she finally surrendered to my kiss, her curves sought support against me.

When I broke away, rebellion flashed in her eyes again.

The low hum of the office ventilation system was the only sound beyond her rapid breathing. The moonlight streaming through the blinds cast shadows across her face, highlighting those wide, fearful eyes that had occupied my thoughts for weeks.

The way her mouth had moved against mine told me everything I needed to know.

That a dutiful girl existed beneath the surface, and I would peel back every layer of hate and fear to find her.

Her fate was sealed the moment I first saw her, when she lied to me in that sweet, honeyed voice before fleeing.

Telling me a false name had been a bold move.

She had invaded my dreams since that day. Every

33

morning I woke aching to sink inside her while she called me "sir" repeatedly.

Her chest rose and fell in rapid, shallow breaths, hinting at generous breasts hidden from view.

My cock stiffened, demanding more.

I crushed my lips against hers, licking the seam, commanding entry.

Her mouth parted, tongue meeting mine with hesitant curiosity.

My little kitten—timid, shy, so easily startled.

Her responses betrayed her.

Maybe she could serve another purpose, one that wouldn't end with her death.

Such a waste to destroy someone so valuable when she could still be useful.

I wanted Alina. Why waste an opportunity?

Artem and Gregor would raise hell, of course.

They had made the rules clear: staff were untouchable.

But they would also demand her death as a witness to murder.

Their solution would be simple. Eliminate the liability.

A problem for another time.

My solution was far more creative—and satisfying.

Rules were made by men who feared consequences. I did not.

Now, this woman trembled against me, prepared to do anything for survival, and those plump lips promised other talents worth exploring.

Breaking the kiss, I pressed the gun against the top of her shoulder, forcing her down to her knees.

The thin industrial carpet offered little cushion against the hard floor beneath.

She winced at the impact.

"You want to live, little one?"

She nodded, lips tightly pressed together.

"Not good enough. I asked you a question." I needed to hear her voice, to establish the pattern of obedience now.

"Yes," she whispered, the word barely audible.

"Yes, what?" I prompted, tapping the gun lightly against her collarbone.

She swallowed hard. "Yes, I want to live."

"Then let's see how prettily you can beg."

Her breath caught, panic rippling through her slender frame.

She shook her head, a plea forming. "Please...please, don't do this."

"Do what, little one?"

Her mascara had run, forming dingy gray circles under her lashes, which only highlighted the golden flecks in the rich warmth of her brown eyes. Those pink lips quivered, begging to be claimed. "I...I...don't..."

My expression remained deliberately closed off.

I craved her fear.

Her desperation.

Her surrender.

My fingers grasped her chin, tilting her face upward.

I wanted her to witness this, to understand her choices —a body bag, or my mercy.

"That's not begging. I want to hear you beg me." A command, not a request.

"Please, I'll do anything."

"What could you possibly offer that I would want?" I ruthlessly taunted, drawing out the delicious suspense as I held her fate in the palm of my hand.

Her porcelain cheeks practically glowed in the moonlit room.

I imagined smearing lipstick across that angelic face.

Her expression shifted—a tiny flicker of something beyond terror. Recognition, perhaps, that this moment was inevitable from our first meeting.

Some women sensed their fate before they understood it.

Someone so pure needed to be ruined.

I would be that ruin.

"What value do you have that I can't find elsewhere?"

"I—I'll work for free." Her eyes darted across my face, searching for salvation.

I laughed, cold and harsh. "Try harder."

"I—please, I'll do anything. Please. I didn't mean to see anything. It was an accident. I was just trying to do my job. It all happened so fast, I'm not even sure what I saw. I'm so sorry."

"How sorry are you?" I asked as I unfastened my belt with a quiet click.

She broke completely—gasping, sobbing, shaking so violently she barely remained upright.

Yet in that moment of complete terror, there was the slightest dilation of her pupils that had nothing to do with the dim lighting.

Even her body betrayed her.

My cock had ached since our eyes met earlier.

After feeling those lips against mine, I would wait no longer.

I needed to discover what else her mouth could do.

Her fate had been sealed the moment she fled from me.

Nothing stirred my blood more than pursuit.

No, that wasn't true.

This—the moment fear transformed into submission.

When natural instinct overrode resistance and she became my good girl, proving her obedience.

I placed my gun on the desk beside us, freeing my hand for her soft hair.

"Take out my cock," I demanded, pulling a knife from my back pocket, opening it. The metallic flick echoed through the silence.

Her sobs still shook her shoulders, but she kept them quiet.

I slid the knife through the elastic holding her tight ponytail and groaned when her dark brown locks tumbled free to her shoulders.

"Your hair is wasted in that severe style," I observed, running my fingers through the strands. "Never wear it up again."

Her eyes widened at the implication that there would be an "again," a future beyond this moment.

"I said take out my cock. Don't make me repeat myself," I growled, fingers twisting into those silky strands, gripping tight.

Her trembling hands reached for my pants, drawing down the zipper.

"Please," she whispered once more.

I tightened my grip until she winced. "You need to prove you can take directions."

"I can. I will," she responded quickly, learning.

Her fingers found my hard length, wrapping around it.

The sensation of her soft yet strong touch drew a groan from my throat.

"Good girl," I praised as she pulled my cock free.

Her eyes flickered up at the praise, a brief moment of confusion crossing her features before she masked it.

Interesting.

She responded to those two simple words in ways she didn't understand...yet.

"Now show me how sorry you are."

Her fingers caressed my length, eyes wide and slightly panicked as crimson darkened her cheeks.

I gave her a minute to explore.

Her touch was exquisite, but she wouldn't get off—*or get me off*—so easily.

My fantasies of her on her knees before me paled in comparison to the reality—her trembling lips, her wide, fearful eyes.

Her blush deepened, and I wondered how far down that flush extended.

Did it reach her breasts? Her stomach?

"Look at me," I demanded.

Her eyes immediately found mine.

I pulled her face closer as she tilted my cock toward my stomach. The sight of her looking up at me, my cock so near her pretty mouth, stirred something dark within me.

"Tell me you're sorry again," I demanded.

"I'm so sorry. I promise I didn't see anything. No one will ever know. You don't have to do this, I will never—"

"Enough of your pretty little lies. Put your hands on my thighs and keep them there."

I should've ordered her to put her hands behind her back, forcing her to arch upward to reveal those perky breasts beneath the thin fabric of her T-shirt.

But I wanted her touch—wanted her unable to escape this moment.

There would be no retreat into her mind while I held her captive.

The second she let go of my cock, it fell forward, smacking her in the face.

She winced, but fuck if I didn't like the feeling of her warm skin.

Keeping one hand in her hair, I moved the other one to the base of my cock, then painted her full lips with my pre-cum.

She said nothing, keeping her lips closed as she looked up at me with fear and a little defiance sparking in the depths of her cognac-brown eyes.

I caught sight of a small photo frame that must have fallen from the desk during her earlier struggle to hide. A family portrait, strangers smiling at a beach. How ordinary their lives must be, how safe and predictable.

Nothing like what Alina's life would become now.

"Open your mouth and suck my cock as if your life depends on it. Because it does."

She closed her eyes for just a second, drawing in a deep shuddering breath through her nose before her lips parted and her pink tongue darted out to taste the tip.

"Keep those pretty eyes open and on me, babygirl." I needed to see her face, to watch that exact moment when the fight drained from her eyes and surrender took over.

Her gaze locked with mine as she opened her mouth.

I kept my grip on her hair tight, thrusting straight to the back of her throat.

She gagged and sputtered, eyes watering, resisting every second.

The way her throat constricted around me nearly finished me right then.

I pulled back, releasing her hair and letting her drop to her hands and knees, coughing and gasping for air while I regained control.

I would have come down her throat, but not this quickly.

"You've never done this before, have you?" I asked, observing how she struggled to recover.

She shook her head, gasping for breath.

"Words, Alina. Always words."

"No," she managed between coughs. "Not like this."

Something possessive and primitive surged through me.

Her inexperience made this capture all the sweeter.

I gave her only a moment before tangling my fingers back in her hair and dragging her up.

Even with tears staining her cheeks, bloodshot eyes, and bruised lips all swollen and glistening, she was beautiful.

A woman created to be claimed and possessed... not by anyone else, but by me alone.

Crafted specially for me to control.

40

What man would ignore such a gift?

With one forceful thrust, I pushed between her lips all the way to the back of her throat, not stopping until her nose pressed against my stomach. I angled her face to keep those beautiful brown eyes in view as they begged for mercy she'd never receive.

"Stop fighting it, *moy kotyonochek*. Give in. Learn to take all of me, to crave it, and you just might survive this night."

Hatred flashed in her eyes, but as her lips stretched around me, I witnessed that spark of defiance transform into defeat, acceptance, then fear and panic as she struggled to breathe.

For a moment, she truly believed I would end her life this way.

An intriguing method of execution, but the risk of biting was too great.

"Good girl," I praised, and something new flickered across her expression.

It vanished instantly, but I caught it.

She responded to praise. Another reason not to kill her.

Women who craved praise often flourished under degradation as well. There was a delicate psychology to breaking someone like Alina.

Praise to create the need for approval, then the withholding of it to intensify desperation. The hunger for validation became its own restraint, more effective than any rope.

A delicate balance, but one that promised entertainment and trainability.

I withdrew a few inches, just enough for her to draw breath through her nose, but not enough to grant control.

"Show me what you can do, *moy kotyonochek*. Suck my cock."

She hesitated.

My hands tightened in her hair in warning.

Her cheeks hollowed and her tongue gently massaged the underside of my cock.

"Mm, I think you can do better, beautiful."

Her mouth felt impossibly soft and warm, the velvet of her cheeks against my flesh overwhelming.

She rocked forward and back tentatively, uncertain of her approach. With my grip on the back of her skull, she moved her entire body to slide her mouth along my shaft.

It was exquisite, but insufficient.

I needed harder. Faster. Rougher.

I needed to watch her struggle.

With one sharp thrust, I pushed to the back of her throat again.

She wasn't prepared.

She nearly toppled sideways, clutching my thighs to steady herself.

I showed no mercy.

I took her sweet mouth harder, forcing my cock deeper.

The muscles in her throat contracted against the invasion, creating a tighter grip.

Fresh tears streamed down her face.

Her eyes glazed as survival instincts triggered resistance.

Her hands pressed against my thighs, her head strained to withdraw.

Her struggle heightened every sensation.

With her hair wrapped in my fist, I pinned her against the wall, driving down her throat repeatedly.

No escape route existed, and she knew it.

When her resistance ceased, I withdrew enough for one deep breath before claiming her pretty face again.

I imagined her other hidden treasures must be equally perfect.

Pleasure surged through me as that familiar tension built at the base of my spine and crawled toward my balls.

Should I finish down her throat? Or pull back across her tongue, making her display my seed before swallowing every drop? Perhaps paint her face across her cheeks and lips, marking her as mine?

No, that would come later.

When I marked her face, I would also cover her breasts, her stomach, all the way down her used body.

Time enough for that later.

This time, she would swallow everything.

"That's right," I said through clenched teeth. "Take it all."

Wave after wave of pleasure crashed through me as I stared into those dark, golden-brown depths, witnessing defeat, humiliation, and a hint of desire.

A knock interrupted us before I could withdraw from her lips.

"Do not come in here," I shouted toward the door before looking down at my sweet captive. I gripped her jaw tightly as I pulled free. "Do not swallow."

She looked up, lips now pressed together, and nodded.

"Say it," I commanded, needing her verbal acknowledgment.

"I won't swallow," she whispered, lips barely moving to keep the contents in her mouth.

The door cracked open without permission.

One of my men paused in the doorway, his gaze scanning the room before finding me, then dropping to Alina.

I snarled, blocking her from view as I draped my jacket over her huddled form.

Looking at her broken state remained my privilege alone.

"Get. Out." The command left no room for argument.

The man stiffened, eyes darting to the ceiling—the only reason I considered sparing his life. "Apologies, boss, but—"

"Out! Now!" My hand moved toward my gun, a clear threat that widened his eyes.

"*Da*, boss," he muttered before retreating, pulling the door shut.

I exhaled sharply, dragging a hand through my hair, patience exhausted.

I wasn't finished with Alina, but I awaited crucial information that would determine my next action against our enemies. I couldn't afford delays.

Gregor and Artem would be furious enough.

If I wanted to keep Alina beneath their notice, I couldn't give them reason to investigate her. But I would be damned if anyone else touched what was now mine.

I crouched down to her level, taking her jaw between my fingers.

"Don't move." My glare ensured she understood. "If you run, I will find you. And when I do, I'll start by breaking those pretty fingers one by one. And do not swallow. We are not done."

I traced my thumb across her lips once more, their tremble fluttering against my skin. "Remember, Alina. You belong to me now. The sooner you accept that, the easier your life will become."

I stood and straightened my clothes before turning and striding through the empty office, yanking the door open to address whatever demanded my attention.

This had better be the news I awaited, and it had better be quick.

My new pet needed training, and I had only begun to show her what her future held.

CHAPTER 6

ALINA

*T*he taste of submission lingered in my mouth long after Pavel was gone.

I had a minute—seconds, maybe less—before he returned to finish what he'd started.

The moment the door closed behind him, I collapsed forward to my hands and knees.

My stomach heaved as I spit all of his come from my mouth, wishing I could purge the degradation just as easily.

The violation had sunk deeper than flesh.

It had branded me, marked me in ways soap could never wash away.

I coughed and gagged, trying to rid my tongue of the bitter taste of powerlessness. The bile and stomach acid made it worse, a brutal reminder of what he'd taken from me—what I'd surrendered to survive.

What terrified me most wasn't just the violation; it was my body's betrayal.

Beneath the fear and disgust, a traitorous heat had

flickered when he called me "good girl" with his fingers twisted in my hair.

That unexpected response horrified me more than the gun against my skin had.

What kind of person did that make me?

My confusion only amplified my panic as I struggled to process what had happened, what it meant. My body quaked in the aftermath, my lungs fighting each inhale, my throat raw, my jaw aching from being forced open.

I wanted to curl into a ball, to disappear beneath the humiliation.

I would have.

Any woman would yield to such crushing degradation.

But I couldn't.

Pavel would return.

That monster would come back to either use me again or kill me now that he'd taken what he wanted.

I needed to move. *Now.*

Survival had to overrule trauma. I could break down later, if there was a later.

I stood on unsteady legs and scanned the room.

No sign of anyone.

A door across the sea of cubicles led to another hallway, then to a staircase that would take me outside.

I just needed to reach it and escape this building.

Pavel knew too much about me, starting with my real name.

Thank god I never gave the management office my real address. It was silly but with all the cloak and dagger warnings about rules and the office building tenants, I'd hesitated to give them too much information.

The only reason why I'd given them my grandmother's name was I figured they wouldn't care about a sweet old lady living in a state-run nursing home. She was listed as my emergency contact, but with a note only to contact her if it were a true emergency...like I was dead.

It was bitterly ironic how that actually almost happened tonight.

But if something did happen to me, I'd wanted at least *someone* to know to call her.

The pathetic sadness that I would have to rely on my asshole boss for that because there was absolutely no one else in my life was a cold stone in my stomach.

That must have been how Pavel found out about my grandmother; he must have looked in my employee file.

I was a fool to think I'd ever been invisible to him.

Now I had to disappear completely. Vanish where his resources couldn't track me.

Fuck, I needed a shower, with water as hot as I could stand it. I'd scrub his fingerprints from my skin with steel wool and empty an entire bottle of store-brand mouthwash until I no longer tasted Pavel Ivanov's essence.

I needed to cleanse him from my body, scour him from my mouth, then retreat to my favorite state: denial.

In the morning, I'd pretend none of it happened.

I was simply dismissed from this job and needed to find another late-night cleaning position.

Therapists probably had some technical term with too many syllables for how I processed trauma. Advanced trauma experience compartmentalization syndrome, perhaps.

I called it doing what I needed to survive.

Sometimes that meant ignoring what couldn't be fixed.

I couldn't fix what happened, just as I couldn't fix that Pavel wanted me dead...or worse.

This job was finished, and I needed a new one.

I glanced around one final time before my gaze landed on the desk beside me.

Pavel had left his gun.

The same weapon he'd used to kill that man, the same cold metal he'd traced against my skin.

Carelessly abandoned.

A murder weapon.

I reached for it, then pulled my hand back.

Taking it would cross a line I'd never imagined crossing. I wasn't a thief. I'd never seen a gun before tonight. What would I even do with it?

But Pavel's face flashed in my mind—the cold calculation in his eyes as he squeezed the trigger, the casual way he'd executed a man, then forced himself down my throat moments later.

Would I use it? Could I?

The metal gleamed in the moonlight, both repulsive and compelling.

If I left it, I'd have nothing to protect myself.

If I took it, I became something else—someone who might have to decide whether to fire it.

My grandmother's face appeared in my mind's eye. She depended on me. If I died tonight, what would happen to her?

I seized the gun, wrapping my fingers around its grip.

The weight surprised me; it was heavier than I

expected, solid and deadly. My index finger hovered near the trigger as nausea and resolve battled within me.

It was either the smartest move or the dumbest decision of my life, but I had no time for second-guessing.

I was leaving one way or another.

I crouched low, staying beneath the cubicle walls as I scurried toward the back exit. The gun bumped against my thigh with each movement, a constant reminder of how drastically my situation had changed. Every creak of the building made me freeze, my ears straining for any sign of Pavel's return.

The door opened with a tiny click, and I peered into the hallway.

The main fluorescents were off, leaving only recessed lighting casting eerie shadows along the corridor. The stringent odor of industrial cleaner—usually just an occupational annoyance—now smelled like safety, like the normal world I was desperately trying to return to.

If Pavel remained on this floor, his men would be nearby too.

I hugged the shadows as I crept toward the stairwell door.

"Yeah, it's done. No, they don't know yet," a man's voice said as he appeared at the other end of the narrow hallway.

I ducked into an office before he spotted me.

Pressing against the wall behind the door, I held my breath. The gun felt impossibly loud in my hand, as if it might announce its presence.

He laughed into his phone. "His head exploded like a

fucking watermelon. You should have been here. Bitch to clean up all that blood though."

The casual tone made my skin crawl as he joked about the man whose brains were splattered across marble.

Static from a radio crackled, and Pavel's voice cut through.

"The cleaner ran off. She's still in the building, probably headed outside. Find her and bring her to me now."

A whimper of fear crawled up my throat.

I barely contained it as the man swore and ended his call.

Silence followed. My fingers pressed against the wall as my legs quivered. I clenched my muscles to stop their movement, remaining motionless.

The door to the office I was hiding in swung open and the man stepped into the room.

I froze, not even daring to breathe as I cowered behind the door, barely concealed.

My gaze was trained on the sliver of space between the door hinges and the wall, sweat trickling between my shoulder blades as I stood braced to run if discovered.

He cursed under his breath then left, slamming the door closed behind him.

I exhaled silently and leaned my head against the wall.

He opened several more doors down the hall, each one slamming shut with a finality that made me flinch.

After a few minutes of quiet, I eased the door open a crack and peeked out.

The man was gone, with no sign of other searchers...yet.

I crept in the opposite direction toward the stairwell

and slipped through, closing the door softly. Voices echoed in the stairwell, but from floors above, moving away. The concrete walls amplified and distorted their words, to the point where they sounded almost inhuman.

"What are we supposed to do when we find the bitch? Kill her?" asked someone with a Russian accent that wasn't nearly as refined as Pavel's.

"Nah. Boss wants her alive, but he didn't say we couldn't take her for a spin first," another replied. They laughed as they climbed another story and exited the stairwell.

A chill washed over me as my mind raced with what they planned. I clutched the gun tighter, suddenly grateful for its reassuring weight.

No time to dwell on it.

I moved quickly but silently, eyes fixed on my feet to avoid tripping on the stairs. The rubber soles of my sneakers squeaked occasionally against the smooth concrete treads, each sound like a scream in the otherwise silent stairwell.

Down, down, down.

I wasted no time descending, not looking up until reaching the large steel door covered in warning signs.

Do Not Open—Alarm Will Sound.

If the Ivanovs were here tonight, they'd disabled the security systems.

Men like Pavel didn't leave electronic trails.

The best way to avoid police involvement was to avoid creating evidence.

I pushed that thought aside, realizing I was now evidence they would need to erase.

No point worrying about what I couldn't control. I pressed the door handle, bracing for alarms in case my assumption proved wrong.

Nothing happened.

I pushed the door open just enough to slip through.

Shifting the gun to my other hand, I ran my sweat-slicked palm over my thigh. The metal seemed to grow heavier with each passing moment.

The cool, crisp air outside helped clear my thoughts.

The distant sound of traffic—ordinary people living ordinary lives—was surreal after what I'd witnessed.

I wasn't free yet.

This building was one among several in the compound. I needed to navigate the loading dock and back alleys without detection. My heartbeat thundered as I darted through alleys, sneakers slapping against wet concrete. The recent rain had left puddles that reflected the streetlights, creating twice as many sources of illumination to avoid.

The area was a labyrinth of twists and turns, but I'd spent countless hours dragging garbage through these same passages. I knew my way.

That meant I also knew where the guards stationed themselves.

With Pavel conducting business tonight, who knew if the regular guards remained or if additional men patrolled?

Jimmy might have been given the night off, replaced by some eager distant Ivanov cousin ready to prove himself. I passed the first guard station at the junction of three alleys. This area, which served as my garbage drop-off point, was wider and more open, making me vulnerable now. The overhead security light cast harsh shadows that seemed to move like living things.

Jimmy's station stood empty.

He normally sat in his booth every night regardless of the weather, listening to audiobooks until he spotted me, then helped with the larger trash bags. Jimmy never missed shifts, because he was saving for his son's college.

His absence confirmed my suspicion—none of the regular guards remained.

Relief surged through me, offering a taste of hope.

My thoughts turned to where I'd go after my escape.

I couldn't return to my apartment. It wouldn't take long for them to learn my real address and then that would be the first place they'd look.

My grandmother's nursing home was too obvious as well.

I needed somewhere temporary, just for the rest of the night.

Marcy from the club might let me crash on her couch.

Or maybe that shelter downtown that didn't ask questions.

My steps lightened as I pushed harder, ignoring my protesting thighs.

One more turn and I'd reach the main street with its businesses and steady traffic flow, busy even at this hour.

One more turn to freedom.

Nearly tasting liberty, I rounded the sharp corner, only to barely avoid colliding with an unfamiliar guard, a massive gun strapped to his chest.

Before he could react, I raised my weapon.

55

It trembled in my hand, but I aimed directly at his head.

My finger moved to the trigger, applying just enough pressure to feel the resistance. For a heartbeat, I saw myself pulling it, saw his head exploding like the man Pavel had killed. The image sickened me, yet something dark inside me whispered it might be necessary.

"Move," I said through gritted teeth. "Or I swear to God I'll shoot."

The guard hesitated, his eyes assessing whether I was capable of murder.

I cocked the hammer, the metallic click echoing between the buildings.

He raised his hands and stepped aside.

"You won't get far," he snarled, his accent thicker than Pavel's. "He owns this city."

I didn't respond.

No reason to. We both knew he was probably right.

I took two giant steps sideways, circling him and leaving plenty of distance between us. I couldn't risk getting close enough for him to seize the gun.

His eyes darted between my face and the weapon repeatedly.

I read his thoughts clearly.

He viewed me as a coward, a pathetic, lost girl. He doubted I would pull the trigger. He believed he could easily overpower me.

Radio static crackled. Pavel's voice cut in over the line: "Goddammit. Who the fuck has eyes on her?"

We both glanced at the radio clipped to his belt.

I raised the gun a few inches even as he lowered his hand toward his radio.

Testing me.

Calling my bluff.

Dammit. He was right. I couldn't shoot.

Instead I ran.

Ran with everything I had.

I pushed hard, my lungs burning with each breath.

The guard shouted behind me, but I sprinted with every ounce of strength I possessed.

I ran as though chased by the devil himself...because I was.

I reached the main road just as a bus stopped less than a block away.

I waved frantically, shouting for the driver to wait as I flew down the sidewalk.

By some miracle, I managed to board just as the doors slid closed behind me. Panting a bit to catch my breath from the mad dash down the street, I swept my arm behind me to hide the gun from the driver as I reached into my back pocket for my Metro pass. I'd learned the hard way after getting mugged a few years ago to keep it and my apartment keys on me and leave my wallet at home on these overnight shifts.

Swiping my card, I kept my body angled away from the few bleary-eyed passengers as I stepped down the narrow aisle before collapsing into the first empty seat.

I tucked the gun between my thigh and the seat.

No one looked twice at me—nothing to see, just another late-night worker heading home.

The normality was jarring.

These people had no idea what existed just blocks away, what I'd just escaped.

Still, I was not safe.

This was merely a moment's reprieve.

The gun pressed against the back of my thigh like a fucking telltale heart.

I'd taken it for protection, but now realized it was evidence too—evidence of what I'd witnessed, what had been done to me.

Taking it to the police and asking for protection wasn't even worth thinking about.

I should dispose of it, but not yet.

Not until I was truly safe.

Because Pavel would come for me.

And when he did—I didn't know if I would survive.

But I knew I wouldn't surrender again.

CHAPTER 7

PAVEL

"Your turn, Durak," Gregor taunted, slapping down an ace on the table. "Defend that, if you can."

I exhaled a stream of smoke and assessed my hand.

Six cards left against Gregor's three. Not promising.

"Fuck you," I muttered, tossing down my only defense —the ace of spades.

Cheers and jeers erupted around the oak table where my brothers and cousins had gathered in the basement of Gregor's house. Leather armchairs, hunting trophies, and vintage vodka advertisements adorned the wood-paneled walls of what his wife Samara insisted on calling his man cave.

Glasses clinked as Damien poured another round of the cheap American vodka they'd selected as part of my punishment.

The liquid burned twice—first my throat, then my pride.

"Perhaps our little brother should request lessons from

his runaway girl," Kostya suggested, deftly rearranging his cards. "She clearly outplayed him tonight."

I gripped my glass tighter, jaw clenched as I absorbed the barbs.

This was tradition—when someone fucked up badly enough, we gathered for Durak.

The card game's name translated to "fool," and tonight, I wore that crown.

"Place your bets for the next round," Gregor announced, gathering the cards to shuffle again. "And while we're at it, who thinks Pavel will track down his runaway before she empties his gun into his thick skull?"

Damien snorted, raising his shot glass of vodka. "I hope she pistol-whips him. Would be a better love story than whatever the fuck this is turning into."

"I'll track her down," I countered, "and unlike some men, it won't take me three years to find her. We all know the only reason you two found Samara and Yelena was sheer dumb luck."

I turned to Damien, enjoying the flicker of rage in his eyes. "Didn't Yelena try to shoot you before you forced her to marry you? At this point, I'm still very much ahead."

"Strictly speaking," Damien corrected, raising a finger, "she never actually shot me."

"Only because you removed the bullets," Artem interjected with a rare smile.

"Still counts," Damien insisted.

"She pulled the trigger," Kostya pressed with a grin.

Damien smirked, pulling on his shirt cuffs. "It was foreplay. You wouldn't understand."

Gregor leaned forward and placed his hand on

Kostya's shoulder. "Says the man whose girl knocked him out while his shriveled cock was still in his hand."

Mikhail pounded the table with his fist as he laughed. "What did she use again?"

"A lamp," offered Gregor with a smirk.

"Fuck you both," Kostya countered with a laugh. "And strictly speaking she hit me before I could get my dick out."

Gregor tossed his head back with a bark of laughter. "Somehow that's even worse."

Meanwhile, Damien raised his glass in mock salute. "To the fallen!"

After we all drank, I folded my forearms on the table and turned to Damien. "In fact, if we're keeping score, didn't Yelena hit you with a fucking brick? Alina stole from me. She didn't try to kill me."

Mikhail reached for the vodka bottle. "Your gun."

My brow furrowed. "What?"

"Alina stole *your gun* from you...not exactly an insignificant detail."

I gave him the middle finger even as I pushed my shot glass toward him to fill.

Kostya gave me a wink. "Give my little brother a break. He wasn't thinking with the right head at the time."

The whole table erupted into laughter.

"You all realize I can kill you, right?" I asked mildly, arranging my deliberately poor hand.

Another aspect of being the Durak—playing at a disadvantage.

"Yeah, yeah." Gregor waved dismissively. "But not before you prove you're not the biggest idiot at this table."

"I'm not the one mistaking a blow job for lifelong commitment, so maybe that point has already been proven. Just because you fell for your bride after she made you come doesn't mean I have the same affliction."

Damien's chair scraped back as he pulled a knife from his boot.

Artem seized his wrist, forcing him back into his seat while fixing me with a warning glare.

Wives were off-limits.

I knew it, but being the Durak made me reckless. I lifted my chin in Damien's direction. *"Izvini."*

He nodded his acceptance of my apology.

Gregor, ever the strategist, opened with a seven of hearts. A deceptively weak start.

Kostya countered effortlessly, dropping a nine of spades on top.

As always, my brother's defense was impenetrable.

Artem leaned back, calculating his move. "You know, Pavel, it was an interesting choice to leave your gun behind for her to steal."

Damien nodded, dropping his card without looking. "Yeah. Nothing screams 'alpha male' like getting robbed mid-blow job."

I exhaled sharply, rubbing my temples. "You would know, asshole. At least I didn't tie her up just so she could slip the knots again and again. At least Alina didn't jump out of a window to get away from me."

"Yelena didn't jump out of a window," he scoffed, then paused. "She just made me *think* she did."

"Right...but we all know she would've if she'd had to.

But getting by you was just too fucking easy." Teasing Damien about Yelena's skill was acceptable.

I was taking the piss out of him, not insulting his wife.

Well, maybe questioning her choice of spouse, but that was fair game.

"At least I didn't hand Yelena my gun," he countered with a raised eyebrow.

"I didn't *give* my gun to her," I insisted, eyeing my useless cards. "I left her alone for less than a minute. She was supposed to stay put."

"I guess you're not as scary as you think if she thought it would be acceptable to disobey you," Gregor countered, tapping the table with blunt fingers.

I had nothing to counter with. Taking the penalty cards, I muttered, "You want me to shoot you, Gregor?"

"You don't have a gun," Damien wheezed, slapping his knee as the table dissolved into uproarious laughter.

"She took *one* of my guns, not all of them," I muttered, but my defense fell on deaf ears.

"You know what the real problem is?" Gregor mused, slapping down an ace. "You're growing soft."

Artem pointed his card at me accusingly. "You let her escape...with your gun. If this were a movie, you'd be the dumb American love interest waiting for his balls to drop."

I wanted to point out this all happened after she'd drained said balls dry, but that would only launch a barrage of jokes. I wasn't making it that easy for them.

"The question is," Damien interjected, "did she at least deserve the gun? Was the BJ good enough to warrant a parting gift?"

I flicked my burning cigarette directly at his smug face.

The bastard dodged, laughing as ash scattered across the table.

Worth it.

My mind drifted to her mouth on me, those eyes staring upward, the blend of hatred and reluctant desire.

The way she yielded without breaking.

Her inherent submission fascinated me—how she followed instructions while maintaining that defiant spark. Stretching those pink lips around me, her entire body trembling. I craved more, wanted to discover every expression her face could form: anguish, ecstasy, and that exquisite threshold where they merged.

Her pleas still resonated in my memory.

I needed her addiction to match my own growing obsession.

I was giving her the remainder of the night.

Not by choice.

If it had been entirely up to me, I'd be between her thighs, sinking my cock deep inside her tight pussy as she struggled against the binds I'd use to tie her to her own bed.

Unfortunately, running defense against Gregor and Artem's fury when they found out the real reason I was at the offices a couple of hours ago was more important... but only barely.

The men surrounding me assumed I was awaiting information on her whereabouts, but I already knew her true address—not the fake one she'd given management.

I'd already sent two of my men to watch the place.

Unlike Yelena or Samara, Alina lacked resources to run far. She didn't possess Viktoria's determination or Marina's understanding of our reach.

Let her cling to a false sense of security for what remained of the night.

I'd let her have that momentary comfort.

It would make reclaiming her infinitely sweeter.

My brothers and cousins hunted their women for ownership or control.

That wasn't my motivation, though I fully intended to enjoy my prize.

For me, the pursuit itself was what held the appeal.

The challenge.

The game.

I craved finding her, chasing her, capturing her.

The others wouldn't comprehend.

I'd deliberately let her escape.

Where was the satisfaction if she simply surrendered?

By the time I'd won the next round, forcing Gregor to choke down an entire shot of bargain-shelf vodka as punishment, the atmosphere had shifted.

Artem tapped his fingers against his cards, dark eyes narrowing. "Enough bullshit. What happened before the girl swallowed your common sense along with your cock? Why were you at the building tonight, and why was the place emptied?"

I braced myself.

Here we go…

"Solovyov is handled," I replied in a deceptively casual tone.

The room fell silent.

Until Gregor and Artem simultaneously slammed their fists on the table, competing for dominance even in their anger.

"What do you mean 'Solovyov is handled'? We told you to wait. It wasn't safe to—" Artem began, his voice dangerously quiet.

"It's safe now," I interrupted, leaning back. "He's dead. Everyone knows he was targeting us, and now he isn't."

"How?" Gregor demanded, cards forgotten.

"I tracked the last of his men, brought him in."

"Again," Kostya pressed. "How?"

"The man I killed tonight was a cousin of Solovyov. He thought he didn't know anything, which turned out to be true. Fortunately the dumbass had Solovyov's current burner number saved in his phone, so we traced the location."

"And how do you know his information was reliable?" Gregor's eyes narrowed to slits.

"I called Roman. Had him handle it cleanly. That's what pulled me from Alina in the first place."

Artem stood and paced a few steps away from the table, then returned, leaning forward on rigid arms and pressing his knuckles onto its surface. "You what? We do not call Roman unless there is absolutely no other alternative."

"There wasn't one." I shrugged, though unease began to creep up my spine. "It needed to be done fast and done right. He sent confirmation."

I pulled out my phone, forwarding the message to their burner devices.

The image showed Solovyov appearing almost

peaceful in his bed—if not for the crimson gash across his throat and the blood-soaked sheets.

Beside him lay a young blonde still asleep, unaware of the horror awaiting her waking moments.

"Fuck," Gregor muttered, tossing his phone onto the table.

Artem set his down with deliberate control, inhaling deeply through his nose.

I recognized that expression. The "I'm restraining myself from strangling my brother" look I'd seen countless times.

"Do you understand why we didn't call Roman?" he asked, voice deceptively calm.

"Because his poor excuse for a human being and more than slightly bigoted grandmother believes he's Satan incarnate and not truly an Ivanov since he's only half-Russian?" Damien suggested, attempting to defuse the tension with sarcastic levity.

"No," Artem replied, pinching the bridge of his nose.

"Because once he's involved, there's no controlling the situation?" I ventured. "But the job's complete, so—"

"No," Gregor interrupted, gripping his glass with white knuckles. "Because Solovyov wasn't intelligent enough to orchestrate this campaign against us himself. He lacked the resources to withstand our pressure for this long from that distance. Someone else pulled his strings, and now that trail has gone cold."

My stomach twisted as realization dawned.

"We'll discuss this later," Artem declared, his tone indicating the conversation was far from over. "For now, what's your plan regarding the girl? She's a loose end."

I rolled my shoulders, irritation transforming into darker intent. "I'm not going to fucking kill her if that is what you're asking."

Damien leaned back in his chair. "Christ, Pavel. We don't kill women. You should know that."

I did, but there were exceptions to every rule.

Like when a woman who wasn't part of our mafia family witnessed a murder and then ran off into the night...with the fucking murder weapon.

I reached for the vodka bottle. It was a small blessing that they didn't know the gun she took was that particular gun. Or none of them would be sitting around this table playing cards and joking over shots.

This was my mess. I would clean it up.

I'd made a critical error because, yet again, Artem and Gregor had withheld crucial information.

Now we faced an unknown enemy, and I had a witness on the loose.

"I'm going to find her," I stated simply.

"And when you do?" Kostya pressed.

A slow smile spread across my face as I collected my cards. "I'll teach her the true cost of stealing from an Ivanov."

CHAPTER 8

ALINA

I didn't go straight home. I couldn't.

Every time I considered heading toward my dingy apartment, a man would get on the bus and eye me a little too hard, or the skin on the back of my neck would tingle in warning.

Was it Pavel having me followed?

Or was he watching me?

Was he lurking in the shadows, waiting until I was trapped in my apartment?

Were his goons hiding in the shadows instead?

Waiting for me to head home. Then they'd send word to their boss?

My skin crawled, and my heart pounded so hard in my chest I thought it was going to crack one of my ribs.

I got off the bus and headed to the Metro.

First, I took the yellow line down into Virginia.

Then I took the blue line back up into DC just to switch over to the red to take me to Maryland.

For hours, I rode that line back and forth until I got on

the green and took that through DC again, connecting back to the red.

Over and over I got off at random stops and switched at different lines, crossing state lines through Maryland and Virginia back and forth seven, maybe eight times.

I wasn't sure.

The count disappeared somewhere between the clammy heat of subway platforms and the numbing exhaustion seeping into my bones.

Every time I thought I might have been safe, I doubled back.

Dodging between train cars, I slid between doors at the last minute and then switched cars.

When I found an empty car, I stood in one of the cramped corners so I couldn't be seen through the windows.

I never sat down.

I never stopped looking around me.

Men like the Ivanovs didn't give up easily.

Thankfully, I knew the management office didn't have my real address. The second they told me the pay, and that I was not to see or hear anything, I knew I was taking a risk.

The pay was too good to turn down.

That didn't mean I had to be stupid.

The address I gave the management office was a PO Box on the other side of town.

Pavel wouldn't be able to find me that way.

But his men following me would make it all too easy.

By the time I reached my neighborhood, the sun was

rising, and DC was waking up, ready for another day of greed, abuse, and power grabbing.

When I finally stepped off the platform and climbed the cracked concrete steps to my street, my nerves were frayed.

My hands were still shaking, and my legs were cramping from all the tension.

I had tucked the gun into the front of my waistband and pulled out my T-shirt to cover it. Which of course didn't really work to fully conceal it, but if I crossed my arms low over my stomach it wasn't as overt.

I wasn't about to attract police attention by being the crazy woman on the DC Metro with a gun.

That would make it far too easy for Pavel to find me.

For a moment in the middle of my travels, I had considered waving the gun around to attract attention and then allowing myself to be taken into police custody where I could explain to a detective or a police chief or whoever what had happened and turn over the weapon.

It was a nice little fantasy, pretending for a moment that I lived in a world where the good guys won.

Where someone would listen to me and take my story seriously.

Sadly, I lived in reality, where a woman was rarely believed over a man, and the Ivanovs probably had every single cop on their payroll.

No, making a scene, garnering attention, or telling my story was just going to make it that much easier for him to find me.

I didn't need to draw attention; I needed to fade into the background until he forgot about me.

I needed to stay alive.

I needed to stay on my feet, working to pay off my father's debts and my grandmother's bills.

Someone needed to take care of her.

My father had disappeared, so I was the only option.

She never let me down, and I wasn't about to do that to her.

The moment I stepped inside my tiny apartment, I shoved the door shut behind me and bolted every single lock.

When I moved into the apartment, it already had three deadbolts.

I had added two more and a chain for good measure.

Now, that didn't seem like enough.

After locking up, I dragged my tiny second-hand Ikea dresser against the door and looked around for anything else I could use.

On a whim, I stacked the pots and pans I found at Goodwill on top, as well as anything else that would make some noise if it fell.

It was a tower of sad, pathetic junk.

Almost everything I owned.

I looked at it, hollow desolation welling inside of me, and just sank to the floor.

The dresser wouldn't stop Pavel, but maybe it would slow him down?

If he found me, maybe that dresser with its mountain of clutter would make enough noise to give me the warning I needed to escape or fight back.

I took the gun out of my waistband and just held it in my lap.

For a moment, I lifted it away from my body, like it might bite me.

Before grabbing this one off of that desk , I'd never held a gun before.

I never even had the desire.

The closest I had come was maybe a paintball gun at Bradley Foster's fifth grade birthday party.

What had happened to that shy little girl who was afraid to shoot a paintball gun at her classmates?

Now she was sitting here holding a pistol that had been used to kill someone just a few hours ago.

I had witnessed a grisly murder and how did I respond?

By sucking the murderer's cock.

More tears burned behind my eyes as I grieved that innocent little girl who'd had such a bright future ahead of her.

That wasn't me anymore.

Somehow, I had become this.

A broken husk of a woman desperately trying to make ends meet and having to deal with mobsters and murderers and...

"Seriously, what the fuck just happened?" I whispered aloud, as if the gun could actually answer me.

The events of the night played in a vicious loop over and over in my mind.

Starting with the first gunshot.

The blood.

Pavel opening the door. Meeting his eyes.

His mouth on mine, the way he tasted of mint and coffee.

73

The strength in his hands when he grabbed me and the way I had let him—

I gritted my teeth, swallowing down the shame burning in my throat.

I should have bitten him.

I should have clawed at him, fought him off.

Anything.

I should've done anything other than let myself drown in the moment.

No, it was so much worse than that. I didn't let myself drown in the moment.

Drowning in the moment would have been acceptable.

It would have meant I was forced to do something against my will, and I shut myself off mentally and emotionally.

Drowning would have meant I compartmentalized and hid my mind from what was happening.

That was understandable.

I could've lived with that.

I was just a girl trapped in an awful situation, and I did what I needed to do to survive.

Survival was acceptable.

What I did wasn't about survival.

I gave myself over to it, to him.

It didn't matter that I hated him.

I didn't want what happened, but I didn't fight it either.

I submitted to him, to his power.

My body responded in ways that it shouldn't have.

I didn't recoil from his kiss.

I melted into it.

Into him.

When he put me on my knees, warmth sparked between my thighs, then grew, spreading to my limbs.

No. That wasn't true.

If I was going to be completely honest with myself, I was aroused the second our eyes met.

My heart caught in my throat, some emotion that I should not have felt at that moment.

That was why it took me a moment to run.

That was why I couldn't escape that moment.

I was struck by him, by his handsome features, his air of dominance and power.

For a second, I was frozen in admiration for the man I saw in front of me.

He wasn't a coward who would sell his daughter and mother out to cover his gambling debts.

He wasn't a loser who would cheat on a woman and then throw her out.

Pavel Ivanov wasn't some little boy who would take from those he loved.

He was a man.

A warrior who would protect his family.

For just a moment, I allowed myself to fantasize what it would be like to have a man wrap me in his arms and tell me that everything was going to be okay. That I didn't have to worry. That he would handle everything.

That I wasn't alone anymore.

That just for one fucking second, I didn't have to be the strong one. The independent one. The responsible one. The one who wasn't allowed to buckle under the weight of all her problems.

That just once, I could hear someone else say "I got this" and be able to believe it. Trust in it.

When he had me cornered under that desk, I was scared, but I was curious too. I wanted to know what he would do to me and then, when he put me on my knees, I didn't fight him.

I preened under him calling me a good girl, and I leaned into it because some broken part of me wanted that praise. I wanted to show him I could be good, I could be worthy of—

No. I shut that line of thought down.

It was just the adrenaline talking, and I refused to believe it was anything else.

The truth gnawed at my gut, and I needed to shut it up. I desperately needed to silence that insidious whisper in the back of my mind, the one that suggested I liked being dominated by a powerful man.

That wasn't who I was. That was not who I wanted to be.

Maybe under different circumstances, maybe in a different life with a different man who wasn't so dangerous I could be that girl, but not like this.

If it were different circumstances, if it was any man other than Pavel Ivanov, then you wouldn't have reacted the way you did.

The voice in the back of my head taunted me with a truth that I refused to acknowledge.

I needed to forget.

I needed to shut that little voice up and pretend that none of this ever happened.

This memory, along with the other ones too painful to

dwell on, would be locked in a vault deep in my mind to never be brought up or examined again.

Crawling across the cramped floor of my studio, I reached for the half-empty bottle of cheap wine sitting on the rickety nightstand. There was only one way to silence that little voice and to make sure that memory never came to the surface again.

The first gulp burned, my throat still raw from the way Pavel's cock was so rough and—

The second gulp went down smoother, dulling the ache. By the time I finished the bottle, my limbs were numb, my eyelids heavy, and my head had finally stopped spinning with truths I refused to acknowledge.

Bright mid-morning sunlight stabbed through the broken blinds and my skull throbbed in protest.

I squinted at the clock.

The bright red numbers read 9:42.

Shit.

I was late.

I shot up so fast my stomach lurched. My head pounded from that ill-advised half bottle of cheap merlot. It was the wine. It had to be the wine. I refused to allow it to be anything else.

Stumbling to the sink, I choked down the last two aspirin in the bottle and swallowed them with a handful of stale tap water before wiping my face with trembling hands.

I could never go back to that cleaning job.

It was a death sentence, or maybe worse.

But I needed money.

Rent was due in five days and the last thing I wanted

or needed was to end up on the street with Pavel hunting me like a dog.

So, I needed to show up for my bartending shift at Velvet Dreams, or as the girls and I liked to call it, Vomit Dreams.

It was the kind of place where the waitresses wore cheap satin corsets, thigh-high stockings, and heels that could double as weapons.

The dancers started in cheap Halloween costumes and ended up fully bare.

The only thing they wore off the stage was a lifeless haze in their eyes.

Hell, management took eighty percent of their tips.

There was a small part of me that had some respect for this strip club, though.

It didn't even pretend to be classy.

It knew what it was, and what it wasn't.

They never pretended the rules couldn't be bent or broken for a price and did nothing to hide the fact that most of the dancers were strung out and just dancing for drug money.

The waitresses were like me, dirt poor and working a few jobs to make ends meet.

Some were runaways with fake IDs management didn't care to check, others were single moms trying to put food on the table while hiding from an abusive ex, or with a record too long for a nine-to-five.

I hated every second of working there, but it paid in cash and no one ever asked me questions, too afraid someone would start asking them questions.

This was the type of job that I needed. I once hoped

that in a month or two I could quit this one and work solely as a cleaner but plans clearly had changed.

I needed to get to the club, get on the good side of my boss, and try to pick up extra shifts until I found something to replace that cleaning job.

I shuddered.

Getting on the bosses' good side was never fun.

It meant making one of the managers think there was a chance I would let him fuck me in the office. If it was the other one, I would have to demean myself even more by boosting his delusional ego, convincing him in a cutesy, almost childlike voice that he was the big, important man.

Both options made my skin crawl.

Before I left, I grabbed a bruised apple from the counter. My stomach twisted at the thought of food, but I needed something to hold me through this shift, and probably the next.

If I was lucky, I might grab some maraschino cherries from behind the bar, assuming they were from a fresh jar and not already molding.

My stomach rolled again, acid rising to the back of my throat.

Half a bottle of wine on an empty stomach was a terrible decision.

Who would have thought?

I cast one last look at the gun, sitting on the nightstand by my bed. I could bring it with me.

God knew Vomit Dreams, and the neighborhood around it, definitely warranted carrying a gun.

I knew nothing about guns. How would I know if that

79

gun was maybe special? Would someone recognize it? Was it some kind of fancy Russian deal that people would instantly know belonged to an Ivanov?

It was too risky, so I left it.

Instead, I grabbed a couch cushion off the futon I had dragged up from the corner and shoved the gun into a hole on the other side of it. I pressed it deep into the worn-out stuffing. Just in case.

Ignoring a fresh spike of pain through both temples and its accompanying wave of nausea, I pulled the dresser away from the door and slipped out. Cringing from the harsh clang from a pot which slipped to the floor that amped up that spike of pain.

It was fine.

Pain meant I was alive.

I'd survived.

If Pavel hadn't found me yet, that meant I was in the clear.

Right?

CHAPTER 9

ALINA

$\mathcal{T}$he only thing worse than nighttime patrons of a strip club were daytime patrons of a low-rent dirty strip club.

Nighttime patrons were frat boys on college student allowances. They were out partying with their bros. Sometimes they were douchebags celebrating a bachelor party by harassing women, pretending that they weren't still going to be back there every Friday night for a "boys' night." Or celebrating their first job.

The girls called them budget ballers.

They were loud, obnoxious, and hell to deal with, but they had an energy that was sometimes infectious. Those men were there for a specific reason; they were there to have fun. They were there to let loose, to party, and maybe pay a little extra for the birthday boy or bachelor to get more than a lap dance in the champagne room.

According to the girls, most of them paid for more but when it came down to it were too shy, embarrassed, or drunk to get it up.

Mostly, they were relatively harmless. Annoying, but fairly harmless.

Daytime patrons were an entirely different beast.

There were two types of men who came to a cheap, crumbling strip club for lunch.

The shady businessmen who got off on the power trip of demoralizing women in a way the other clubs wouldn't allow, and they couldn't afford, anyway.

And the men who used to be those businessmen, now retired, divorced, their kids refusing to speak to them. They came here because they had nowhere else to go.

There was something seedy, almost demoralizing about them.

Those older men weren't there to party, they weren't there for a night of debauchery and fun. They were there out of habit, routine.

They watched the women and made lewd comments, but behind their eyes they were dead.

We called them the zombies.

Going through the motions of life, but despite their animation, they were soulless, rotting corpses.

It was almost like they were trying to grasp a sliver of what the night patrons had but which was just out of their reach.

It would have been depressing and I would have pitied them, if they didn't work so hard to grab my ass every single time I walked past them.

There were only so many times an old man could call you a bitch for refusing to show him your tits or blow him in the bathroom before you lost all sympathy.

The zombies were all old men, who stank of alcohol, sweat, and a life of regret.

As for the shady businessmen, we called them vampires because they sucked every ounce of the will to live from the girls and gave nothing in return.

They were young, hungry, and always out to make a quick buck.

These assholes would talk big like they were high rollers but then visited low-end strip clubs, maybe cashing in ten-dollar bills for ones. They would talk like they were spending big money, and about how much they were going to make by selling counterfeit bonds or threatening some low-level senator.

They came to celebrate over lunch and to degrade the dancers. It made them feel big and powerful to boss around women with their tits out, or to put their hands on my thighs while ordering expensive whiskey and then leave a two-dollar tip.

As if two dollars made up for the way they treated me or the girls.

They thought that two dollars meant we owed them something. Like they were being magnanimous, and we needed to fall all over ourselves, display our gratitude on our knees.

Fuck them.

Those two-dollar tips didn't mean shit, and they knew it. They weren't really here to spend money, they were here to be treated like big shots as cheaply as possible, while bragging about the money they made taking from "suckers and losers."

If the FBI ever wiretapped this strip club, they were

going to be in a lot of trouble. But the FBI would never come here. The men on their radar would be at any establishment other than this one.

These men were criminals that not even the feds cared about.

Whether it was the vampires or the zombies, they were all like roaches creeping out of the walls when the city wasn't looking. The worst of the worst who, despite the shit they did, the lack of value they added to society, just never died.

Even if someone — or liver failure — killed one, another would take their place. And it was my job to make these assholes feel like men, like they had a shot so they would keep giving the club their money and I could keep taking home pennies on the dollar.

I pushed through the door of Velvet Dreams, the weight of exhaustion already dragging at my body. I needed more sleep, but in order to get sleep, I needed a roof over my head, so I needed to work.

The dim interior smelled like cheap perfumes, stale beer, and regret.

I made it two steps inside before my boss, Lou, clocked me, giving me an angry scowl as he lumbered over to me. I was hoping Chad would be in today. Lou was harder to manage.

"You're late," he barked.

"Not now, Lou," I said in a sickeningly sweet voice.

Bile rose in the back of my throat. I hated using that voice. It was demeaning, placating this man. Acting like he was doing me a favor made my stomach roll. "I had a really rough night."

He didn't give a shit.

He never did, but by putting on that sweet, almost childlike voice, he wouldn't fire me.

Instead, his beady eyes dropped to the denim shirt I had thrown over my corset, and he gestured toward it like it was insulting him personally. As if I could ride the Metro and the bus across town in my uniform without getting arrested for indecent exposure or solicitation.

"Take that off when your shift starts."

I gritted my teeth, then plastered the fake smile on my face.

"You got it, boss."

"I mean it, Alina," Lou said, narrowing his eyes at me.

My sugary sweet act must not have been as convincing as it usually was.

"Don't make me tell you again. Our guests like to see some tit from the girls serving their beer. If you don't give them what they want, they will go somewhere else, and you are out of a job."

Guests.

The way he said it—like the drunken degenerates and washed-up losers who came here at noon were some kind of elevated clientele—made me want to roll my eyes.

Lou knew exactly the kind of men who came in here, he counted on it. Especially since today was two-for-one-on-the-first-round Wednesday. He wanted everything perfect. As if these degenerates would ever spend their dollar bills anywhere else.

Still, I really needed this job right now.

So I plastered on my fake smile. "Sure thing, boss man. I'll keep them happy."

I bit down on my frustration and turned toward the bar, setting up everything for the oncoming rush. Every muscle in my body was wound tight with nerves, and no matter how hard I tried to put it out of my mind, I was sure I was going to flinch every single time someone came into the place.

Was someone coming for me?

What would happen if Pavel found me?

Would he find me?

Could he find me?

The thought made me nauseous, and I had to constantly remind myself that he did not have my address. Yet. He only had my name. There should have been no way that he could find me.

Just like the FBI, there was no way that a man like that would even think of looking in a place like this.

Still, once we opened, every single time the door opened I would be looking up, expecting to see him.

My skin crawled, my stomach twisted, and bile burned at the back of my throat. That I could understand. I could live with terror.

What I couldn't live with was what was underneath it.

Under that terror, something worse lurked.

A dark, shameful heat.

I shoved it away time and time again, burying myself in prep work, scraping the mold off of the fruit garnishes, rinsing the glasses and polishing them enough to look clean, watering down the fresh bottles of liquor for the few well drinks our patrons ordered, and even switching out the kegs under the bar.

I kept myself distracted, busy so I wouldn't think

about that dark forbidden heat that burned in my core every time I thought about Pavel walking in.

Part of me wanted him to come in and take me from this hell.

Common sense told me that if he came in here to find me, it wouldn't be to save me.

It would be to kill me. But then why did my stomach drop at the thought he wouldn't come at all?

Ignoring everything, I lost myself in the tediousness of preparing for my job.

"Alina," Lou called, venom dripping from his voice. I looked over and he tapped his watch. It was just a few seconds till noon.

I nodded and with a deep breath, I slipped my denim overshirt off and tucked it away under the bar.

The cheap satin corset was a size too small, which was intentional to make my tits almost spill out. The ribbon lacing had broken a few weeks into working here, and Lou not only refused to fix it, but docked my pay.

A shoelace was in its place. The rest of my uniform consisted of black shorts that did not cover my ass and fishnet thigh highs with non-slip strips that were holding on for dear life. Soon they would have to be replaced, or I would have to figure out how to adhere more of that non-slip rubber myself. Would hot glue work?

I fluffed up my hair and adjusted my corset to push my tits up even further, and Lou gave me a single nod of what I was sure he considered approval. Then he opened the door, and the first wave of creeps stumbled in.

The usual hollow-eyed zombies had a bit of a pep in their step today, knowing that they could get two beers instead of their usual one. Most of them were already half drunk and their fingers twitched on the bar top as they watched me move.

I focused on my work, filling beers, sending lunch orders that consisted of little more than grilled cheese and fries back to the kitchen. I ignored the pangs of hunger in my stomach, the last echoes of my hangover throbbing in my temples, and the fear that made the hair at the back of my neck stand on end.

I poured beer after beer, delivered greasy fries, and avoided grabby hands as I stared at the clock like it was a countdown to freedom.

Six hours in this shift, then I was off to find a new second job.

I'd been working almost an hour, losing myself in the familiar rhythm of pouring drinks and riding the line between flirting and being professional with the patrons, when Lou came barreling out of the back room. "Take a bottle of vodka to the champagne room. Now."

"Brand?"

"Whatever is on the top shelf," he said, then stopped and walked over to me, his meaty hand grabbing my arm, squeezing hard enough to make me wince as his thumb caressed my breast.

Lou pulled me closer to him, so he could whisper in my ear, my nose curling at his wretched breath. "Go to the back and grab a bottle of the good shit, not the stuff that we've already watered down for the zombies and vampires that don't know any better."

"Yes, boss," I nodded.

Delivering to the champagne room was not my job.

But I didn't argue.

The faster I got it over with, the sooner I could go back to pretending I was invisible.

Just the woman behind the bar that served their drinks while they stared at the women dancing on the center stage.

I grabbed the bottle and walked toward the private lounge, pushing past the curtain.

Where I froze.

He was waiting for me.

Pavel sat there, dressed in a black suit that was probably more expensive than anything that had ever stepped foot in this establishment. He was lounging in a leather chair, all cocky power, like he owned the fucking place.

Dark.

Dangerous.

Arrogant.

A knowing smile pulled at the corner of his lips.

He'd been expecting me and was enjoying seeing me shaken.

My stomach dropped.

I hadn't seen him come in.

How had I not seen him come in?

My body moved before my brain could catch up.

I took a step back toward the curtain, ready to drop the bottle, turn and run.

I barely took half a step before his arm shot out and grabbed my hand, stopping me.

With a rough yank, my balance shattered and suddenly I was tumbling forward, colliding with a wall of muscle.

A sharp gasp poured from my throat as I landed in his lap.

His firm hands locked around my waist as I tried to scramble up.

A low rumble of laughter vibrated from his chest as he leaned forward to whisper in my ear. "It seems I've trapped a little kitten."

CHAPTER 10

PAVEL

"What the fuck are you wearing?" I growled, looking Alina up and down, taking in the trashiest outfit I'd ever seen.

Her tits were practically spilling out of the corset, and her round, perky ass was barely covered by tiny black shorts. I wasn't even sure they could be considered shorts.

She shouldn't be wearing shit like that.

This woman should be wrapped in the finest designer silks, cashmere, and wool. Clothes that whispered status. Power. Claimed.

INSTEAD, every time I saw her, she was dressed like someone disposable.

Her so-called cleaner uniform—black T-shirt and yoga pants—wasn't just cheap, it was insulting. A deliberate attempt to disappear into the background like a broom or a bucket. But a body like hers was impossible to hide. The fabric clung to her curves in all the wrong ways, like an afterthought that somehow demanded attention.

And then there was this second offense.

This pathetic excuse for a strip club costume. A bartender's outfit designed to humiliate.

She looked like a walking target.

Cheap. Unprotected.

Like no one gave a damn what happened to her.

It made my blood boil.

Because if she were mine, the only thing the world would see when she walked in a room was that she was untouchable.

The fact that other men could see this much of her, that she willingly put herself on display like this, had my grip tightening around her waist until she let out a little squeak.

Anger burned in my veins, pushed harder by a tinge of jealousy, or maybe possessiveness.

I wasn't mad because she had run, or because I had gone to her apartment and found it empty.

I wasn't even mad that I was forced to track her down like prey through the city.

That part I kind of enjoyed.

I was impressed by the chase she had given my men throughout the night.

She lost an entire team.

The first man she lost when she ran off the bus to the Metro, but the rest were able to follow her for a bit.

Then she darted away, out of their sight, jumping off one train to get on another.

More than once she ran through a train to hop one on the opposite track.

It took all night, but she lost every single one of my men.

Alina was far cleverer than I had originally given her credit for.

She had even lied on her work application, giving a false home address and listing a second job at a rat-infested strip club in a shitty neighborhood. I figured if the home address was fake, the second job had to be too.

It would have been a dead end if only she remembered that part of her onboarding included a background check.

I wasn't pissed about the amount of energy that I had to expel to catch her only to find out that my intel about her second job had been right all along.

No, I was pissed because I should have known better.

I shouldn't have underestimated her.

The girl who fascinated me more than she should have, the girl who stole my gun, stole my time, and stole my fucking patience was standing in front of me wearing nothing but cheap satin, fishnet, and a goddamn corset.

She belonged to me.

She was mine, and where did I find her?

In a trashy, run-down strip joint dressed like a hooker and selling herself to fucking nobodies.

"Answer me. What the fuck are you wearing, Alina?" I growled again, the warning clear in my tone.

"My uniform." Her breath hitched as I ran my hand from her throat down her body.

Clenching my jaw, I let her go so she could scramble off of my lap.

I stood and took off my suit jacket.

Then lifted it up, offering to slide the jacket over her bare shoulders. "Put this on."

She shook her head, her lips parting as she took a step back and glanced behind her at the heavy, dark-red curtain that separated us from the rest of the club.

She was going to run again.

I wasn't about to let her get away from me this time.

It didn't matter how many games of Durak I won, I would never live a second escape from me down.

"I wasn't asking." My warning clear.

Her sweet lips parted as she took another step away from me. "I don't want—"

Her words fell silent when she turned to look at me and saw the anger in my eyes.

"Don't argue with me," I said, before she could refuse again.

The curtain to the champagne room ripped open and the sleazy manager, Lou something, stormed into the tiny room.

"Alina, where the fuck have you been? The guests need to see your sweet ass out—"

I barely turned my head before pulling my gun and leveling it at the sweaty, obese rat bastard. The click of the safety was deafening in the cramped space, even with the muffled bass from the music playing on the stage.

Her boss's face drained of color as he skidded to a halt.

"Fuck off," I said.

The man raised his hands, his eyes darting between Alina and me. "I was just looking for—"

"I'm coming right out," Alina said.

The fuck she was.

My thumb pressed against the hammer, sliding it back with another audible click, and his words died in his throat.

"Go serve them yourself or find someone else. Alina no longer works for you."

"Wait, no. I'm coming right out, Lou, I promise. Everything is okay."

I didn't know if she was trying to convince him of that, or herself. Either way, she was very wrong.

"I. Said. Fuck. Off," I repeated, aiming the gun at a new spot with every word.

He shook as I started at a kneecap, then his groin, then his heart, before landing on his head.

Lou's eyes went wide, and a dark stain appeared on his pants as he stared directly into my gun. Jesus, he was pathetic.

"Now," I added.

He opened his lips to say something, then thought better of it. He practically tripped over himself as he turned to run, pawing the curtain back and forth in a struggle to find the opening.

Despite Alina's wide-eyed protests, he was gone, and now it was just the two of us.

"Please. You don't have to do this."

I tilted my head, looking at her still not wearing the jacket I had offered. I pressed it toward her again and this time she took it, her hands shaking as she wrapped it around herself.

"What exactly do you think I'm doing?"

Her throat bobbed, and she pulled the lapels closer together to cover her body.

I gave her a slow, deliberate once-over.

The jacket was far too big on her frame. It swallowed her, hiding everything that I wanted to see.

"Killing me." Fear filled her eyes, but she didn't look away from me. She was terrified, but brave. Far braver than her boss.

"Well," I said casually, as I sat back down in that cheap pleather chair. "That is certainly one option."

She stiffened and I could practically see her mind race as she tried to figure a way out of this.

"I know there are those who would prefer it if I were to kill you. It would be quick, clean, and you would no longer be an inconvenience."

It was kind of amusing watching her eyes dart around. I could see her heart racing in the vein at the base of her neck and a fresh sheen of sweat made the skin of her brow shine.

"Killing you is definitely on the table, but I am entertaining…other options."

God, taunting her was so much fun.

She stood there shaking as she weighed her options, and I couldn't wait to see what she was going to do next.

"Give me money," she blurted out.

Out of all the things that she could have possibly said, those words hadn't even crossed my mind. Maybe that was what I was so enthralled by with my little kitten. She kept me guessing. It was refreshing.

Everyone else was so predictable. So boring.

"What?"

"I just need enough to leave town. You'll never see me again. I won't be an inconvenience at all. It will be like we never met." The words tumbled out of her lips and slammed into me like bricks.

Never see her again?

Like we had never met?

The idea tightened my chest, my heart beating a little faster.

My teeth ground down, and my fists tightened over the arms of the chair.

That was not a fucking option.

Alina was a loose end. Loose ends didn't survive in the Russian mafia.

I knew this. Killing her was the best option. Her suggestion, the second best...though it was missing an element of mutual destruction.

Still, after what she saw, paying her off wasn't enough.

There was too much at stake, too much damage she could do if she talked to the wrong person.

I could analyze it all day, but I knew that wasn't the real reason I wasn't going to let her go.

I leaned back, spreading my arms along the top of the low chair and kicking my legs out, making myself comfortable. "No."

Her face crumpled. "Please."

"I do so love it when you beg. Maybe I'll consider it. If you dance for me."

She blinked at me, stunned for a moment. "What?"

"You heard me," I said.

The corners of my lips pulling into a sly smile, I

gestured to the small, raised stage surrounded by mirrors. "You want me to consider paying you and letting you go. I want a dance. Maybe you'll convince me the world would be a dimmer place without your beauty to illuminate it."

Her eyes widened again, the tops of her cheeks flushed, and her lips parted. Teasing her was just too much fun.

Alina shook her head violently, her brown curls bouncing around her face, the sweet scent of her shampoo filling the room. "No, I'm not one of the—"

As she argued, I picked up the remote for the sound system off to the side and made my selection. The first twangs of a familiar song drifted from the speakers behind her.

Bruce Springsteen's *I'm On Fire*.

I gave her a cocky smirk.

She was stuck.

There was no escaping this.

The sooner she realized it, the easier her life was going to be.

I had caught her.

She was mine. That meant she was going to do as I demanded.

"Dance."

Alina hesitated for a moment. Then her eyes flicked down to the gun that was resting on my thigh, my hand still gripped around the base, my finger laying along the slide.

Fear flickered across her features. Her hands trembled at her sides, but she lifted her chin and swallowed before stepping onto the platform.

The only sound in the room was the music coming from the speakers, and the low thump from the music outside the curtain. Otherwise it was quiet.

I didn't want it too loud. I wanted to see if I could hear her heart race from across the tiny room.

The bass line thumped softly, hypnotic and compelling as she tentatively lifted her arms, unsure of the movements or what to do. Then her hips swayed. It was barely noticeable at first, my jacket hiding most of her movements, but she followed the rhythm of the music.

As the music pulsed through the room, something changed. Her eyes closed briefly, surrendering to the rhythm despite herself. My gaze locked on the gentle sway of her hips, the way her throat worked as she swallowed nervously. Despite her fear—or perhaps because of it—my cock strained against my pants, demanding attention I refused to give it. Not yet.

Watching her dance was exquisite torture. Each small movement revealed another glimpse of the curves I intended to claim. The slight arch of her back, the way she bit her lower lip in concentration—all of it stirred something primal in me. The way she moved wasn't practiced like the whores in this place. It was innocent, vulnerable...and infinitely more arousing.

Her moves were clumsy, unpracticed. I got the distinct impression that she was just copying moves she had seen the other girls do.

There was something about that fact that pleased me. I didn't want to know that other men had seen her dance for them. I should be the only one ever seeing her like this.

My body ached with the need to touch her, to pull her down onto my lap and hold that heat against me. But I restrained myself. This game was too delicious to rush.

I tilted the gun slightly, making sure she knew it was still in play.

"The jacket," I demanded, my voice rougher than I intended.

Her fingers clenched the fine Italian fabric and her breath came out shallow. Slowly, achingly slowly, she slipped the jacket from her shoulders and let it fall to the floor.

I could see more of her body move now, the thigh highs and tight shorts leaving absolutely nothing to the imagination. My mouth went dry at the sight of her curves, fully revealed in the dim light. My gaze trailed hungrily over her exposed skin, lingering on the swell of her breasts against the cheap corset. My hand tightened on the gun, knuckles white with the effort of restraining myself.

It still wasn't enough.

"More," I demanded, the word coming out like a growl.

A stifled sob escaped as she reached behind her back, fumbling with the corset strings. Then she turned her back to me and I realized they weren't the corset strings at all. She'd tied the cheap satin together with what looked like shoelaces.

What the hell kind of establishment was this?

As she struggled with the makeshift ties, my eyes traced the delicate curve of her spine, the soft dimples at the small of her back. Heat pooled in my groin, my cock throbbing painfully as I imagined pressing my lips to each vertebra, working my way down her body until she trembled beneath me.

Her shoulders shook and her hands trembled, but eventually she got it, and the corset slipped lower.

"Turn around," I prompted, my heart racing with anticipation.

She did as I demanded. As she faced me, her hands gripped the cheap satin and held it to her chest.

My expression darkened, and the way she took a shaky step back told me she picked up on it.

"Let it go."

Her eyes slid closed for a moment as she sucked in a deep breath and then let the cheap satin fall to the floor.

Her arm snapped back to cover her full breasts. I only caught a hint of a pale pink nipple, but even that glimpse sent a jolt of pure desire through me. My breathing quickened, nostrils flaring as I took in her scent—fear mingled with something else, something sweet and undeniably feminine.

"Put your hands over your head."

She hesitated.

"That wasn't a request, *moy kotyonochek*." My voice hardened nearly as fast as my cock did.

Tears slid down her cheeks as she raised her arms, her pale pink nipples tightening in the cold air, goosebumps scattered along her skin. I ached to taste them. The sight of her bare breasts, perfectly sized for my hands, made sweat break across my brow. I wanted to capture those tears with my tongue, taste the salt of her fear before claiming her mouth.

"Now the shorts."

God, this woman was going to look so fucking beautiful stretched out bare in my bed.

She sucked in another deep breath, lifting her tits up further in the air.

This time, she didn't hesitate. Her thumbs went to the tiny shorts and hooked into the waistband, and she slid them down her hips and over her thighs until she stood there in nothing but the thigh high fishnets, a garter, heels, and a thong.

The sight of her nearly naked body sent a surge of lust through me, so powerful I had to grip the chair to keep from lunging at her. My gaze devoured every inch of exposed flesh—the gentle curve of her stomach, the flare of her hips, the soft mound barely concealed by thin fabric. My mouth watered, imagining how sweet she would taste against my tongue, how her thighs would tremble as I forced them apart.

"Kick them to me," I demanded, my voice husky with need.

She looked so fucking perfect bared to me.

Visions of her nude like this down on her knees, choking on my cock like she had last night flashed through my mind.

Had she been a good girl and stayed, I would have taken her back to my hotel room.

Spread her out in my bed and had her over and over.

By the time I was finished, she would have had a new meaning for the word satisfied.

She hooked the toe of her shoe into the black fabric and kicked them to me. The shorts slid across the floor. I stood and Alina moved back, her ass hitting the mirror behind her.

Without taking my eyes from her, I bent down and picked up her clothes, then tossed them through the curtain into the main bar area, before snagging my suit jacket and shrugging back into it.

Her eyes widened, and her jaw dropped in horror.

"You bastard!" she hissed.

I smirked.

"Now that my little kitten has no fur, I think she'll be much more cooperative."

Her body tensed, then coiled like a spring.

She lunged for the curtain to get to her clothes, but I was faster.

My hand snapped out, wrapping around her delicate throat before I yanked her body back to mine.

Her bare skin pressed against my suit, my breath hot against her ear.

The softness of her curves against me, separated only by the thin fabric of my shirt, nearly undid my control. Her pulse hammered against my palm, her skin hot and alive beneath my fingers. Every breath she took, every tremor that passed through her body, elevated the experience.

"Careful," I whispered, tightening my grip. "I'm not a patient man."

She struggled in my grip, her teeth gritting as she tried to get away from me. The friction of her body against mine only inflamed my desire further, my erection pressing insistently against her hip.

I tsked. "You're going to learn to behave one way or the other."

"Get off of me," she grunted.

"Not until you learn what it means to be mine."

I reached for my belt.

She wanted to learn the hard way, and I was happy to teach her.

CHAPTER 11

PAVEL

"*P*ut your hands on the table," I demanded, and Alina froze against me.

"What are you going to do?" she whimpered.

"You ran from me last night. And even now, when I have you trapped, you fight me." I brushed her hair to one side of her body, revealing her breast to my gaze in the mirror.

Her soft skin and delicate curves were a contrast to the hard lines of my black suit.

"You haven't quite grasped the severity of your situation," I said, placing my hand on her hip and running my fingers from the cheap fabric of her garter up to the soft skin of her stomach.

I traced the line of her curves. The hollow of her stomach was a little concerning, but not surprising. Any woman having the money for a good meal wouldn't be working here.

Slowly, methodically, I smoothed my fingers up

higher, over her rib cage to the swell of her generous breasts.

"What are you going to do to me?" she said with a gasp as her nipple hardened even more under the attention of my fingers.

"Whatever I want," I answered honestly, and a low whimper sounded in the back of her throat. "Right now, I need to make sure you understand what happens when you are a bad girl."

Her lids sank closed for a moment, and I studied her expression in the mirror. Her fists were clenched at her sides and her thin stomach flexed. She was scared and trying desperately not to show it.

She was so brave. Too bad it was too late for that to help her.

Her wide, shimmering brown eyes flashed open and darted to the mirrors lining the wall, focusing on her own reflection, as if she could somehow disappear into it. She gave a tiny, barely perceptible shake of her head.

A silent plea on her lips.

Soon she would realize the only plea I would ever accept would be the one where she begged for more.

I exhaled, slowly and deliberately, as I unbuckled my belt with an unhurried flick of my wrist.

The soft leather slid free, the sound slicing through the thick pulsing tension in the room. "I won't repeat myself, *moy kotyonochek*. The more you fight it, the worse it'll be."

She let out a tiny whimper, still staring at herself in the mirror. Still not moving.

"But by all means," I leaned down and whispered in her ear, "let's make this much, much worse."

Her breath came in short, uneven gasps as she turned, her movements stiff and mechanical as she pressed her palms against the cool wood of the low table.

The muffled bass from the club beyond the curtain, more noticeable now that our sound system fell silent, was a constant reminder of how exposed we were.

Although I knew no one would dare enter.

Not unless they wanted a bullet between the eyes.

Her back arched down in a graceful slope, as she bent practically in half to rest her weight on her palms.

The tiny black G-string was the only thing preventing me from seeing her pussy and that tight little hole between her cheeks.

I stepped behind her, absorbing the sight of her submission—or at least what she was willing to give for now. I would break her soon enough.

Her feet were together, her thighs tensed and clamped closed, as if that was going to save her. With her head angled up as it was, her hair fell over each of her shoulders, shielding her breasts, and her eyes never left my reflection, tracking my every expression and movement.

Good. Let her see my appreciation, my hunger for her body. Let her see what was coming. It wouldn't stop a damn thing.

I lifted the belt, folded it in half and then ran the smooth edge down the center of her back, tracing the delicate curve of her spine.

She shivered, but refused to make a sound, or look away.

My little kitten was still trying to act brave.

"You were a very bad girl," I said, dragging the leather

lower, just along the small of her back. "You were told to stay where you were. Instead, you disobeyed my command, running from me like that last night. And you took something that wasn't yours."

Alina's shoulders tensed.

"I'm sorry," she whispered. Her words were sweet, innocent, and so very fake. She wasn't sorry, yet. But she was about to be.

"And what are you sorry for?"

"Taking the gun and running?"

"Oh?" I taunted. "Not sorry for hiding in a closet?"

I pressed the belt flat against her lower back, the slight tremble in her frame sending small vibrations through the leather. From the way she clenched her fists against the wooden table, she seemed to be bracing for the inevitable.

"That too," she gasped. "I'm sorry I ever took that job."

"That's not good enough. You and I have a little problem, Alina," I said, caressing the soft leather over the tight swell of her ass.

"No, we don't." Her voice quivered, even though the sound was barely more than a whisper. "I promise I'll be good. I won't tell anyone."

I leaned down, letting my lips graze the shell of her ear. "You saw something you shouldn't have seen."

Her breath hitched. She held it for a moment before letting it go in a shaky exhale. I ran my hand over the impossibly soft skin of her hip, loving the way she flinched under my touch but already knew enough not to pull away.

"And now," I continued, keeping my voice soft, but my

tone firm like silk-wrapped steel. "Now it's my job to do something about that little problem."

I stared at her reflection as she squeezed her eyes shut again and another tear fell, leaving a gray, mascara-stained trail down her cheek.

I reached out and caught it with my thumb, tracing that damp path. A gentle touch. A touch that from another man would soothe, would show some type of caring affection.

That wasn't what I was doing.

"Shhh," I cooed, my grip tightening around her hip just enough to remind her who was in control. " I'm not going to kill you…yet."

Her entire body stilled. I wasn't sure if it was fear, anticipation, or maybe something else?

I straightened, gripping the belt once more. Her bare thighs clenched in her fight against that instinct to run from me.

"Do you want to live, Alina?" I asked, stroking the belt over her delicate flesh.

She mumbled something.

"I can't hear you. Do you want to live?" I dragged the belt against the backs of her thighs, her muscles twitching in response.

"Yes, I want to live."

"Good girl, then take your punishment."

My hand snapped forward, and the belt cracked across her ass, leaving a beautiful pink stripe.

She cried out, arching forward, her nails digging into the wood.

I tilted my head, admiring the instant blush blooming

across the pale skin of her ass, and when I looked into the mirror at her, the same blush graced the tops of her cheekbones.

I left stripe after stripe across her ass cheeks and her thighs, but it wasn't enough. I wanted to leave more marks on her lower back, but that fucking G-string and garter were in the way. With one hand, I reached out and grabbed the flimsy fabric and ripped it from her body.

She had been hiding secrets.

That flimsy little G-string pulled away from her and it was soaked.

Alina would never admit it. She didn't need to; her body revealed all of her shameful little secrets. She liked this, or at least a part of her did.

I held the damp panties up to my nose, breathing in the sweet musky scent that was all her arousal, then tucked the fabric into my pocket for later.

My attention back on her, I left another series of lashes across her body.

God, I wanted to take out my cock and fuck her right there. Hard and fast until she screamed my name so loudly the entire building knew she was mine.

But I didn't.

The first time she came on my cock, I wanted her looking me in the eye and begging for it.

Part of me wanted to shield her from prying eyes, yet here I was, marking her in this semi-public space. The contradiction gnawed at me, but my need to dominate her overrode everything else.

A drop of arousal slid down her pussy lips, glistening in the low light, and my cock demanded I take her. She was ready. She needed to be fucked hard. Alina needed my cock deep inside her, and she needed it strong and brutal.

Instead, I grabbed the gun. The long, thin barrel would work perfectly. I stood behind her and waited for those beautiful, gold-flecked eyes to open and watch me again.

When she looked at me, she moved to stand, and I put my left hand on her back to keep her in position. I lifted the gun with my right and showed her the barrel.

Her eyes went wide as I lowered it and placed the muzzle against her soaked opening.

She shook, and her thighs trembled as she started to cry again.

"Push back onto the gun," I demanded.

She shook her head no.

"It wasn't a question. Do it now."

She pushed back a little, then leaned forward. The barrel barely breached her lips. I doubted it went inside of her.

"Take it all. You can do it, or I can fuck you with it. I would hate for my fingers to get slippery."

Her shoulders trembled and she pressed her lips tight to stop another sob from breaking free.

To my complete fascination, she pushed back. The muzzle disappeared deep inside her, then she rocked forward.

Fuck, this was the hottest, most fucked-up thing I had ever seen.

"Spread your legs," I demanded, kicking her feet apart. "I want you to take it all and take it deep."

The movement lowered her body a few inches but put

her hips in a much better position. Her ass cheeks spread wide, and I could see everything. Everything from her tight little puckered hole to her cunt greedily pulsing around my gun.

God, this greedy little pussy was going to feel so good milking my cock.

She could fight it all she wanted, but I knew the truth.

My babygirl liked this. I needed to be sure she couldn't deny it later. The shame needed to mark her, just as intensely as my belt had. I angled the gun down so the muzzle pressed against her G-spot. She was going to come apart for me.

I knew the second I had the gun in the right position.

Alina's body shuddered with a deep moan she wasn't able to hold in.

"That's right, fuck this gun, pretend it's my cock pushing deep inside you."

Her face screwed up tight, her lips clamped together, and her nails pressed little divots into the cheap wood varnish on the table.

"I think you would prefer my cock, wouldn't you? You swallowed it so well last night. If you had done what you were told, I would have let you have it. Now you have to earn the privilege of my cock."

I knew she was getting close.

"Show me how badly you want it. Show me you can be a good girl and earn it."

She pushed back harder, her juices dripping onto my hand. The smell of her sweet sex was maddening. I wanted to drop to my knees and lick up every drop. But I meant what I said. She was going to have to earn it.

Instead, I ran my hand over the curve of her ass, her skin still hot from the spanking she endured. Her back arched harder and when I pressed my thumb into a particularly red-hot spot, she pushed back onto the gun harder.

It was like the pain spurred her on, making her work harder for the pleasure. I was going to have to remember that.

When she came, it was with a shuddering scream that bowed her back. Her lips parted and her eyes were wide open, staring straight into mine.

I knew my reflection revealed the hunger in my eyes to her, the demand for more.

Keeping the gun buried deep inside her, I reached forward and grabbed her hair, pulling her back hard enough she had to arch her back. Her shoulders almost reached my chest.

Slowly pulling the gun out, I leaned forward and traced the shell of her ear with my tongue, making her shiver.

"If you want to live, you have to learn how to obey. Can you do that? Can you be my good girl?"

She nodded.

It was time to move, time to utilize a necessary tool for what came next.

No one could see her face when I moved her.

I released her hair and after tucking the gun away, pulled the hood out of my back pocket and swept it over her head.

CHAPTER 12

ALINA

*E*verything went black.

I screamed, but it was muffled by the thick fabric covering my face.

I might as well have been crying out underwater.

The hood blocked out all light and most sound.

The fabric didn't cut off all my air, but I had to strain to get oxygen in, my head swimming with the effort.

Or maybe that was panic? I didn't know.

Pavel was still behind me, his body pressed to mine, against the hot, painful welts left by the belt's sting.

The pain was a godsend.

It grounded me. Told me which way was up, and that I was still alive. I was in danger, but I was alive. As long as I drew breath, even if it was thick and smelled of my shame, there was a way out.

Temporarily deprived of my sight, the mirror was of no use in helping me figure out what he was doing. That somehow made everything so much worse when he secured what felt like a buckle around my throat.

I raised my arms to undo it, my fingers clawing at the straps to rip it free from my throat so I could breathe.

He quickly wrenched my hands down, pulling them behind my back and securing them with something cold and hard that bit into the delicate skin of my wrists.

Fear clawed through me as I tried to fight him, tried to pull my wrists away, but it was no use.

He'd handcuffed me!

I screamed out in frustration and fear, and I swore I could hear his low laugh, muffled by the hood.

"Calm yourself, little kitten. You'll only make it worse. You can't stop this, so you may as well enjoy it." His voice sounded so far away.

Then his hands were on me, pulling my head to the side so he could press his face to the hood.

I could just make out his muffled words from the other side of the thick fabric, but it didn't distract me from his hands running from my back, up my arms and around to my breasts where he pinched my nipples, sending a sharp shock of pain through me and straight to my still-pulsing core.

"I know you enjoyed coming on the gun you stole from me. I can see how wet your cunt is, and you completely lost yourself to the adrenaline and fear."

He'd found the gun. Which could only mean one thing: he'd not only been to my apartment but had searched through my meager possessions to find it.

"No," I denied. Over and over, I rejected his words and the truth they held.

Seconds later, I was lifted off the floor.

His broad, warm shoulder pressed into my soft skin as my body was turned upside down.

He threw me over his shoulder like I was a sack of potatoes or something. Blood rushed to my head, and my ribs ached with every step he took, jostling me around.

Oh, my god. Oh, my god.

He was carrying me out of the club—naked and handcuffed.

Everyone was going to see the evidence of what we had done... no, what he had done to me.

My ass was still hot from the belting, my thighs still wet from what he had done with the pistol. It didn't matter how hard I clenched my thighs together, they would know.

Panic clawed its way up my chest when I realized it didn't matter what they saw.

It was going to be the last they ever saw of me.

Pavel was taking me to a second location.

I had listened to enough true crime podcasts to know what that meant.

There was absolutely no way this ended well for me.

All the times I had cursed my wretched lot in life crashed over me. But no matter how bad it sometimes got, I wanted to live. I didn't want to die in some ditch, discarded like trash. That was not how I was going to die, at least not without a fight. I thrashed and kicked, but it only earned me a sharp smack on my already sore ass.

"No," I cried out, ignoring the pain and the way the hood over my head muffled everything. He probably couldn't hear me, but I didn't care. I had to try. "Please, my grandmother depends on me. I have obligations, responsibilities. You can't do this. My grandmother needs me."

Breath sawing in and out of my lungs, I tried to kick out, succeeding only in prompting his arm to tighten around my knees, pressing my legs to his body.

I tried using my shoulders and what little core strength I had—anything to make it impossible for him to keep a hold on me, but it didn't matter.

My skin was suddenly covered in warm fabric before a rush of cold air hit me.

He was taking me outside.

Muffled voices reached me through the hood over my head, but the words were indiscernible.

Then I was tossed onto a car seat, the leather soft and cool against my bare skin. It even soothed the fiery heat across my ass. The hood felt tighter; the way I landed pulled at the buckle around my throat.

It became harder to breathe. Beads of sweat ran down my face, stinging my eyes as I tried to wriggle myself to the other side of the car.

The seat below me vibrated as the engine started, and the doors all slammed shut with deafening thuds. Someone was in the back with me as the car pulled away.

There was no escape.

Despite that, I tried to talk, to plead, to beg for my life. I couldn't make out any response.

"Please, I'll do anything. Please, don't kill me."

Warm hands wrapped around my ankles, and I was pulled back across the seat.

Then, I was lifted onto a lap and forced to straddle a man's hips.

I thought it was Pavel, but there was no way to be sure.

I could barely smell some kind of cologne through the hood, but I wasn't sure if it was Pavel, or his cologne still on my skin, or even the hood itself.

The only clue I had was the hard cock, barely contained by his pants pressing between my thighs.

Warm breath ghosted over my throat, and then—a wet mouth was on my nipple, sucking and pulling at the sensitive flesh gently, almost reverently.

I lurched backward, trying to break contact, ignoring the way my blood heated at the touch.

The move cost me a hard slap to one breast, then the other, before a hand grabbed the collar holding the hood to my throat and pulled me back against my assailant.

I felt rather than heard the growl vibrate through his chest. His hands dropped down and gripped my waist, strong and possessive.

It was Pavel.

It had to be.

No other man could growl like that and have my body respond with tight, hard nipples, softening stomach muscles, and a warming core.

The man was dangerous, depraved, and had a control over my body that defied logic and every survival instinct I had.

Why did that thought calm me?

Why did it matter?

The mouth returned to my breast, his lips, teeth, and tongue sucking and nipping at the puckered flesh while his thumbs rubbed small circles on my hips, making my body buzz with heat.

It was strange to be unable to see or hear and be left only with touch.

His warm hands running up my back.

His hot mouth on my breast and the subtle growl as he pressed his cock against me.

My body pressed down.

I didn't mean to.

I didn't want to, but still my hips rocked, looking for the friction that would satisfy us both.

My mind spiraled in a thousand directions. Was this it? What was he planning on doing to me? Was he planning on fucking me before he killed me? Was he planning on keeping me? If he kept me, what would he do with me?

Surely, he didn't need me to be some kind of arm candy or bed warmer.

Pavel was attractive, powerful, and seductive.

If the whispers from the other cleaners were true, then he could get any woman he wanted. Willingly.

Why would he take me? Why was this happening to me? What was he going to do?

The more thoughts that raced through my mind, the harder it was to breathe.

A cold sweat broke out over my back as I tried to slow my thoughts.

My skin was over-sensitive, every soft touch of air, every shift of the car, every movement of his hands or his tongue against my flesh—it was all too much. Too overwhelming.

I wanted to scream but couldn't.

I wanted to fight past him, but there was nowhere to go.

There was nothing I could do but endure and pray for a quick end.

Would some poor, unwitting soul come across my body in a year chained in some long-forgotten basement when Pavel tired of me? Or would he do something else, something as threatening as making me fuck a gun, but that ended in death before the orgasm?

Was this how I died?

In some kinky fantasy that could only be born in the mind of a madman, the brain of a monster?

Something pushed inside of me.

I stiffened. It was thicker than what I experienced before, still firm, but more giving, and warmer.

When it curled to press into my G-spot, I realized it was his fingers and not his gun again, or some other weapon. Still, his fingers were merciless, the way they stretched me, pressed in deep and rubbed the most sensitive parts of me.

Once more, I held my breath.

Before, I had feared losing my virginity to a weapon.

Now, I feared he would discover I was untouched.

He was going to feel how innocent I was, and I didn't know how he would react.

Would it make things worse?

Men like him valued virgins in the world of sex trafficking.

Would he keep me alive just to sell me?

I didn't know what would be worse—being killed and left like trash on the side of the road, or being sold into sexual slavery.

Tears soaked the hood's fabric as my body betrayed me

by tightening around him, my arousal coating his fingers, making them slick and their intrusion so much easier.

He said something. The rumble of his voice pressed into my breast before his teeth pressed into my skin. I had no idea what he said. A part of me was desperate to know.

Did he call me his good girl again? Did he say something about the way I took his punishment? Or did he like the way my pussy was pulsing around his fingers? Had he figured out that his gun was the first thing that had ever penetrated me?

Why did this damn hood have to be so thick?

With a shaky, hard-won breath, I shut those questions down and tried to distance myself from all of this. There was nothing I could do yet. I needed to save my strength.

I tried to think about anything else. The dancers had told me how they survived working in the club, doing the shit the vampires paid extra for by not really being there.

One girl said that while she was on her knees, in her head she was on a beach in the Caribbean sipping on a pina colada. Another said she was at home, in her bed, her kid in their own room, safe and asleep. They let their bodies go on autopilot while their minds were somewhere else, anywhere else.

I tried to dissociate.

I tried to think about being anywhere else, to let my mind roam free, but every time I pictured myself somewhere, he was there, too.

He was there, one hand holding a belt, the other between my thighs with three fingers buried deep inside of me, his mouth licking at my breast.

No matter where I tried to be in my mind, Pavel followed me.

I couldn't believe this was happening. How did I end up here, and was there even a single hope of escape?

The car stopped.

Warm fabric was draped around my body, and I was lifted out of the car and thrown over his shoulder again.

I had no idea where we were.

The hood muffled everything but there was no mistaking his arm wrapped around the backs of my thighs, holding me in place.

He stopped and turned around, and by the sudden g-force pressure that made my head swim, my stomach drop, and my ears pop, I assumed we were in an elevator.

His hand moved up higher on my thighs, sliding underneath the fabric he had wrapped me in.

I twisted my wrists, testing the bonds of the handcuffs. There was no escape.

His fingers toyed with the seam of my pussy, just petting the sensitive skin. Warmth and pleasure spread from his touch and shame filled my veins.

It was several minutes before he started walking again. We must have been really high up.

A skyscraper or really any kind of tower meant there were people around. A hotel? An apartment building? Hell, even an office building meant there were people. It was a Wednesday afternoon. There had to be people coming and going.

Right?

Maybe someone would hear me scream?

A kernel of hope blossomed in my chest as I tried to

pull enough air into my lungs to scream. I would only get one good one, so I had to make it count.

Pavel set me on my feet, and my head swam as I struggled to stay upright.

I knew better than to run.

I couldn't see and I had no idea where I was. Instead, I took another deep breath, preparing to let it all out in one horror movie-worthy scream that would shatter his eardrums, curdle the blood of anyone nearby, and call for help.

I had no idea if I could pull that off, but I had to try.

A metal clasp clicked, freeing one of my wrists.

Before I could react, I was shoved backward. The air being pushed from me was more of a gasp than a scream.

I was on a bed, where firm memory foam cradled my body and silk sheets soothed my heated skin but made crawling away impossible.

He was going to find out I was a virgin; he was going to take that from me, and then he was going to kill me.

Despite knowing it would be muted, I opened my mouth and screamed.

I screamed until my lungs burned and my head swam, and I struggled to get him away from me.

My arms were stretched over my head, and the handcuff was re-secured to my wrist, chaining me to the bed. I pulled, but the chain held strong. I wrapped my hands around the chain to pull it free from whatever held me, but it was no use.

Pavel straddled my hips, pinning me down with his weight.

I held my breath. Tears ran down my face as I tried not to think about what was going to happen.

It was only then that the hood was removed.

It took my eyes several minutes to adjust, and Pavel's face came into view, hovering over mine.

His hands were on either side of my outstretched arms.

He caged me in with his body.

Making sure I knew I was under his control, was his captive.

I was his toy to play with.

"Hello, beautiful," he said with a sinister smile. "Want to play a game?"

CHAPTER 13

PAVEL

"*The* rules are simple. You play nice...and I won't kill you...yet."

I said it with a smirk.

There were so many things swirling in her big, beautiful brown eyes.

Fear and arousal, but I expected those.

The fear was warranted.

Death threats had that effect on people.

Especially people who watched me kill someone right in front of them.

Alina knew I was a cold-blooded killer.

I had earned that fear swirling in her eyes.

In fact, I would say it was right on the edge before turning into pure terror.

The arousal was something I expected, too.

Her body responded to my touch, and although I hadn't intended on touching her in the car, how could any man resist those beautiful tits? I knew how addictive the taste of her kiss was. Those delectable breasts made my cock ache and my mouth water. Soon I was going to know what every inch of her tasted like.

I was going to devour her whole, and she was going to love and loathe every moment of it.

Maybe her nipples being hard had to do with the cold and not her attraction to me, or even the adrenaline and post-orgasm hormones surging through her after her pistol fuck.

But the way her impossibly tight cunt gripped my fingers, how her arousal coated every digit, like thick creamy honey...there was no hiding that.

My sweet captive was just as depraved and fucked up as I was.

She may not have known it yet, but she was absolutely fucking made for me.

There was also something else... panic, maybe? Panic was definitely reflected in her eyes, the golden flecks more pronounced, but there was something more. Something I couldn't quite name.

She rattled the handcuffs. "Let me go, you sick bastard!"

Anger.

I smiled to myself.

Of course. It was anger in her eyes.

Maybe I had pushed her too hard. Or maybe I hadn't pushed her hard enough.

"Tsk, tsk, tsk. That's not playing nice," I taunted as I skimmed my mouth along her jaw. "Maybe I need to show you how."

I bit down on her lower lip, pulling on it, tasting her,

before releasing it. Still straddling her hips, I leaned back to pull a knife from the holder in my boot.

She inhaled sharply.

"Let's see if I can make you more comfortable," I said as I slipped off the bed and stood hovering over her form.

The silk sheets beneath her gleamed in the low light, her pale skin luminous against the dark fabric. Her breasts rose and fell with each erratic breath. Her stomach was sucked in so hard it was hollow. While her fingers, and even her toes, clenched.

Alina was scared. Good. She should be.

Using the blade of my knife, I sliced through the fishnet stockings, stripping them from her body and pulling off the cheap heels. It wasn't until I pulled them off that I realized they were scuffed to hell, the marks haphazardly covered in Sharpie ink.

She was dressed like a street rat. That was going to have to change, and I was just the man for the job.

Or perhaps her new wardrobe should comprise nothing at all. What use did she have for clothes when she was meant to be my fuck toy?

I couldn't for the life of me think of a single reason she needed to leave my bed. The hotel my cousins owned had everything she could need, and it would be brought to her, delivered right outside that door where I would fetch it.

There was no reason she needed clothes or shoes when her entire purpose would be to satisfy my cock.

The dark thoughts twisted inside my mind.

I hadn't brought her here with the intention of keeping her imprisoned, just like I hadn't chased her down in the office with the intent of forcing my cock down her throat... but here we were.

The contradiction gnawed at me. Part of me wanted to shield her from the world's cruelty, yet at the same time I was becoming her greatest threat. She just had to keep running, keep fighting me and making me punish her. Speaking of which...

"What the fuck were you thinking? Working at a place like that?" I demanded, throwing the cut fabric and shoes aside. The shoes landed on the thick carpet with a dull thud as I looked down at her. Her skin erupted into goosebumps as my gaze caressed her form.

Between her job as a midnight cleaner and the fucking strip club, my anger rose.

Did she not know what could have happened to her? A beautiful, innocent woman had no business putting herself in such dangerous situations.

She risked running into murderous sociopaths... like me.

Case in point. She was now chained to my bed, and I had no intention of letting her go.

She licked her full lips.

Tempting the devil.

I was going to taste those sweet lips again very soon. But first I wanted to hear her answer.

"I was thinking I needed to eat and pay rent."

"Well, you don't have to worry about that anymore." I ran the flat of the blade down her body.

Her body jerked as her eyes widened.

I was fully aware she assumed I meant I was going to kill her.

I wasn't going to. At least I was pretty sure I wouldn't.

A better man, a good man, would have reassured her that she would survive our little encounter.

I was many things; a good man was not one of them. In fact, many have called me everything from an evil son of a bitch—which if they knew my mother, was not unwarranted—to a sadistic asshole.

Most of the men who had dared to say such disrespectful things to me were dead. They died slowly and painfully, which may have proved their point.

I was content being a sadistic asshole, and it suited my purposes to keep Alina thinking that her life was on the line. Her fear was sweet, and it brought a serrated edge to her submission that made my mouth water.

It gave me a hunger I was going to satisfy very soon.

I rested the knife on her hip. With her hands handcuffed, it was nothing more than a taunt. A tease. A threat. Keeping my gaze trained on her, I kicked off my shoes and started unbuttoning my shirt.

"You could have worked anywhere. Why there? What did you do for the... patrons of that club?"

I didn't want to know.

The club had a reputation with my men. Velvet Dreams wasn't where you went for a lap dance. It was where you went to get your cock sucked for cheap. The dancers strutted around, and every single one of them was for sale at bargain basement prices.

Apparently, for an extra hundred bucks, a few of the girls would let the men fuck them raw.

More than one of my men had to see the doctor we

kept on staff to treat what they now called the "velvet rash."

Was my girl for sale too? Did she let those dirty fuckers touch her?

I would kill every single man who dared touch her.

"Normal jobs don't pay enough," she said, her voice shaking. "And I don't have the experience they need. I'm just trying to support myself."

"How long?" I asked, undoing another button. Her eyes were focused on my hands as I worked each button free.

"How long what?"

"How long have you been supporting yourself on your back?"

Her brows furrowed in confusion, then cleared as a fire lit in her eyes.

"I am a bartender, not a whore."

"Is there a difference in that place?"

"Yes," she said between clenched teeth.

Maybe it was only because I wanted to, but I believed her.

"Why not? You would make more money that way than emptying garbage cans and slinging stale beer."

"Because that's not who I am," she said, meeting my eye. "Unlike some, I make an honest living."

I tipped my head back and laughed, letting the amusement pour from my lips and my shoulders shake with each chuckle.

She had spirit, I'd give her that.

When I looked back down at her, I slid my shirt off of my shoulders and tossed it to the side.

Her eyes widened at the sight of my tattoos. The

violent imagery sprawling across my chest and arms told their own story of blood and brutality. The look of terror that crossed her face told me she understood exactly what kind of man she was dealing with. I reached for the zipper of my pants.

"An honest living, really? You serve watered-down drinks in a shithole meant to suck every last penny from a bunch of losers to line the pockets of the greedy, and to keep those women addicted to their drug of choice. Where is the honesty in that? Where is the honesty in cleaning office buildings when we both know that every trash can you empty is destroying evidence?"

"I—"

"You are no better than I am, Alina. You think you can look down on me?" I ran my hand over her chest, squeezing her breast until she let out a soft, pained whimper.

"Baby, you are just like me. You may think you can dance in the gray and not get dirty, but by the time I am done with you, you're never going to want to see the sunlight again." I leaned down and took her breast in my mouth, biting on her stiff nipple, loving the way her panting pulled at the sensitive flesh.

Then I stood up straight and fisted my cock.

Tears filled her beautiful eyes and spilled down the sides of her face. Soon they were going to stain my silk sheets.

She was so pretty when she cried. All big shining eyes and pink cheeks.

"Let me go," she gritted out. Her tears told me she was scared, her tone suggested anger. It was adorable.

Ignoring her outburst, I yanked off my pants and Calvin Kleins and moved to straddle her again. Her eyes slid shut as she turned her head away from me, trying to bury it in her arm.

I let my hard cock brush the silky skin of her abdomen.

"Look at me," I demanded.

She kept her eyes squeezed shut and her head turned to the side.

I grabbed her by the throat with one hand while I fisted my cock with the other.

"I said look at me." It was a warning, a threat.

Her lips trembled as she faced me and opened those eyes. I ran my thumb over her lips before pushing it inside her mouth.

"Suck it, like a good girl."

She sniffed, her mouth remaining motionless.

"I said suck it. If you want to live, you will obey me. Obedient girls do as they are told."

Her lips wrapped around the base of my thumb, her hot, wet tongue cradled it as she sucked.

I was already remembering the soft press of her tongue along my shaft from earlier.

Christ, the girl could suck cock.

Her mouth would be on my cock day and night.

She was so fucking good at it, I had to wonder where she had learned.

The thought instantly ignited my jealousy like gasoline on fire.

There was no reason to be jealous of any man between her thighs before me...and yet I was.

I despised any man who knew how talented that tongue was, who knew what her cunt tasted like.

There was no way a man could fuck someone like her and not spend the rest of their life thinking about her every time they jerked off.

Every one of those bastards deserved to die.

Any man who knew what sounds she made when she came apart at the seams deserved a bullet between the eyes.

I couldn't change the past, but I could erase her memory of them.

The only cock she was ever going to ache for, ever dream about, let alone remember, was going to be mine.

Something dark and twisted rose in my chest.

I was overwhelmed with a primal need to fuck her so hard, so fast, so painfully, that all thought of any other man was literally pounded out of her head.

Pulling my thumb from between her lips, I moved down her body, spreading her thighs open with my shoulders. First, I wanted a taste of her sweet cunt. To know what her arousal tasted like directly from the source.

CHAPTER 14

ALINA

$\mathcal{M}$y body trembled as Pavel captured my gaze.

He held me with his dark eyes as his head lowered between my thighs.

A breath caught in my throat as he opened his mouth and pushed his long tongue out, licking the seam of my lips.

The monster was teasing me, toying with his food.

"Stop," I said, the word sounding weak to my own ears.

"Ask nicely," he taunted, lifting just enough that I could see his wicked grin before he made a show of sticking out his tongue and running the point over the seam again, this time pushing in just enough to make my skin erupt into goosebumps.

It wasn't just the tip of his tongue; it was the cool silky sheets at my back, his soft warm skin against my legs. The strength of his hands on my body and his shoulders under me. It was his warm moist breath ghosting across my skin, even the cold metal biting into my wrists somehow adding to everything.

It was all too much and not enough at the same time, and he knew it.

He shouldn't have had this kind of control over me.

"Please," I gasped as he parted my folds with his thumbs, spreading me out for him. Exposing the most vulnerable, intimate parts of me to the cool air.

"Well, when you beg so beautifully, how can I not make you feel good? God, your cunt even smells sweet." He flicked my clit with just the tip of his tongue.

I cried out, and Jesus wept as a shock of pure bliss shot through my body.

What the hell was that? I didn't know he could make my entire body jump with the smallest flick of his demonic tongue. That was it. That had to be it.

He was literally a demon. No mere mortal man should have been able to do that.

I may have been a virgin, untouched until Pavel got me in his sights, but I had heard the stories. Except no one had warned me about that.

He ignored my pleas as I begged him to stop. Over and over again, he stretched out his tongue and flicked my clit while holding me with his dark gaze.

He was enjoying the pleasure and the torment dancing across my features. I tried to school my face, to keep it blank, unaffected, so it wouldn't encourage him. It simply wasn't possible.

The urge to scream overwhelmed me. My hips wanted to buck against his mouth. The sensation was too much, too intense. Every instinct told me to kick him away.

But I couldn't move beyond the trembling that wracked my body.

I wanted to rattle the handcuffs until people in the next room heard. Surely someone would hear? From what I could see of the hotel room it was big, but did not take up the entire floor. The wall behind the bed had to be shared with another room on the other side. Right?

I did none of those things. I couldn't.

He had me right where he wanted me, and I was powerless to escape his pull.

If I kicked him away, or drew the attention of someone else, he could stop. Or worse, he could keep going. I didn't know how I knew, but I was sure this was only the beginning of what he could do to me.

I was locked under his spell.

He tortured me with his tongue, lash after lash, building the most intense and delicious pleasure in my core.

"Please," I chanted, not sure when my begging switched from asking him to stop to urging him to continue. I didn't understand it. I didn't understand how he could make me feel like this when I didn't want to feel like this.

How could he build so much pleasure in my veins, too much pleasure, pleasure to the point I wanted to scream, when I didn't want to be here? Why was my body betraying me?

His eyes slid closed as his devilishly long tongue slid inside of me, tasting where only he had ever even touched.

My eyes rolled to the back of my head and my hips arched up.

It only encouraged him.

He pushed his tongue in deeper then drew it out only to thrust back inside of me.

It was better than the gun, and not just because I wasn't afraid his tongue could kill me. Though that fear added something to it.

This was different from his fingers.

His tongue didn't stretch me to my limits like his fingers did. There was no stinging strain or even the same hard pressure against my G-spot. The pressure built like it did before, but this was different. Better. Less intense yet more overwhelming.

When my thighs trembled on his shoulders, he moved back to licking my clit.

He kept me on the edge of oblivion but never let me tumble over.

He was ruthless. Working me until I was ready to scream and see God just to force me back down to earth, denying me that pleasure.

"Beg," he demanded.

I clamped my jaw shut, refusing.

I was not going to beg for him.

That wasn't who I was.

I was lying to myself. I had already begged him to stop, to never stop, but I didn't want to let him know he was breaking me.

He may have been violating everything I knew about myself, changing me in ways I couldn't understand, but I was not going to give him that.

Not again.

He let out a dark little rumble that I felt as much as heard.

Damn him, that rumble pushed me even higher. Until my thighs ached and I needed it. If he didn't relieve that pressure soon, I was sure my body would just spontaneously combust.

"Beg," he growled again, his intense dark eyes on my face.

There was something so erotic about making eye contact while his tongue was inside me. I just knew that I would remember this moment for the rest of my life. It didn't matter whether I lived only another few hours, or a few more decades. Nothing was going to top this moment.

Every time I closed my eyes, I was going to see those dark eyes staring up at me from between my legs while he held my life in the palms of his hands.

"Please." The words escaped my lips unbidden. I pressed my lips together, sinking my teeth into them to stop them from betraying me like the rest of my body was.

Amusement sparkled in his eyes as he drew my clit into his mouth and sucked, flicking his tongue over the sensitive bud over and over until I gave him the orgasm he demanded.

My back bowed hard enough to lift my shoulders and my hips off of the bed, my weight balanced between my heels digging into his back, and my wrists pulling at the handcuffs.

Even the sharp shock of pain from the metal clamped

around my wrists, radiating down my arms into my spine, just added to the overwhelming waves of pleasure. An edge that seemed to intensify each wave so much more.

I didn't know if I screamed, or if I cried out, or if my beautiful agony was completely silent. I knew that it took what seemed like an eternity for the waves of pleasure to finally subside enough for me to release the tension in my back and land softly back on the mattress.

The moment I did, I was filled with shame.

This man had threatened to kill me...multiple times.

He was a murderer and a villain.

More than that. He'd stripped me of my dignity, forcing me to suck his cock in a dark office. Then he stalked me to my second job, where he bent me over to spank me, tortured me in the most intimate ways, shamed me in front of everyone at that club, and then kidnapped me.

Not just kidnapped me. He put a hood over my head, making sure I couldn't see or hear anything as he paraded my naked form out of the privacy of the champagne room. He only covered me to go outside, and I suspected that was less about my modesty and more about making sure a cop didn't try to take me from him for indecent exposure.

I'd never been so scared in my life.

He pushed me past my limits and there was no sign of him slowing down.

No one had been this controlling, this terrifying in my life. No one had ever stripped me of my agency so completely.

Even when those thugs broke down my apartment door to threaten me over my father's gambling debts.

They allowed me to act as an adult. They pretended like I had some control over my actions, my body. Even as they demanded I pay my father's debts, locking me into a life of misery, but still. They treated me like a person.

Pavel treated me like a thing, a thing he could control, a thing he could steal with no repercussions. And then he showed me how little control I had—not only over what happened to me, but over how I responded.

How was it even possible for me to freaking come? How could he make me feel things that were so depraved and yet so intense? I should have been too terrified to respond to him at all, but here I was. Naked, chained to a bed and instead of shaking in fear, my body was shaking with the aftereffects of the second orgasm he had pulled from my unwilling body.

The man really was sent straight from hell. Another punishment I suffered in place of my father.

My fingers curled into fists as I fought my bindings even as each delicious aftershock rolled through me.

Reality crashed over me when he reared up, keeping my ankles balanced on his shoulders and positioning his massive cock at my entrance.

"My turn."

"Wait!" I cried out, not ready for that, not wanting him to take my last shred of innocence, of dignity.

Maybe if I could tell him before, he wouldn't—

He thrust in deep, cutting off my thoughts completely.

He impaled me on his cock, taking my virginity in one harsh push.

A single intense, white-hot spike of pain tore through me, disintegrating whatever pleasure was still flowing through my veins.

"What the fuck?" He dropped my legs, forcing them apart so he could drape his body over mine, pinning me down as he grabbed my hair and forced me to face him.

"Are you a goddamn virgin?" He growled the question like he was enraged by the anticipated answer.

Probably mad he didn't realize he could have sold me for a higher price.

I was so scared I couldn't answer.

I couldn't confirm what he had just taken from me.

Tears trailed down my face as his features twisted in anger.

I didn't need to answer him.

He pulled out of me, and the evidence was there in the smeared blood on my inner thighs and his cock.

He stared down between us for a moment, then turned back to me.

Slowly, his fury melted away, shifting into something far more sinister, far more dangerous.

Pleasure, pride, and possessiveness masquerading as affection.

"That's my beautiful girl," he purred, leaning down to place a kiss on my neck. "Saving this sweet cunt just for me."

I wanted to scream and yell that it hadn't been for him.

That he had taken something important from me with force.

But I was too afraid of him.

What else was he going to do to me? The way he was

looking at me now was... intense. Not just with desire, but something deeper, more sinister and unhinged. Something closer to obsession.

Bracing his forearm on the side of my head, he leaned down and placed a wet kiss over my nipple. "Brace yourself, baby, this is going to hurt."

My hips bucked as I cried out, "No!".

Ignoring my plea, he thrust in again.

Hard. The pain was still there, still intense, but less so.

This time, he didn't stop. My body rocked with each punishing thrust. The pain morphing into something more. Another sign that I couldn't even control my own body.

All the time, he sucked and bit my breasts while whispering to me in Russian. It was cruel that his deep, guttural voice sounded so fucking sexy. For all I knew, he was telling me all the ways he planned to dispose of my body afterward.

Or he was describing in horrific detail the things he was going to do to me before selling me as a pet to some sadistic animal.

But I couldn't help my response to every guttural word and every kiss or bite to my breasts.

Just like I couldn't help the way my core tightened around him, pulling him back in every time he pulled out. I couldn't help the way the pain had completely dissolved and pleasure took over. Deep-seated, intense pleasure.

Like everything else was to get me ready for this. For his cock to reach the itch inside of me I didn't know needed to be scratched as he pushed in deeper and harder than I thought possible

God help me, I came again.

Screaming as my hips rose to meet his thrusts. Obviously, I had very little sexual experience, but I couldn't imagine anything beating this for its dark intensity.

Everything about this was wrong, but no matter how much my mind screamed that I hated it, my body loved it.

I couldn't deny the way my body tightened around him, pulling him deeper, never wanting to let him go until he gave me what his thick cock promised with every thrust.

It promised more.

More pleasure, more satisfaction.

He ground down, angling his cock to press against my G-spot while he angled my hips so every thrust pressed against my clit as well, making my head spin.

Using both his forearms, he rose above me as he increased the pace of his thrusts.

"That's right. Take it all. I am going to be the first, the only man to come inside this tight little cunt and mark it as mine. You were made for my cock."

"Oh, no! Please don't come inside of me! I'm not on birth control!" I panicked, pushing against his chest, trying in vain to push him away from me.

"Too late, babygirl." He gritted his teeth before throwing back his head.

Veins strained in his neck as he roared something in Russian and came deep inside of me.

I could feel it. Rope after rope of his hot come shooting straight into my womb.

How much worse could this day get?

CHAPTER 15

PAVEL

*F*uck. That was the most intense sex of my life. I thought I knew what a good fuck was, but that had just given me a new high.

I should've known she was going to be spectacular.

After the way she took my cock down her throat, I should've known that was just the start.

And knowing that they were all her natural responses, not ones that were trained over several lovers and tailored to what she thought I wanted, but her actual instinctual responses were just...Fuck me.

There was something about knowing that I was the first, the only man who had ever claimed her.

I had planted my flag in uncharted territory.

I was the first and I would be the last.

No other man would ever know the unbridled ecstasy that existed between her milky white thighs.

The power of claiming her innocence sent dark satisfaction through my veins.

Feeling her tight, virgin body fight against me just to give in to my power.

No, she didn't just give in to me. She got off on it.

I made that virgin pussy come… again.

It tried to fight me just to be consumed by me.

God, she was so fucking tight, her muscles gripping me like a fist as she went from trying to keep me out to pulling me in deeper.

Fuck if that didn't make a warm pride settle in my stomach and my spine straighten so I would stand a little taller.

I still wasn't sure what I was going to do with her, but one thing was certain.

I wasn't giving her up anytime soon.

Before, I was mostly joking about leaving her naked and chained to my bed.

But the more I thought about it, the more I thought it was a good idea.

I couldn't just let her go. She was a liability, and I was having way too much fun.

Lifting off the bed, I left her still panting, my come leaking from her freshly fucked cunt. God, she looked so perfect lying there trying to catch her breath and wrap her mind around what had just happened.

What happened was simple, sweetheart. You became my new fixation.

I padded into the bathroom and ran the bath, filling the large porcelain tub with steaming water and adding an obscene amount of bubble bath. Then I rummaged in the bag I'd purchased earlier while I hunted her down.

After that incredible blow job, I knew I couldn't just scare her into submission or kill her.

Well, I could've, but it would've been such a waste.

Even before I knew her skill was more of a natural talent, I had already planned on capturing and playing with my new pet.

New pets required new toys.

From the same store I purchased the sensory deprivation hood to cut off her ability to scream or hear, I got a whole slew of toys that I planned on exploring with her.

I opened the plastic packaging that held a mid-size metal butt plug and placed it on the edge of the tub. Had I known she was innocent, I would have gotten a smaller one, but she could take it.

It wasn't too long, and at its thickest, it was still smaller than my cock.

I moved it to behind a candle. Not wanting her to see it before I was ready.

The tub was full, and fragrant bubbles spilled over the rim, filling the bathroom with the scent of vanilla and amber. I lit the three candles perched on the corners of the tub and dimmed the light.

It was time to retrieve my new toy.

She had curled up in the fetal position. It was awkward, given her arms were still stretched over her head. The sight tugged at something unexpected in my chest—an unfamiliar discomfort that I quickly pushed aside. I didn't care that she was crying, emotionally wrecked after I stole her virginity.

What bothered me was seeing her uncomfortable.

The contradiction annoyed me. I'd just brutally

claimed her virginity yet seeing her in pain from the restraints made me want to fix it.

Her ass still showed the marks from my belt, beautiful pink lines crossing in intricate patterns. The top of her right breast held the impression of my bite mark and her thighs showed the shadow of a bruise. I liked that.

I liked that she wore my marks, not just the lashes from my belt, but the bruises from my bite.

Considering she was a virgin, I had definitely played a bit rough.

Guilt—an emotion I rarely entertained—crept up my spine. I shoved it down, focusing instead on what came next.

Unlatching the handcuffs, I swept her into my arms.

She whimpered as her head fell back against my chest. "Please, no more."

"Shhhh, I'm going to make it all better," I comforted, holding her to my chest as I took her into the bathroom.

The massive two-person marble tub full of hot water and suds seemed to glow in the dim candlelight. The bubbles almost sparkled.

I stopped for a moment and set her on the edge, testing the water temperature to ensure it wouldn't scald her delicate skin. It was hot, just on the verge of scalding. Not hot enough to burn for more than a moment. If anything, it would soothe her muscles.

Picking her back up, I stepped over the edge with her still in my arms. There was plenty of room to put her on the other side of the tub or even next to me. I didn't want her next to me; I wanted her close, skin to skin. My instincts demanded I hold her, or she might just slip away from me.

I settled her on my lap with her back resting against my chest.

She hissed in a breath as I lowered her into the water, but after a moment, her body relaxed against mine.

Alina's head rolled to the side, her eyes closed.

No doubt she was exhausted.

She did good.

She took her punishment well and then took my cock even better.

Good girls got rewarded, so I would let her rest... for now.

I lifted the natural sponge from the side of the tub and took my time washing the day from her body. I started with her shoulders, massaging them in slow, even circles. Then I moved down her chest and swept the sudsy sponge over her breasts.

Her lips parted with a small gasp, but her eyes didn't open.

I took my time letting the bodywash and sponge glide over her wet skin, leaving a trail of bubbles glittering in the low light.

I knew her breasts were sensitive. I wondered if I could make her come just by teasing these delectable mounds? I bet she would love it when I slid my cock between her tits, fucking them before spraying all over her face.

I moved the sponge down to her stomach, washing away the sweat, dirt, and stench of that fucking club from her skin, then moved down between her legs.

She hissed another breath between her teeth and her thighs snapped closed.

I tugged on a lock of her hair.

"Open," I said in her ear, a quiet demand, but a demand all the same.

With another low whimper, she let her thighs fall to the sides, opening for me. I swiped the sponge over her swollen and sore pussy.

I considered rubbing her clit again, this time in slow, soothing circles to guide her to a gentle, relaxing orgasm, but decided not to.

Good girls got rewarded, but she was going to have to prove herself a lot more before I spoiled her.

I'd let her rest for now.

I kept my movements gentle as I washed away my seed from her delicate flesh and let the warmth of the water soothe away some of her ache.

Once she was clean, I set the sponge aside and leaned my head back against the rim of the tub. Alina sighed and relaxed against me, our bodies almost melting together as I let the water soothe her while her small body resting in my arms soothed me.

The moment was unexpectedly peaceful. Dangerous territory for a man like me.

Almost half to myself, I murmured, "What am I going to do with you now, babygirl?"

She twisted on my lap. I opened my eyes to find her own gaze, heavy-lidded and glassy, on me. "I promise I won't tell anyone anything. Please, you can trust me. Just let me go."

I stroked her cheek, leaving a trail of soapy bubbles on

her face. "That's not an option. Even if it was, I don't want to."

Her eyes filled with tears. This time, she didn't let them spill. "Then are you going to kill me?"

I smiled. She was so sweet when scared. "Not yet."

She rocked forward, trying to leave the tub, but I wasn't done yet.

I pulled her back against my chest, stroking her hair as I kissed the top of her head.

"No. None of that. If you're a good girl, this will all work out. Trust me."

I knew there wasn't a chance in hell she'd trust me.

She was innocent, not stupid.

Just like I had no intention of trusting her.

I was a monster, not a moron.

The moment I released her, she would scamper straight to the cops.

I knew she saw me kill that bastard. But there was no telling if she knew who he was, or if she had seen other things. She was a liability. There was no way around it. She would have to be dealt with, but not today.

She shimmied on my lap, trying to get free or comfortable, I wasn't sure which. But she was teasing my cock, rubbing her perfect ass against me. It responded, swelling against her ass, pressing between her cheeks, already up for round two.

I knew the moment she realized what she'd done by her small moan and the way her body tensed.

"Time to be my good girl," I said against her ear before sucking the lobe between my teeth, loving the way it made her shudder.

"Please no. I'm so sore," she whimpered and tried to get up again. She was trapped in my arms, so all she did was splash some water onto the marble floor and rub that sweet ass against my hardening cock.

I whispered against her wet hair. "I promise I won't push my cock into that tight pussy of yours."

Her shoulders relaxed slightly. She trusted too easily.

"Grab the far side of the tub," I said as I grasped her thighs and arranged her body to straddle my hips with her back still turned.

Fuck me, this put her in the perfect position. Her ass sticking up from a sea of bubbles, giving me the perfect view of her puckered opening.

I picked up the metal butt plug and ran it down the center of her back.

She arched into it like a cat. When she tried to turn around and see what I was doing, I grasped her hair to keep her head forward.

"No peeking." I kept running the plug up and down her spine, getting closer to her ass with each pass. With my other hand, I spread her cheeks and leaned forward to run just the tip of my tongue around her tight, puckered hole.

Her entire body went rigid. Then she let out the most adorable moan.

I only teased her for a moment before I replaced my tongue with the plug between her cheeks and teased her ass even more.

"Oh, god! No. Not there," she said as she tried to get away from me.

One firm slap to her ass had her freezing in place.

"When are you going to learn? You're not allowed to tell me no."

Over her objections, I pressed the butt plug deep inside of her. Listening to her objections lessen each time I pressed a little more in and pulled back. It didn't take long until I was able to work the thickest part of the mushroom shape past her tight rim, and the plug was seated tight in her ass.

"Good girl," I praised as I lifted her out of the tub and let it drain. "Now you are going to take a shower, and you are going to wash any trace of that strip club from your body. Do you understand?"

She nodded, her eyes never leaving the floor.

"I'm going to sit right here, and you had better leave that plug where it is. If you try to take it out, or push it out, I will replace it with my cock. Do you understand?"

She nodded again.

I leaned over to turn the shower on.

Once she was inside, I sat down on the bamboo bench across from the glass chamber and leaned back, enjoying the view.

I watched the way her thin, delicate fingers brushed over her body as she cleaned herself. The way she stood under the showerhead with the hot spray aimed at her shoulders.

Every movement was graceful, unconsciously sensual. She had no idea how captivating she was.

When she emerged, I was still naked, sitting on the bench, my cock hard against my stomach and tenting the towel I wrapped around my waist.

I took her hand and guided her to sit on my lap as I

brushed the wet curls away from her cheek. The gesture was surprisingly tender—more intimate than anything I'd done in years.

If I had been anyone else, this would be a perfect moment. The kind that normal couples cherished. If I were a different man, a good boyfriend, this would be the kind of intimacy that would make her swoon.

I was not a good man, and definitely not boyfriend material.

That was the last fucking thing I was.

My cock throbbed as it pushed against the backs of her thighs. It demanded access to her body, to that tight greedy cunt, that still-virgin ass, or even her talented mouth. I wanted to indulge it, but I had work to do.

Alina had already taken up far more of my day than she should've.

I carried her back to the bed wrapped in a warm towel, then tucked her under the covers.

She needed rest.

Then I lifted her arms to the headboard.

She let out a whimper of protest. Despite it, I still re-attached the handcuffs.

She watched me as I held up the hood. Her eyes went wide but were still cloudy with exhaustion. "You don't have to do that. I'll be good. I promise."

Her eyes pleaded with me.

For a moment, I considered it.

Then I shook my head. I leaned down to give her a quick kiss. "Sorry, babygirl, maybe I'll let you earn some freedom later. Right now, this is how it's going to be."

CHAPTER 16

PAVEL

I didn't want to leave her, but I couldn't stay.

I had obligations that required my attention.

My brothers were already here, ready to discuss what they had found.

Neither one of them were staying in the hotel our family owned. They both preferred houses and seclusion for their wives. Maybe they were worried their wives would try to run away again.

I laughed to myself.

Normally, I would've been annoyed that Kostya and Artem just showed up and let themselves into my penthouse. But they had been with me when we found Alina's apartment.

They stayed behind while I hunted her down to find her at that fucking strip club.

They had gathered the fragments of her life, ready to piece together who she was and what they wanted to do with her. A lot of it depended on what they found in her apartment.

Was she spying on us? Did someone send her? Was that why she was at the office when everyone else was told not to come in?

I closed and locked the door behind me.

Alina would be safe in the bedroom.

My brothers wouldn't touch her.

They wouldn't even go to the bedroom.

They had found out the hard way what was in my bed was none of their business. A naked girl chained to the headboard wearing a sensory deprivation hood would be a new level of what they found waiting for me...but not by much.

Whatever we discovered about her life, her motivations, she was my problem to deal with. If they decided she had to go, getting rid of her would be my responsibility.

I also knew there was no way she was getting out of those handcuffs, and she could scream all she wanted. That hood would muffle the sound.

Still, whatever we were about to uncover, I wanted that extra layer of protection between her and the rest of the world.

Kostya and Artem had been waiting a while.

As I passed through the penthouse's dining room, the air was still thick with smoke and the tangy, salty scent of caviar. The remnants of an earlier conversation still lingering, I wondered how much they had brought with them.

I strolled across the open living space, past the dining

room table that hadn't been cleaned. I made a mental note to myself to have the hotel housekeepers come and straighten up while I was here to ensure they didn't go into the master bedroom.

Or maybe I could put Alina in a closet with the hood on while the maid changed the sheets and scrubbed the bathroom. The last thing I needed was some nosy maid looking for shit to pawn to stumble across a naked woman in a sex dungeon hood.

That would cause more problems.

Hell, a maid seeing something she wasn't supposed to was what landed me in this mess in the first place.

I joined Artem and Kostya in the lounge, where the low hum of classical music played in the background, and the sunlight flowed in from the floor to ceiling windows, bathing the room in light.

Both of them were seated on leather couches, wearing custom fitted Brooks Brothers' suits and sipping from dainty porcelain cups, with a full English high tea set up on a cart next to them. They drank their tea while looking over the folders piled on the coffee table in front of them.

Just dignified businessmen having refreshments while looking over a new business proposal.

Fuck that shit.

Before sitting down and joining them in their oh-so-dignified display, I moved to the bar cart and poured myself a drink—vodka, Russian, smuggled, because fuck those tariffs—served neat.

I downed the first glass, the bite of it settling deep in my chest. I closed my eyes and savored the smooth burn, letting the familiar warmth settle me, before pouring a second glass and gesturing toward the boxes on the coffee table. "Are these from Alina's apartment?"

Kostya nodded, his sharp blue eyes flicking up from the documents he was already sifting through. He drank the rest of his tea in a single pull and held out the delicate porcelain cup for me to fill with vodka.

I grabbed a few of the tea sandwiches from the tiered silver tray and brought the bottle of vodka to the table with me.

I hoped Marina knew she was never going to completely civilize Kostya, no matter what she tried. After spending a little time with my sister-in-law, I was starting to think she preferred him a little rough around the edges.

"The boys cleaned it out earlier." His tone was casual, but I knew better. If Kostya had taken an interest, it meant there was something worth finding. They were only supposed to gather everything and make me sift through it.

Part punishment, part responsibility.

The fact that they were still here meant something had caught their attention.

Artem, ever methodical, thumbed through a thick accordion file that seemed to contain financial documents, old receipts, and some legal paperwork, W-2s and the like.

His brows furrowed, his signature frustrated look.

"Not much here. Standard shit. Rent payments, bills, some past-due notices..." He flipped to another section, his expression darkening slightly. "But there's something interesting."

"Student loan debt from Georgetown," Kostya said, inspecting a printed-out schedule. "But she dropped out."

He pulled out a financial aid document, and I snatched it from his fingers.

He kicked a worn-looking bag toward me. Textbooks spilled from the opening.

I picked up the pile of well-used textbooks, skimming their broken and taped covers.

Law and economics.

I started pushing them back in the bag when I spotted something more personal—a stack of photographs wrapped in an elastic band.

Something twisted in my gut.

Personal items always revealed more than financial records ever could.

I tore off the rubber band and flipped through the photos. There was no reason for me to care about these pictures, but something kept me going.

Some nagging sensation in the back of my throat and in my gut told me there were answers here. Answers that I needed.

The first few were innocent enough—Alina as a child, standing uneasily beside an older man with sharp features. He had the same sharp nose she did, the same eyes. Her father, perhaps? He had a large, cheesy grin for the camera and he looked like he would be a normal, caring father. But something was off.

The way Alina positioned herself told a different story.

She was shrinking away from him, like his hand on her shoulder physically hurt her. Even as a child who couldn't have been older than seven, maybe eight, Alina was afraid of him.

The next few photos painted a different story. Her father wasn't in them. In his place was an elderly woman. Alina's grandmother, most likely.

The woman's eyes were kind, her arm wrapped protectively around Alina's shoulders in almost every picture, and Alina looked...content in the first few.

But then her smile widened, and she looked happy.

The transformation was remarkable. Under her grandmother's care, the timid child blossomed.

If I were to guess, I would say the love and attention her grandmother gave her was what she needed to come out of her shell. But as I went deeper into the stack, the images grew...unsettling.

Her father was in more photos, same cheesy smile, but in each photo he was in, Alina's and her grandmother's smiles were tight and didn't quite reach their eyes. In more than a few, the grandmother and Alina wore long-sleeve shirts even though they were outside, while the father wore a T-shirt and shorts.

My jaw clenched as the pattern became clear.

Then there was the one that stood out and made my teeth clench.

Alina looked like she was maybe fourteen. There were banners all around them for the Fourth of July. Some kind of cookout. Her father wore that same stupid grin and a T-shirt.

The grandmother was looking off-camera, unable to smile, and Alina was wearing a long-sleeve shirt with a high neck and her hair down, in front of her eye. I could just see the outlines of a bruise under her hair.

Rage, pure and vicious, surged through me.

If I ever got my hands on the son of a bitch, I was going to kill him.

The pictures got happier again. Alina as an older teenager, in weather appropriate clothing. No bruises and a genuine smile. The grandmother's face looked serene, at peace, but there were shadows in her eyes, and in each picture, she seemed to age faster and faster.

The old woman had sacrificed everything to protect Alina. The toll was written in every line of her face.

I wrapped the rubber band around the pictures again and set them aside, removing more things from the backpack.

My fingers stilled when I found an envelope marked "Evidence." The word was scrawled in bold, jagged hand-writing across the front.

My blood turned cold, and instincts screamed at me as I slid my thumb beneath the flap and began to pull out some of its contents.

Did she work for the feds? She wouldn't have been the first one of our civilian employees to get into trouble with the feds and turned into an informant.

Several years ago, Artem had a gardener that got pulled over for drunk driving, and the police had tried threatening him with everything to turn against the family. Thankfully, he was smart enough to come to us, and it was dealt with accordingly. The gardener never saw the inside of a cell, and the police got absolutely nothing.

163

The few who tried working with the government did not fare as well.

If Alina was working for them...I wasn't sure I could protect her.

Sucking in a deep breath, I held it until my lungs burned, making a silent wish that it wouldn't come to that.

Then I focused my attention on the first photo.

The image made my blood run cold.

Alina stood beside her grandmother again—but parts of the grandmother's face had been burned away in perfect circles. A cigarette had been placed on the photo, blackened holes where the old woman's eyes should have been.

I flipped it over, and my stomach twisted at the words scrawled in red ink.

"Do as you're told, or she's next."

The federal government might be ruthless, but they didn't operate like this. This was personal. Intimate. Designed to break Alina's spirit.

Well, unless the FBI had grown a fucked-up pair of balls in the last few years, I didn't think they were the ones threatening my girl.

Kostya peered over my shoulder and let out a low whistle. "That's not good."

"No shit," I said as he took the photo from my hands, passing it to Artem.

Artem took one long look, then grabbed the envelope from my hands and poured the rest of its contents out onto the table.

We sifted through the remaining pictures.

Each image was a masterclass in psychological torture.

Each photo was worse than the one before it.

Artem's lip curled as he looked through them.

Bile rose in my throat, burning its way up and leaving a sour taste in my mouth as nausea rolled through me.

The methodical cruelty behind each threat spoke of someone who enjoyed the process as much as the result.

Each image we found only added to the growing storm inside me. One photo had Alina's face violently scratched out. Another had her entire head burned away, blackened and distorted, the photo paper melting and twisting.

So many threats, telling her that her debts were due, threatening her grandmother, her life.

More than a few even suggested that if she didn't pay, they would collect what was owed another way.

The worst one made my fingers tighten around the edge of the paper, as red filled my vision.

Someone had cut my sweet girl's face out of another photo and taped it onto the body of a naked, mutilated woman. The carnage was depraved even by my standards. I was no stranger to gore, but the shit we did was to send a message and was never done to women.

Whoever had cut up this woman may have started with that intention, but at some point, they liked it. This wasn't a job, it was the work of a rabid madman who needed to be put down like a dog.

The message on the back was clear.

"You know what happens to disobedient girls."

A red-hot rage pounded through my veins. My grip on

the glass in my other hand tightened until the glass cracked.

Artem exhaled slowly, his fingers tightening around the edge of another particularly disturbing photo. "What the goddamn fuck?" he muttered.

Kostya, ever composed, leaned back in his seat and rubbed his jaw. "Looks like you weren't her first, brother."

"Excuse me?"

At first, my mind immediately—stupidly—went to the memory of taking her virginity, of the feel of my cock crashing through her delicate maidenhead, of her body yielding to mine for the first time.

I knew I had been her first.

There was no denying the way she had clenched around me, the little gasps she had made, the physical evidence.

My possessiveness flared, a primitive response I couldn't control, as my hand tightened into a fist ready to defend her honor.

Then I caught the way Artem bared his teeth in disgust as his eyebrows lowered and seemed to pinch together as he nodded toward the photos, and I realized what Kostya meant.

This wasn't about sex. None of this was about sex.

This was about power.

Control through fear and ownership.

Someone else thought they got to play their sick little games with my girl.

The realization hit me like a physical blow.

Alina had been marked long before I ever laid a hand on her.

Someone was making a claim on what was mine.

And that was unacceptable.

And that made me mad enough to want to burn the entire world to the ground to stake my claim.

I hadn't spent my life clawing my way to the top just for some nameless bastard to think he could touch what was mine. Threaten what was mine.

The glass in my grip shattered. Vodka mixed with my blood dripped down my fingers, but I didn't feel it.

The only thing I could feel was the slow, calculated rage curling its way through my veins.

Kostya set his glass down with a sigh. "Looks like we're not the first dangerous people your girl has pissed off."

"No shit." Artem was still eyeing the photos like they could reach out and pull him into their depravity just by existing. "Looks like they are making her pay a debt."

"Seventy thousand," I growled.

Remembering what she told me last night about her father's gambling and abandonment.

Like the vicious bastard that I was, I'd only been interested in the information to manipulate her into doing what I wanted. Goddammit. I should have asked more questions. At the time I just assumed she was paying back a fucking casino or maybe a credit card company.

And here my sweet little kitten was being threatened by some low-life thugs. Fuck.

The fact that I was also threatening her was different.

These bastards were sadistic animals who got off on terrorizing innocent women.

At least when I used leverage, it served a purpose beyond cruelty.

Kostya shook his head. "I know what we paid her, and the strip club pay was decent considering she wasn't on the pole, and since her grandmother qualifies for assistance the nursing home cost is practically covered. But the place she lived in was a shithole. Her bills are past due, and she has no savings I can find. Unless it's going up her nose or in her veins, which I doubt... the math doesn't add up. Someone's bleeding her dry."

My vision narrowed as the full picture crystallized.

Their words barely registered.

My mind was already working, already planning the kind of pain that was both creative and absolute.

I would find every person involved in terrorizing her. And I would make them understand that touching what belonged to Pavel Ivanov came with consequences that lasted lifetimes.

I would find the bastard responsible for this, and I would carve him apart, piece by agonizing piece, until he understood what it meant to truly suffer.

Alina had secrets.

But so did I.

And mine were about to become someone's worst nightmare.

I was going to uncover every single one of hers, and someone was about to learn just how dark my secrets could be.

CHAPTER 17

ALINA

*T*he cold metal of the cuffs bit into my wrists as Pavel unlocked them, leaving behind raw, irritated skin.

I resisted the urge to rub at the lingering sting, blinking against the sudden brightness as he yanked the hood from my head.

My eyes stung as I tried to think through the disorientation while everything around me seemed to shift and blur.

After hours—days?—spent in darkness, my senses struggled to adjust.

I thought I slept some, but I couldn't be sure.

All I knew was that my head pounded, my throat was painfully dry, my stomach empty, and my arms ached from hanging above my head for so long.

Every muscle in my body protested from being held in the same position for too long. A fog seemed to cloud my thoughts, making it hard to focus on anything beyond the physical discomfort.

Before I could orient myself, Pavel reached for me.

I shrank back, away from his touch, curling my knees to my chest, trying to make myself smaller.

Harder to grab.

His eyes darkened, his lips curling into a scowl. "Come here. Now."

He ordered me like a dog.

My stomach twisted at the command, but I stayed frozen in place.

My muscles were too heavy with fear and indecision.

Did I follow his orders and come to him, ever the obedient pet, or did I run?

What else was he planning on doing to me? Would running make it worse? Could it get worse?

"Where are you taking me?" I asked hesitantly.

"Don't ask questions," he bit out, reaching for me again.

I jerked away from him, acutely aware of how naked I was. "Can I at least have something to wear?"

"No."

"Please, I'm cold." I asked again, and he gave me a flat look. "Can I take out the...the...thing?"

My cheeks burned with humiliation, as my core ached from his brutal cock and my ass was still stretched around the...I couldn't even say the words—butt plug.

"No." His word was final. "Come here and do as you are told, or I will get a bigger plug for your pretty little ass."

Before I could react, his fingers closed around my ankle, and he yanked me across the smooth sheets.

I tried to claw at the bed, to grasp onto something to stop him, but the silk gave me nothing to grip.

A startled gasp escaped me as I landed in his lap, my body colliding with his chest.

My legs spread over his thighs, giving him access to whatever he wanted.

He grabbed a fistful of my hair and held me in place.

For a moment I thought he was going to kiss me, then for another, longer moment I thought he was going to take out his cock and make me ride him, taking me again like the brute he was.

The room was eerily silent.

No movement. Just the two of us.

Like we were the only two people left in the world.

My skin prickled as I waited to see what he was going to do. What did I want him to do?

The tension broke when he let go of my hair and pushed me off of him just to sweep me off my feet, literally.

He carried me effortlessly into the dining area, settling me onto his lap at the large, elegant table.

A lavish feast stretched across the polished surface—decadent dishes, some familiar and others… less so. There were a few bottles of wine with pretty labels that looked expensive. It was an overwhelming display of indulgence.

Despite not having eaten properly in days, nausea threatened.

The sight of so much food should have made my mouth water, should have had me starving.

Instead, my stomach churned.

There were so many chairs around this table. It could

easily fit ten to twelve people. Why did he have me on his lap? Why wasn't I allowed to put on clothes? What was he going to do with me?

"Are you hungry?" he asked.

I shook my head. "I ate before you kidnapped me from the club."

My stomach betrayed my words with a low, angry growl.

Pavel smirked. "When was the last time you actually ate?"

I eyed the food warily, knowing full well I had no intention of eating.

"I had an apple," I muttered absentmindedly.

His smirk vanished, replaced with a cold, hard line.

"An apple?" He grasped my jaw, his grip firm but not cruel, forcing me to meet his gaze. "That's it?"

I blinked. "More like half an apple, kind of."

A muscle in his jaw ticked. "That's not good. You need to eat."

My lips parted, a sharp retort slipping out before I could stop it. "Sorry, I guess being kidnapped and assaulted messed with my eating plans today."

Silence. Heavy. Suffocating.

The words hung between us like a loaded weapon.

Pavel's fingers tightened just a fraction before he slowly reached for a piece of buttered black bread.

"Careful, babygirl," he murmured. "I may not let the next outburst slide. Do not let those pretty lips get away from you, unless you want another punishment. Is your ass already missing the sting of my belt?"

I stiffened, clamping my lips shut and staring at the

wood grain on the tabletop. I meant to stay quiet, I really did. Apparently, the brutality I had suffered, the endless orgasms and being tied to a bed for who knew how long, made me a little more hangry than usual.

I scowled, my lower lip pushing out in a slight pout.

Pavel chuckled, a deep, rumbling sound. It should've been reassuring, but it wasn't.

His laugh was laced with something dark.

Amusement.

He was laughing at me. His amusement was at my expense.

My shoulders tensed, my body reacting with pure survival instinct. I wanted to get off his lap, to walk away from him, or turn and tell him how I didn't enjoy being the butt of his jokes.

There were enough vile men in my life who laughed at me, belittled me. I didn't want another. Not that he was giving me a choice in the matter.

He must have noticed, because the laughter stopped just as suddenly as it started.

His expression turned unreadable.

The mood in the room shifted once more.

Back to a thick tension, while I waited for the next shoe to drop.

Without warning, he sighed, standing abruptly.

He set me aside on my own wooden chair. I was grateful until I shifted, and the hard, cold wood pushed the plug even deeper into my abused behind.

He brushed off imaginary dust from his expensive slacks before turning his back on me.

"Stay here. Be a good girl and don't move." His voice lowered. "Or you'll regret it."

My heart pounded, but I didn't dare challenge him.

Not yet.

There was no actual way for me to escape. I wasn't just going to run out of the room naked with this thing sticking out of me. I needed to bide my time. Make a plan, then escape when the time was right.

The easiest way to make him loosen the reins was to make him think he had already won.

So for now, I would take this disrespect and swallow the humiliation that left me cold.

Pavel disappeared into the bedroom, only to return moments later with a charcoal-gray, cable-knit sweater draped over his arm. He held it out expectantly. "Arms up."

I hesitated, staring at him. It was a trick. It had to be a trick. Right?

When I didn't comply fast enough, he rolled his eyes and simply pulled it over my head himself, the thick fabric settling warmly over my shoulders. For the first time in hours, I exhaled a shaky breath of relief.

It smelled like him—clean, woodsy, expensive. It shouldn't have comforted me. I should have felt stifled, trapped. Instead, I felt warm, protected, and almost cozy.

The contradiction disturbed me more than I wanted to admit.

He wasted no time pulling me back onto his lap.

Again.

This time, he held up a delicate blini topped with caviar.

"Eat."

I wrinkled my nose at the pungent, fishy smell. "No, thank you."

Pavel's grip tightened on my waist. "Eat."

"But I don't like caviar."

His brows lifted. "Have you ever had it?"

It's fish eggs. Who could possibly like it?

"Well, no, but—" There were lots of things I hadn't tried that I knew I wouldn't like. I didn't say the last part out loud. God only knew what kinds of depraved ideas it would give him.

"Then eat." He pressed the bite against my lips. "Trying new things is the spice of life."

I huffed, pushing away his hand. "My life is already spicy enough, thank you very much. I think we both know I have tried plenty of new things since meeting you."

Pavel gave me a dirty smirk, and I knew exactly what he was thinking.

I glared at him, but he didn't remove the fishy monstrosity from in front of my face. His silent demand was clear.

Reluctantly, I took the bite.

The instant the salty little bubbles burst on my tongue, I regretted it. The briny, fishy taste flooded my mouth, making my stomach lurch. I would rather starve to death than ever eat that again.

My nose scrunched, my gag reflex hit hard as the rest of my body tensed.

Everything about it was wrong—the texture, the over-whelming saltiness, the way it seemed to coat my tongue.

But I didn't dare spit it out.

Not in front of him. I had seen how much this awful stuff cost. Would he yell at me for wasting such an expensive... delicacy?

Pavel watched me closely, his sharp gaze missing nothing.

After a moment, he held up a napkin, silently offering me an out.

Hesitant, embarrassed, and terrified of angering him, I spat it out, quickly muttering an apology for not appreciating his expensive taste.

But then the words slipped out—

"It tastes like a salty dead fish."

Instant regret washed over me. Why couldn't I keep my mouth shut? Bracing myself, I waited for his reaction. For his hand to slam across my face or for him to grab my shoulders and slam me down on the table before getting his belt again.

But Pavel laughed.

Not just a smirk. A real, amused laugh. It sounded pure and spontaneous, like he couldn't help himself.

It unsettled me more than anything else he'd done. Laughter like that only came from joy. Could a man that evil experience things like joy without his emotions being contaminated with malice?

The entire situation was unsettling.

I was trapped with a man who could kill me in an instant, and every instinct in my body screamed at me to run. Nothing good could come after that laughter.

My eyes darted around the penthouse, flying over the

luxurious space, scanning for anything—anyone—who might help me.

There was no one. No allies. No escape.

We were alone, and I was trapped.

My fate was tied to this treacherous man, whether or not I liked it. The weight of it settled like lead in my chest. I was stuck, and my time was running out.

My fingers twitched as I tugged at the hem of the sweater, wishing it were longer, thicker, and I could just hide from the world in its thick threads.

The movement sent a sharp ache through my body—a painful reminder of just how thoroughly he claimed me. Another small jolt and the plug nudged deeper inside me. Every time I thought I was used to it, something would remind me of its full weight.

Pavel watched my reaction, his amusement fading. His gaze turned sharp.

He wasn't finished with me. There was something more he wanted. What was left?

"Now. Tell me about your grandmother. And your father."

I shook my head, refusing.

Pavel could do whatever he wanted to me, but I wouldn't put my grandmother in danger. Not again. I wouldn't betray my family like my father did.

His expression darkened.

With slow, deliberate movements, he stood and placed me on my feet, so he was hovering over me.

I took a shaky step back, and he followed me.

Every time I retreated, he advanced until my back hit the wall.

My pulse spiked, and it became impossible to swallow as he pressed his forearms to the wall, caging me in.

His presence was overwhelming. Suffocating. Inescapable. And just a little intoxicating.

"Tell me, Alina."

I swallowed hard.

But no matter how close he got—

I wouldn't give him what he wanted. I couldn't.

"No." Not yet.

Pavel didn't like that answer.

Slowly, deliberately, his patience snapped.

He reached beside him to a drawer in the long buffet table and pulled out a wooden box. Flipping open the lid, he dumped out a pile of loose and bundled photographs.

The sight hit me like a physical blow.

My stomach plummeted. He knew.

"Where did you get those?"

He didn't look up. "Your apartment."

A chill raced down my spine. Of course he did. I wondered what else he had found.

"I emptied it. So I have everything."

The blood drained from my face, and my hands shook.

"You—"

"You no longer live there. It isn't safe."

No longer caring if he retaliated, I pressed my hands to his chest and tried to shove him back.

He must not have been expecting it.

I managed to move him back a good foot and a half, just enough to duck under his arm and escape the cage his body had me in.

The sweater slipped past my knees, drowning me in warmth I no longer wanted.

"How dare you go through my things?" I hissed, hands trembling.

Pavel ignored my outrage, lifting one of the photographs. "You said you were paying back your father's debts. You didn't fucking say anything about this."

I froze. Staring at the photo with my grandmother's eyes burned out.

His voice dropped to a dangerous murmur.

"Either tell me what is going on… or I get my belt."

CHAPTER 18

PAVEL

*A*lina was going to tell me everything I wanted to know—whether she liked it or not.

Soon enough, she was going to learn that I was not someone to be fucked with.

She needed to understand that I was a man to be obeyed, without question.

My hand snapped out, wrapping around the base of her throat, not hard enough to cut off her air, but firm enough she knew I could.

I pushed her against the wall and caged her in again, hovering over her so she couldn't miss the differences in our bodies. I wanted to impress our height disparity on her, how her thinness contrasted with my muscular build, and to remind her how my hard cock could impale her sweet little cunt over and over.

She was being a brat, and I needed to put an end to that immediately.

Things would not turn out well for her if she forgot for even a moment who she was dealing with.

I couldn't keep her safe if she didn't respect what I could do and fear the monster that I could become.

I caressed her cheek, my touch deceptively gentle as I leaned into her, pressing my body against her, my cock already hard as it settled against her soft stomach.

"Remember, sweetheart, I have very creative ways of making people talk. I'd rather have a civilized conversation over dinner, but if you would prefer a more... interesting way, that can be arranged."

She still refused. Her lips pressed together in a firm line, her jaw clenched so hard that her cheek twitched.

Her stubbornness was impressive, but there was still fear in her eyes. Her hands still trembled at her sides.

My patience was running thin, and I didn't know what pissed me off more—that someone was hurting her, threatening her, or that she was protecting them.

Neither was going to work for me.

All she had to do to end this suffering was tell me everything.

I knew that you attracted more flies with honey, and if I had the time, maybe I would coax the information from her. Maybe I'd be inclined to be gentle, earn her confidence, or just tie her to the bed again and edge her until she broke. I rather liked that idea. My cock throbbed with the need to do exactly that.

Too bad it wouldn't work. Not because I couldn't break her with pleasure and pain, but because I had already tested the limits of my control.

There was no way in hell I could see her cunt wet and dripping for me again, feel it gripping my fingers, my tongue, or my cock without losing my mind and fucking her so thoroughly neither one of us would be in any position to ask or answer questions, let alone form coherent thought.

Work first.

Lose myself in her tight body second.

I wrapped my hand around her throat again, tilting her head back, forcing her to look up into my eyes. I wanted to see the truth in those pretty, golden-flecked eyes.

She was a captive.

I was the monster holding her here, at least for now.

"Your disobedience is making me angry."

Her pretty eyes reflected the exact moment her resolve cracked. The tears that welled in them spilled down her cheeks.

I could see it—the moment she realized what she needed to do to survive. That was what she was, a survivor, and a natural submissive.

She wasn't weak, far from it. But what her mind wanted and what her body wanted were at odds.

I could use that.

She wanted to please me. Even if her mind fought it with every fiber of her being, her softening body, her hitching breaths as she hesitated were all I needed to see to know she liked the way I made her feel.

Her lips opened and closed a few times, like she was searching for the words.

I loosened my grip on her throat and leaned in to whisper into her ear. Coaxing the information from her lips. "It would please me for you to obey. I think you would much prefer the way I treat you when I'm pleased."

Finally, she broke.

Her body relaxed against mine, and her eyes slid closed.

The confession poured out of her, and I knew the words were true.

"It's my grandmother," she gasped. "She's all I have in this world."

"Were you telling me the truth last night that you've had no contact with your father?" I asked, thinking about the man in the photos that clearly made her uneasy.

She nodded. "He used to just show up when he needed something. Usually money. He would bring gifts—things he had stolen—and he would act like a provider. Like Grandma and I were living off his generosity. Then he would disappear as soon as his debts caught up to him. They always caught up to him."

Alina's voice trembled as she continued her confession.

"My grandmother was diagnosed with early-onset dementia. I couldn't take care of her, so now she lives in a nursing home in Virginia. I go to visit her as often as I can. At first it was fine, better even. She had Medicaid and a pension to pay for her housing, and I was living just off campus. I missed her, but she was doing so much better."

"Then what happened?"

"One day, she told me about these men dressed in black who came to see her. They were asking questions about me and my father, how she paid for the nursing home, and where I spent my time."

Her eyes cast down as she swallowed. I gave her only a

moment to gather herself. Just as I was about to say something to urge her on, she kept going.

"At first, I just dismissed it as paranoia, or maybe some delusion, or something from the TV she thought was real —just the dementia talking. But then the staff confirmed it. They had asked the nurses about me too, and a few of them were scared of the men. There were three of them, and at least one of them had a gun."

"And the staff just let them in?"

"They claimed to be cousins. I don't think the nurse saw the gun until they were leaving. They asked strange questions about my father. How often he visited and things like that. I didn't think much of it until later that night..."

Her words trailed off again. I tilted her chin up for her to look at me. Her eyes flicked up to meet mine.

She was terrified of whatever had happened.

Something twisted in my chest at the sight.

"I came home to find my apartment trashed. Before I could take out my phone to call the police and make a report about what happened, three men burst through my door. They told me that my father had debts. If I didn't pay them off, there would be consequences—starting with my grandmother. They wanted to take more than just money... but I agreed to pay the debt if they didn't hurt my grandmother."

A long, shuddering breath left her body, and I took my hand off her throat and instead cupped her cheek, wiping away the tears with my thumb.

"What aren't you saying?"

She swallowed. "I had a roommate at the time. She

came home, and I think if she hadn't, things would have ended...very differently."

The implication hit me like a physical blow. I fought the urge to pull her into a protective hug and promise her everything would be okay. That wasn't who I was. I wasn't the man who held a woman close to comfort her.

But I would be the man who ended the lives of everyone who hurt her.

"I had no choice. I dropped out of college, started working as a cleaner and bartender under the table. The debt was so large, I was doing anything I could to earn as much cash as possible."

The more she talked, the more my anger rose, like a deadly heat snaking up my spine.

I let her go and took a step back.

She kept telling me about every time they demanded more, adding fees for collection, and interest on the interest. She paced the room, her nerves on edge. But all I could feel was the burn of something vicious and unfamiliar inside me.

Rage. I thought I had felt it before, but this was different.

This wasn't a hot, uncontrollable fire. This was cold, hard, and all-consuming.

This rage wasn't aimed at her, it was for her.

Fueled by the trauma she had endured at the hands of others.

This rage was aimed at them.

The contradiction should have bothered me more than it did.

And I couldn't explain why.

Why did I want to rip these men apart for doing things I had done a hundred times? Hell, I had done significantly worse and reveled in it. I had only just met this woman. I shouldn't give a fuck what some other family did to recoup their losses on a bad loan.

But I did.

I cared, because she was mine.

If anyone was the monster in her life, it was me.

And yet…

From the moment I saw her, from the moment she looked up at me with those big, defiant brown eyes, I'd known. I didn't understand it then, but I understood it now.

She needed protection.

And I wanted to be the one to give it to her. It should've meant protecting her from myself. Resisting the urge to go after her, to take her, strip her naked and chain her to my bed.

But that was not how the real world worked.

Without another word, I grabbed a notepad and a pen, slamming them onto the table. "Sit."

When she hesitated, I picked her up and then forced her into the chair.

"Write down everything."

"Why?"

"Because I said so. Now. I need details. Your father's name. The names of the men who threatened you. The names of the group your father owes money to. How you paid them. Your grandmother's full name. The name of her nursing home. Everything."

"No. I can't."

She didn't want to do it. She was protecting them from me. They wouldn't get mercy from me, and they didn't deserve her protection.

Standing behind her, I wrapped my hand around her throat again, tilting her head back so she was looking up at me. The way my large hand covered her delicate neck felt right. It just fit, and I couldn't help wanting to feel it over and over. Her soft skin, her life in my hands, the way her pulse fluttered against my fingers as her heart raced.

I wanted her to see the malice in my eyes, to know what I was going to do with that information.

"Do it. It wasn't a question, it was an order."

"And if I don't want to obey?"

My grip tightened.

"Then I'll fuck you into submission. I will take you hard and fast, bent over this goddamn table, and then you will do it, anyway."

She picked up the pen with a shaking hand and started writing.

When she finished, I grabbed the pages and skimmed over the details.

She didn't know a lot. Her father's name, her grandmother's name. She paid in cash. They would just show up demanding payment at least once, sometimes twice a month. She knew the first names of the men who came: Carlos, Tony, and Rick. No mention of who they worked for.

It wasn't enough information to hunt down the debt, but it was enough to start.

Satisfied, I fixed her a plate of food, avoiding the caviar and anything too decadent or strong. She needed her strength, so I loaded the plate with simple, hearty foods. Black bread, roasted meats, carrots and parsnips roasted in a honey glaze.

Then I poured her a vodka and set both the plate and the glass down in front of her.

Alina looked at the food and made a face.

"Eat. You're going to need your strength, and we both know you haven't had a good meal in a long time."

"I'm not hungry," she said, pushing the plate away.

"I wasn't asking." I pushed the plate back toward her and crossed my arms.

Her shoulders slumped and she took a single bite, struggling to chew and swallow.

Her face twisted like the decadent food tasted like sawdust in her mouth.

"It's not that bad." I rolled my eyes. Actually, the food at this hotel was excellent. My cousin had stolen the chef from a top restaurant in Moscow, providing papers and a home for him and his family.

Alina barely moved, barely breathed, as she stared at the notepad like it had betrayed her.

"What is wrong with you?" I snapped. "Is the best food in this country not up to your moldy apple and dollar store ramen taste?"

Her eyes turned to me, that familiar fire sparking in their depths.

"Excuse me for not being hungry after signing my grandmother's death warrant. Not all of us can see death so casually. Not all of us regularly put a gun to someone's head and pull the trigger, figuratively or literally."

Her words were heavy, but even with the emotion I

could see the fire dimming and her eyelids drooping. She was exhausted.

That hit me harder than her thinking I would kill a defenseless old woman.

The old woman was valuable to me precisely because she was valuable to Alina. That connection would ensure her compliance. Alina cared about the woman deeply. It wasn't herself she had been protecting; it was her grandmother. This leverage would prove handy.

"I can't just eat like nothing is hap—" Her voice cut out mid-word as her jaw stretched in a deep yawn.

"Did you poison me?"

I sighed.

How was this girl even still alive? She had no idea how to take care of herself.

I lifted her into my arms, my grip firm and possessive as I held her to my chest.

"I didn't poison you, Alina." I tried to soothe her. "You're just exhausted. You've had a long day after what I can only assume were several long years."

I carried her into my bedroom.

I peeled off the sweater, leaving her naked and vulnerable before I tucked her into my bed, pulling the covers up over her then quietly leaving the room.

Resting my head against the door, I took several deep breaths.

Letting my heart break for her and then letting the cold, relentless steel slip back into place.

Alina was mine.

Mine to take, mine to fuck, and mine to protect.

She was being threatened, as was everything she loved, and it wasn't by me.

That wasn't going to work.

I wanted to be the only villain in her story.

I was the only man she should've been worried about.

With my rage taking over, I picked up my phone and dialed.

The line rang once before someone picked up.

"I have a job for you."

CHAPTER 19

PAVEL

I heard his screams before I saw him.

Damien and Mikhail worked fast.

I knew what I'd see the second I opened the door to the hangar.

My cousins never disappointed. They were almost as fierce and ruthless as I was.

Almost.

I walked into the large, nearly empty space to see a man dangling from a chain like a slaughtered pig, trembling and pathetic. I watched him swing upside down, unmoved by his cries for mercy.

Richard Russo, Alina's deadbeat father.

There were many things I was willing to give this man.

Mercy was not one of them.

He didn't deserve mercy.

Especially given how easy it was for my men to track him down. Finding him at a blackjack table in Atlantic City, racking up more debt even as his only daughter put herself in danger bearing the burden of his old debts.

As I stepped further into the warehouse to check on the progress Damien and Mikhail had made, the stench of sweat stung my nose. A far cry from the delicate florals that graced Alina's skin.

She was the reason I was here.

It didn't have any deep meaning.

This bastard hurt a vulnerable woman.

That was as deep as I needed to go to unalive him.

And why not?

No one was going to miss him, least of all his daughter.

At least that was what I was telling myself.

The fact that I'd never gone this far to track down someone who hurt one of my past lovers didn't matter.

That there was something special and innocent about Alina that made me want to be the man who sheltered and protected her...well, that was something to consider another time.

As was the fact that I wanted nothing more than to be with her now, forcing her to eat more, to drink and regain her strength before I punished that sweet pussy again.

Instead, I got to watch this pathetic excuse for a man— filthy, trembling, and utterly powerless.

Yet, he was the one who caused Alina so much pain and suffering.

I despised men who abused those they were supposed to protect.

This wasn't a man at all, but a snake, a coward, and really not worthy of the air he breathed.

Damien and Mikhail moved to stand beside me, their

gazes sharp with disgust as they shoved the chain, making Richard swing like a human pendulum.

His screams echoed off the metal walls, making my ears ache.

We were miles from civilization, surrounded by corn-fields and the private airport that was only ever staffed when a flight was expected. He could scream all he wanted, and I might have let him get it out, but I was eager to get back to the hotel.

Grabbing him by his greasy, thinning hair, I forced the swinging to stop with a violent jerk.

"Please, please," he babbled. "I'll get you whatever you want. Just let me go."

"That sounds reasonable," I said, looking back at Damien and Mikhail. "What I want to know is simple. Just one little question, and we'll let you go."

"Anything," he panted, his face turning red as he struggled to breathe.

"What kind of garbage human being forces his own daughter to pay off his gambling debts?"

"What?" Richard asked, confusion sliding over his red, sweaty face.

"One that deserves to die," Damien replied coldly.

"Slowly," Mikhail added.

The fear hit him then, real and immediate. Richard stammered, trying to form words, but terror strangled his speech. Or maybe it was the way he was hanging, the blood all rushing to his head. Then his panic manifested in the worst way—his body betrayed him, and a dark stain spread across his pants, seeping into his belt and down to his shirt.

Damien took a step back with a sneer, glancing down at his expensive Italian leather shoes. "You better not get any piss or blood on my shoes, fucker."

I remained focused, not letting his disgusting display of weakness distract me.

Drawing a knife from my motorcycle boot, I tested its weight.

Unlike Damien, I came dressed for the occasion. My tailored suits were safe in my closet; instead, I was dressed in black cargo pants and combat-ready attire. If the look the hotel staff gave me was any indication, I looked like a man ready to deal in death.

That was exactly what I was.

With a simple command, I had my men lower the wretch to the ground. His body landed with a wet thud and my men all grimaced as they hoisted him to his feet and dragged him toward a rickety card table set up in the dimly lit hangar for questioning.

I would've preferred to leave him hanging, but there was a good chance the weak fuck would have passed out on me. This needed to be over quickly, and waiting for him to wake up wasn't something I was willing to do.

They slammed his head down onto the table as he gasped for breath. His face turned from red to a mottled shade of purple, a single string of saliva dripping down from his mouth onto the green felt.

I could've shown him mercy—given him a moment to catch his breath. But mercy was something he'd never shown his daughter.

I gripped his wrist in my fist and slammed his trembling hand onto the table, the knife hovering just above his fingers.

"How many years have you been destroying your daughter's life with this gambling bullshit?" My tone was almost casual. I didn't betray the rage that was coursing through me. I wanted him to be surprised at what was coming.

Richard looked like he needed some more excitement in his life.

Slowly, deliberately, I put the tip of the blade between his pinky and ring finger.

A clear warning. His eyes widened as he fought to pull back.

"It wasn't my fault. I never meant to involve her. I owed too much money," he cried as he tried in vain to jerk his hand back.

I didn't have the time or inclination to listen to his lies. Instead, I turned to Damien, who had a file in his hand, looking over Alina's finances.

I didn't need him to tell me what they said.

I already knew. Every line item, every betrayal. I had them memorized.

"How many years has she been paying off your debts?" I demanded.

"A few months," he choked out, and I removed the blade. Richard sighed, taking a moment of relief as he thought his lie worked.

I knew better.

Alina dropped out of college three years ago.

Still, my brothers and cousins didn't need to know how much I knew.

I looked at Damien, who shook his head.

The confirmation was all I needed.

I placed the tip of the knife in between Richard's ring and pinky fingers again.

He tried to scream out, to tell me to stop. I didn't hesitate. The knife came down with one satisfying cut. Precise and clean through the bone. I severed the man's pinky finger, leaving it on the table in front of him.

A scream ripped through the warehouse, blood spurting onto the worn green tabletop.

He tried to sit up. Two of my men stepped forward, guns pulled. I waved them off as I placed a hand between Richard's shoulder blades, forcing him back down, making sure his severed finger was right in front of his face as I leaned in. I wanted the fucker to smell his own blood, to know the stench of his own rotting flesh.

Richard shook and screamed again. I waited, unbothered by the blood, or the ringing in my ears. It would stop when he died. My momentary discomfort was nothing compared to Alina's.

Finally, Richard took a breath, and I tried again.

"I'm only going to ask you one more time. If you lie to me again, I'll take more than just a finger. How many years?"

Richard sobbed, snot running down his face. "Three years! Three years! That's it. It was only for three years. I was going to…"

I stood up and took a step back, saying nothing as his words trailed off and he stared at his finger laying on the table. His face flushing an unnatural green.

Then his gaze shifted back to his hand, where the

finger should have been. He screamed and cried, carrying on like a toddler who fell off his bike and thought the world was ending.

The pathetic display disgusted me.

Comparatively speaking, his daughter had lost far more than a pinky in the last twenty-four hours, and she didn't carry on like this.

My brave girl was far stronger than her father.

Damien tilted his head, feigning confusion. "Math was never my strong suit, but I think that means two additional fingers."

I nodded. "You'd be correct."

It should have been far, far more. But I needed more information before I could kill him, and he deserved the pain.

Alina's father stopped, looked up, his cheeks tearstained and his brows furrowed as he tried to understand what Damien meant.

Perfect. The confusion would make this hurt more.

I took the opportunity and lashed out with the knife.

The blade struck again, slicing off another finger. His ring finger. Then again, for his middle finger.

He screamed while I wiped the blood from the blade onto his shoulder. No reason to dirty my clothes if I didn't have to.

Richard howled in agony, his entire body convulsing from the pain. But we were far from done.

"Shut up," I ordered over the man's wails. Immediately, his cries silenced, but his body still shook. "We are only just getting started, so you might want to save your strength."

There was a lot of information I needed from Richard, and I had to act fast if I wanted to claim it before he lost too much blood and fainted or, worse, just up and died from a heart attack or a stroke or some shit.

Not that it would've been a significant loss.

Slamming the knife on the table in front of his face, I focused on the task at hand.

"Who do you owe money to?" The question hung in the air like a blade.

He shook his head, refusing to answer. Maybe Richard had more balls than I thought. That meant it was time to make them shrivel.

"Grab his hands," I ordered.

Mikhail raised an eyebrow as my men grabbed Richard's hands and held them to the table. Richard tried balling the one fist he could still make, but my men straightened out those fingers pretty easily.

He sobbed harder as I took my place in front of him and pulled the revolver from the holster tucked at my side. Slowly, methodically, I unloaded it. Then pulled another two bullets from my pocket and stood them up in a neat little row on the table, like soldiers awaiting orders.

"You have seven fingers left, my friend. We are going to play a little game. Seven bullets for seven fingers."

"There are eight bullets," he said, his voice barely a whisper.

"The bonus round," I said, the corners of my mouth pulling into a sinister smile as I took the first bullet and slid it in the chamber before spinning it and clipping it closed.

He tried to pull away as I held the muzzle to his right index finger and repeated my question.

"Who do you owe money to?"

"I can't—" he cried, and I fired the gun.

The hollow click echoed in the hangar, and Richard's shoulders sagged as he sobbed.

"Lucky you, you get to keep pushing buttons and pointing at things, for now." I opened the gun and placed another bullet in the cylinder and spun it again, placing it against his thumb. "The first time you had a one-in-six chance, it's now a two-in-six. Do you like those odds?"

"No, please."

"Tell me who owns your debt," I yelled.

He let out a strangled sob, and I pulled the trigger. The shot was loud, and his blood and bone sprayed over the table. He screamed, his entire body jerking.

"Uh, boss." One of my men nodded under the table. I looked below and saw the bullet not only blew off his thumb, but blew through his shoe about where his big toe would have been.

"Hey." I turned to Damien and Mikhail. "I got a two-fer."

"Nice." Damien nodded.

"Bonus points." Mikhail lifted his chin in approval.

"Next hand," I said, turning back to Richard and loading in another bullet. "Still a two-in-six."

"The Colombians," he screamed. "*Los Infideles*. They are the ones I owe the most to. They are the ones getting paid by Alina. Please, I need a hospital."

"Fuck," Damien groaned behind me.

Ignoring Richard and his pathetic cries, I turned to Damien to see the exasperated look of annoyance.

"What?"

Damien gave a wry smirk. "Let's just say we don't have the best relationship with them. After all, we slaughtered their leader and half their enforcers when we rescued my wife."

Because, of course, this couldn't be as simple as paying off some street gang.

The implications hit me immediately. I thought about Alina and the power struggle between Artem and Gregor.

I carefully weighed my options.

Alina was just some cleaner who had seen something she shouldn't have. Or at least that was what she should've been.

She was more, so much more. I wasn't sure what she was, but I knew I wasn't ready to let her go.

The others wouldn't understand, and I really wasn't sure I understood either.

I should've just washed my hands of the entire thing.

Killed this asshole and his daughter. The Columbians need never know I was ever involved. They would probably assume that Richard owed someone else money. Hell, he probably did.

It would have been so easy to kill him and Alina, let the old woman face whatever consequences life and death had for her, and move on with my life.

But then images of Alina flooded my mind—the way she'd yielded to me, fought me, surrendered to me.

Then I thought of how hungrily her cunt clamped onto my fingers, how sweet her cunt tasted, and how good it felt when her wet, sultry heat milked my cock as I pushed through her innocence.

I came to one simple conclusion.

Fuck it.

"Well, it's about to get worse, because I intend to kill every one of those fuckers," I said with a twisted smile.

"Is it worth it, starting a war over this woman?" Damien asked quietly as he rubbed the edge of his jaw.

An unfamiliar wave of possessiveness crashed over me as I thought of Alina—my Alina.

I thought of her dainty softness against my body, how her eyes slid closed as she tried not to give in to the passion just before she came, the way fire flared in those same eyes when she felt cornered.

"Yes."

I couldn't explain it, but there was something fragile and vulnerable yet feisty about her that deeply intrigued me. I wanted more, and no one was going to take her away from me.

Damien cleared his throat. "You know we're going to have to make a decision about her. Loose ends and all that."

"She's my problem," I said too quickly.

"She can directly implicate our family in a murder. She's all of our problem," Mikhail said, with a knowing look in his eyes. "One way or another, she will have to be dealt with."

"It's about the only thing Artem and Gregor agree on. Something will need to be done about her," Damien added.

The reminder sent cold dread through my veins.

The Ivanovs didn't kill women...unless it was absolutely necessary.

Mikhail crossed his arms over his chest. "You could just marry her."

He and Damien laughed at the joke, but I said nothing.

The suggestion wasn't as absurd as they thought.

Marry Alina?

Marry Alina.

I turned the idea over in my head. The words should have sounded foreign, strange—bitter even. Never once in my whole damn life had I ever considered taking a wife... or having children. My world was violent and unpredictable. There was no room for a woman in it.

Or so I thought.

But these last few months, seeing my brothers who used to feel the same way go from making fun of my "Americanized" cousins and their domestic bliss to sharing in it, had changed something.

The other night they invited me to stay for fondue... whatever the fuck that was.

Apparently, the wives had planned a "fun" night of food and games at Gregor's house. I'd been there for a status meeting on tracking down Alina's piece of shit father, when we broke up early because Samara had entered the room to gently remind him that dinner was ready.

The transformation was startling.

It was jarring to see the change in Gregor.

He'd gone from the ruthless man I knew who ruled over our bratva with an iron fist, to a charming, doting husband right before my eyes.

I'd seen the same change in both of my brothers. There was something about their women that softened the sharp edges of their lives.

It had me questioning my own life.

In the end...what was the fucking point of it? All of it.

The money. The violence. The crude brutality of my world.

If there wasn't someone soft and warm waiting for me at home.

Home. Not a house. A home.

A woman could make a home. Children could make a home.

And if my brothers and cousins could wash off the blood and achieve some semblance of a real life...one filled with meaning, love, and laughter...then why couldn't I?

The concept solidified in my mind.

Take Alina as my wife.

She would be mine completely—legally, socially, under God, irrevocably mine.

Mine.

My wife.

Marry her to keep her, protect her...build a life with her.

If there was one thing the men in my family had in common, it was that they married fighters. Strong women who were filled with fire and sass. A woman would need those qualities if she were to survive in my world.

Alina was a fighter.

Right now, she was tucked safely in bed. My bed.

If I married her, it would solve the issue of her being a dangerous liability.

But more than that—she would belong to me in every way that mattered.

The thought of calling her my wife sent an unexpected thrill through me.

Something twisted in my chest, an unfamiliar eagerness to return to her.

I wondered if she would still be asleep. Her eyes closed and her lips barely parted—

My reverie shattered as a different realization crashed over me.

Ice shot through my veins and a sharp, immediate panic hit me.

I forgot to cuff her back to the bed. *Fuck.*

CHAPTER 20

ALINA

I was warm, comfortable and though it defied all logical reasoning...safe.

The silk sheets were so smooth against my skin as I rolled over and buried my head into a soft pillow. The scent of warm spices and a masculine cologne filled my senses and urged me to fall back into a restful sleep.

God, these pillows smelled so good. They smelled like...him.

I jerked awake.

My bed was not warm or comfortable.

My apartment was anything but safe.

Every night was filled with shouts from my neighbors, screaming matches, and gunfire.

My sheets might as well have been made of burlap, they were so rough, and my pillow smelled faintly of cloyingly sweet strawberry dollar store conditioner, poverty, and mildew.

Where was I?

Memories of what we had done flashed through my

head, and I started shaking. I was being held against my will in some high-end apartment—or maybe hotel—God only knew where.

Pavel Ivanov, one of the most feared men in the Russian mob, freaking kidnapped me.

Closing my eyes for a moment, I listened for any noise, any sound that would tell me if there was someone else in the apartment.

Nothing.

No movement, no breath, no footsteps, no music or television. Nothing.

I didn't know where he was, how long he would be gone, or when he was coming back.

I did know that this was my only chance to escape.

A sharp jolt ran through me, and I couldn't tell if it was panic or determination.

All I knew was that if I wanted out, now was the time.

I still didn't trust it.

Why would he just leave me here like this? He didn't put the handcuffs or hood back on me. He just left me sleeping peacefully in his bed.

It didn't make sense. What if it was a trap?

Still, I slowly, quietly crept to the bathroom, not trusting that he wouldn't pop out at any moment.

When I peered into the large, white-tiled room, there was nobody there. I stepped inside and closed the door behind me, going straight to the mirror to stare at myself.

I looked the same—no, worse than that.

I looked well-rested, and my skin had a glow that it didn't before. Sure, some of the glow was the warm-to-the-touch pink stripes left by his belt. And I had several faint bruises forming on my thighs from his fingers.

But I looked more alive than I had in years. What did that mean?

It was just from the silk sheets, I told myself as I ran my fingers through my hair, trying to make it look less like I'd grabbed onto a live wire. Then carefully I went to remove the metal plug.

Taking it out stung even more than when he'd pushed it inside of me. Still, I gritted my teeth and gripped the jeweled base to pull the oblong orb out.

It took a few moments, but once I finally got it out, the relief I expected didn't come. I felt somehow empty. Like I was missing something. It was like he was no longer touching me.

The small voice in the back of my head urged me to put it back in; to go back to that bed and wait to see what sinful delights he had in store for me.

That little voice begged me to be a good girl, to bend to his will and let him show me all the things I was too afraid to experience before he made the decision for me.

Memories of his lips and tongue on my breasts while his cock gave me the most incredible pleasure filled my mind.

My fingers brushed the pink stripes he had left across my ass in the club. They were sore and still a little warm to the touch, but the pain just kindled thoughts of the pleasure. The way he touched me, tasted me...even the way he put me on my knees and made me take him in my mouth.

Part of me wanted to give in to it all.

To savor the domination, and know that whatever I needed, he would take care of. There was a kind of peace in not having control, in giving all that responsibility over to someone else.

Why did I always have to choose?

Why was every problem mine to solve?

For a moment, the thought of going back into that bed and letting him handle everything was so unbelievably tempting that I almost caved. Just the idea of being able to give up my control, my own responsibilities, and the responsibilities that were thrust onto me by others was almost overwhelming.

So should I put the plug back? Go back to bed and let him find me without it just to see how he would punish me again?

I shook my head, clearing the silly idea of staying here with him. Of giving up my freedom to be, what? His pet? His whore?

No. That wasn't who I was.

I didn't want to be his toy.

I wanted freedom.

Freedom from him.

Freedom from my father's debts.

Freedom from obligations that never should have been mine.

Leaving the plug on the counter, I cleaned myself up as best as I could before creeping back into the bedroom.

It was still eerily still. Quiet.

The only sound in the room was my heart hammering in my chest.

I still didn't trust it.

It didn't make sense, but I didn't want to look this gift horse in the mouth, either. If he wasn't going to be here to make sure I stayed, then there was no reason for me to stay.

I just needed clothes, and I would be gone. No one would ever hear from me again. I'd figure out how to buy a new identity, how to start over somewhere where Alina Russo didn't exist.

It was going to be hard, if not impossible. But it couldn't be worse than this.

It couldn't be worse than demeaning myself by serving drinks in that hellhole. Nothing was worse than getting groped by old men who reeked of desperation and piss.

It couldn't be worse than scrubbing bloodstains out of carpets and mopping them up from tiled floors while pretending I didn't recognize the smell.

It couldn't be worse than having to watch my grand-mother slip further and further away from me, her mind almost completely gone, and seeing the signs of neglect on her body and not being able to do a damn thing about it.

All I had to do was take this opportunity and run. When I was safe and settled, I would return and sneak my grandmother out as well. Maybe I'd find a state with better senior facilities. At least hope was free.

I rushed to the wardrobe, opening it to see designer suit after designer suit, all in the finest fabrics, all whis-pering wealth and decadence.

I could take one. I would bet sliding one of his jackets on would feel like I was wrapped in his powerful arms.

That wasn't what I needed. I slammed the doors and

went to the dresser, ignoring the pang of regret and longing in my body.

The first drawer had more than I expected.

Thousands of dollars in cash, all neatly stacked and wrapped with paper strips labeled $5,000, $10,000 or $20,000.

The stacks were all made of fives, tens, twenties, or fifties. Small, unmarked bills.

What the hell?

Pavel had cost me two steady jobs and taken my virginity.

This was the least he owed me.

The next drawer down had T-shirts and the one below that had workout shorts and a pair of gray sweatpants. I thought about what he would look like in the gray sweatpants, how they would cling to his thighs, the outline of his cock visible. Mental images of him coming back into the room wearing nothing but these sweatpants hanging low on his hips, his abs glistening with sweat from an intense workout, came unbidden to my mind.

"Get yourself together," I whispered, shaking the images out of my head.

What was wrong with me?

I slid on the sweatpants, tightening the drawstring as much as I could before tying it off. Then I grabbed one of the white T-shirts. It was so soft and smelled like him.

As I slid the shirt on, I realized I had been right about the jacket, because just wearing this shirt made me feel like his arms were around me. Unfortunately, the fine fabric was also too thin to be completely opaque.

I needed something more.

I rummaged around and found a winter coat that hit my knees. It was huge, but it would keep me well hidden, and it wasn't going to be the strangest thing people saw in DC.

One quick glance out the window had confirmed where I was. The Washington Monument was easy to see in the sprawling cityscape.

Quickly I shoved money into the pockets of the sweatpants and more stacks in each of the pockets I could find in the coat.

My phone and purse were nowhere to be found, but I really wasn't expecting to find them. Either Pavel had them and I was never going to see them again, or they were left at the club, in which case I was still never going to see them again.

It was a pain, but if I was going to survive this, Alina Russo was dead. I didn't need her ID.

Finally, I needed to find something to put on my feet, but one look at the monstrous shoes that were lined up on the bottom of his closet told me that wearing those would draw more attention than I needed.

Ignoring a woman in clothes that were too big was one thing, since she could be making a fashion choice, or was possibly a tourist making do after their luggage went missing. Regardless, most people went out of their way to not notice other people. But when you added tripping around in clown shoes, staring would be unavoidable.

Instead, I went back to the dresser and searched until I found socks. Two thick pairs of wool socks pulled over my feet and halfway up my calves would have to do.

One last peek in the mirror told me I looked ridiculous, but no more or less ridiculous than any other person walking the streets of Washington, DC.

There really was something magical about a place where a crooked politician in a four-thousand-dollar suit, probably on the prowl for a sex worker, could walk down the same street as a woman who looked like a fashion school dropout, and people would avoid them both as if they had the same disease.

I would at least blend in enough that no one would take notice.

The coat was really nice, maybe oversized, but I didn't think anyone would really pay any attention. If they did, they could easily assume I was making a statement of some sort.

Creeping into the main room, I looked around, expecting to see Pavel sitting in a chair staring at his phone, or pacing around with a glass of vodka in his hand.

Nope. He wasn't here.

The stack of papers was still spread out on the table, and I took the chance to grab the photos that he had of my grandmother and me from when I was a child. They weren't much, but they were all I had left.

With each step I took to the front door I grew more convinced I was tempting fate. When I peered through the peephole, there was nothing in the hall, just a crisp white wall hung with inoffensive art across from the door.

With my breath catching in my chest, I slowly pushed down the lever and opened the door just a sliver.

And there he was. Some man, standing with his back

to the door. Broad shoulders covered in a dark blue suit jacket.

The way he stood told me who he was.

Security.

Whether he worked for Pavel directly or was hotel staff, I had no idea. Either way, he'd stop me, and then God only knew what he would do. I couldn't imagine Pavel would hire anyone unless they were at least as unscrupulous as him.

Did he even know I was in here? I could pretend to be a call girl or somebody he picked up, doing the walk of shame. But would he want a turn? I didn't want to risk it.

Carefully, my breath still caught in my throat, I closed the door and set the latch back without a sound.

Hope bled from my body as my shoulders slumped enough that the coat almost fell off of my shoulders.

No, I refused to give up that easily.

I straightened my spine, lifted my chin in the air, and walked around the apartment, searching for another exit. There had to be another way out. This suite was too big for there not to be a second door somewhere.

I headed toward the back and found a living room area. It still smelled of smoke and had two teacups and glasses sitting on the coffee table.

On the other side of that room was a small door, designed to blend in. A servants' entrance.

Hope blossomed in my chest, but I pushed it down just as quickly. While I had to try—there was no doubt about that—what were the chances that Pavel would leave something so obvious completely unguarded?

I ran to the door, first pressing my ear against the

wood. It was cold to the touch and there was no sound on the other side.

With one final glance behind me, my hand trembling on the handle, I inhaled sharply and pulled the door open.

I waited for a yell, a guard telling me to get back inside, or threatening me. There was nothing.

Only a dingy, off-white hallway, with no natural light, no art, and no signs of life.

Every nerve in my body screamed at me to run.

I was free—for now.

Taking one last breath, I gripped the handle, pulled the door closed behind me, and stepped into the cold hallway.

I didn't know where I was going—only that I had to run.

CHAPTER 21

ALINA

*T*his was probably the stupidest, most reckless thing I had ever done.

But I didn't have a choice.

The entire time I was in the elevator, I was sure that I was going to hit the bottom floor and the doors would open to reveal Pavel standing there waiting for me. He would have a sadistic grin on his face, the hood in one hand and his belt in the other.

The elevator landed on the ground floor.

There was an excruciatingly long pause before the doors slid open.

My breath locked in my lungs as I squinted, my eyes half-closed.

The breath I'd been holding rushed out of me in a whoosh.

He wasn't there.

No one was.

I crept down the back halls, and I didn't see a single soul until I passed an office where a manager was giving the cleaning staff a lecture about tight corners when making beds.

He berated them about the importance of ninety-degree angles, and it sounded like everyone was too terrified of the man with the thick Russian accent to look away. For a moment, I wondered if the cleaning staff knew what kind of men were in this hotel?

The staff at the offices were never told, but we still knew.

Thanks to my stolen socks, I was able to creep past the door with no one noticing. It wasn't until I slipped out by the loading dock that I realized I had nowhere to go.

I was out. Completely free, with pockets stuffed with more money than I knew what to do with and nowhere to go. There were no close friends I could turn to, no boyfriends or confidants.

The only person I had was my grandmother, and I couldn't bring this to her nursing home doorstep.

With nowhere else to turn and worried that Pavel was going to find me at any moment, I went to the only place I could think of.

My apartment.

I walked several blocks, through the winding maze of DC streets, keeping my head down and avoiding people's gazes. I couldn't risk making eye contact. What if someone stopped me and asked if I needed help? Or worse, what if they stopped me and mugged me, finding Pavel's cash?

People had died on these streets for far less.

I considered stopping for food, but there was no way I was going to flash that kind of money in this neighborhood. The nicer places where it would be safe would never let me in without shoes, and they all had CCTV, anyway.

It was probably best if I wasn't on camera.

When I got to the block of run-down apartments, I looked around and there was no sign of anyone who shouldn't have been there. No fancy cars, nothing out of place.

Pavel had told me he'd cleared out the apartment, but maybe he was bluffing? Or maybe his men weren't as thorough as he thought. Surely there was something still there. My hidden emergency fund? Some clothing. Clothes that fit me would definitely help. Shoes would have also been great.

The socks only worked until I accidentally stepped in a puddle.

I just needed something, anything that could give me a sliver of control in this world where I clearly had none. Just something of mine.

I climbed the four flights of dirty stairs to my door, before I realized I didn't even have my keys. It didn't matter; the door was open. Pavel's men must have left it unlocked. I meant, why not? It wasn't like I had anything of value to steal.

One step inside was all it took for my stomach to plummet at the realization that there was absolutely nothing here.

His men had been very thorough.

The space was a hollow shell of what it once was. The only things that were left were my cheap, impersonal furniture. Most of which I had inherited from the last tenant or rescued from the trash heap when someone else abandoned their apartment.

There was nothing of me in this space. It was like I had never been here.

My breath came out in ragged pants as realization set in.

He had erased me.

Pavel had taken absolutely every sign of me, everything that proved that I had lived here and that I existed. It was all gone.

Tears stung behind my eyes as my stomach rolled, and heat flashed over my cheeks.

How could he?

Pavel had stolen my existence.

How dare he!

Before I could really understand what had happened and figure out if I could or even wanted to do something about it, a shadow moved. I wasn't alone.

"Did you really think you could escape me so easily?" Dark amusement danced in his eyes, but the threat in Pavel's low voice didn't quite mask something raw underneath it. Something that sounded almost like...pain? Concern?

But he wasn't asking a question.

He was rendering a verdict.

Just by stepping through that door I had proven that I was guilty. I had sealed my fate.

He was my judge, my jury, and he would be my executioner. Was he going to put me on my knees and shoot me in the head like he had the last uncooperative man?

"Why?" The bitter word left my lips before I could stop

it. Did I even want to stop it? What was the point in holding my tongue? He had already wiped me from the face of the earth. It would make it that much easier to kill me if no one, not even a landlord, was looking for me.

"What did I do that was so horrible that you had to erase my existence?"

"You are a very bad girl," he said. There it was again; as he looked at me, really looked at me, something flickered across his features so quickly that I almost missed it.

Could it be relief he'd found me?

No. Stop it. Don't romanticize him...this.

I was nothing more than a doll he could torment before tossing away.

That was all I was...entertainment.

"Fuck you," I spat, the words venomous. More contempt rose from my chest, hatred accelerating the already rapid pounding of my heart.

He clicked his tongue in disappointment as he took a large step toward me.

I took an equal step back, some of my survival instincts still intact.

"Fuck me? Oh, little kitten, you are going to regret those words." His voice dropped. "Do you have any idea what could have happened to you out there? Walking these streets alone, defenseless? I didn't erase you. I was spoiling you, keeping you safe. And how did you repay me? You stole my clothes, my money, and abandoned the gift I gave you."

"Gift?" I took another step back, my legs shaking as the bravery that had carried me this far evaporated into icy terror.

He took the metal plug out of his pocket and sat it down on the dresser.

Why did my body clench with need at the sight of that thing?

"You're going to regret giving that up."

"How is that a gift?" I scoffed.

He took another step toward me, the corners of his mouth lifting and curling into a sinister smile. "You're about to find out. Because you have no idea what men like me do to girls like you. The only reason you're still breathing is because you belong with me."

My back hit the kitchen counter and in a flash he was on me. His hand was warm around my neck as his lips devoured mine.

I tried to fight him; I tried to push him away, but he was too strong, and his pull was just too powerful.

My lips parted for him, and he deepened the kiss.

I almost gave in when he pulled away from me and took a step back.

"What am I going to do with you, babygirl?"

Beg. Apologize. Tell him you'll be better.

"Let me go," I said, sounding much stronger than I felt.

He tipped his head back as he laughed.

"I don't think so. No, you need to understand." His hand cupped my face, thumb brushing my cheek with surprising gentleness before his grip tightened. "I almost hate that I have to do this to make you see. Now strip."

"No." I looked around. I was maybe six steps from the door. He was only four.

Could I get around him? Could I make it out of that door and run into the city?

I'd only have to make it maybe two blocks to get to a busy street. But then where would I go?

Did it matter?

No. It didn't.

I bolted toward the door.

My fingers just brushed the edge of the door before he yanked me back. He kicked the door shut as he tore the winter coat from my body.

"Get off of me," I screamed, and he laughed.

He fucking laughed, before yanking my hair back and sealing his lips over mine again.

His hands tore at my clothing, ripping the shirt from my body and pushing the sweatpants down to my ankles, exposing my flesh to the cold air without a care.

His hands were all over me, groping my breasts, pinching my nipples, and sliding between my legs to stroke my clit. He was everywhere all at once. It was too much and not enough.

It wasn't fair. It wasn't fair that he could so easily make my body betray me. It wasn't fair that he could make me want to run from him and kneel for him at the same time. I didn't understand.

His fingers stroked my clit in tight little circles when he broke the kiss and started biting a path down to my shoulder.

"You make me fucking crazy," he rasped. "You can't just run out into the world trying to throw yourself away."

His astonishing words barely registered as I struggled to fight the familiar pressure building in my core.

"Why can't you just be a good girl? I could be so good to you. Make you come over and over until the only thing you know how to say is my name as you scream it."

"Yes," I gasped, my hands gripping the cracked countertop. I was so wet, and even though I was still sore, I needed him again.

"Maybe this time you'll learn your lesson." His hand gripped the back of my neck as he pushed me down, bending me over the table. The sound of his zipper was loud as he freed his cock, running the head over my folds.

"Please," I begged, hating myself for giving in so easily.

"Let's see if you're still begging in a second."

I was confused by the hint of malice in his words until he kicked my feet a little wider apart.

He teased my entrance with his cock, circling his head over my clit, then rubbing his shaft through the humiliating wetness pooling in my cunt. He was everywhere but deep inside me, where I needed him. Then he moved his cock up, past my aching pussy, to my ass.

"Wait—" I said, trying to stand up.

He held me down, one hand pressed between my shoulder blades, the other stroking my hair almost tenderly before lightly gripping the back of my neck. "Shhh, I've got you," he whispered against my ear as he pushed his cock into my ass.

It burned, but the deeper he went, the fuller I felt.

This feeling was different from having him in my pussy.

It was darker, forbidden.

It hurt, but there was something else there, too.

Something deeply satisfying.

He was claiming me, the last piece I had just for me.

He was taking it as his.

"That's right, baby. Take every fucking inch."

I put my hand over my mouth, trying to muffle the scream rising from my throat.

"Bad girl," he said, giving me a swat on my ass before grabbing both of my hands and twisting them behind my back, his grip firm but not rough. "You belong with me, which means I own every single delectable sound I pull from your sweet body. You will not take them from me."

He pressed in harder, seating himself as deep as he could go.

"Tell me you want it," he growled.

I bit my lip, refusing to make a sound.

He pulled out slowly, then slammed back into me. A deep-seated groan left his lips, and I screamed, silently.

It was my last little act of rebellion.

He fucked me harder, faster, slamming in and out of me, even as I could feel him checking my responses, making sure I was with him. A fine sheen of sweat coated my back and I was panting, trying to hold back, to make sure I didn't come apart for him. Not again.

"Give in to it," he said, punctuating his words with deep thrusts.

I couldn't. I wouldn't.

"Admit you like being used by me. That you like the way my cock stretches your tight little body. Tell me you're mine to protect. And maybe I'll let you come."

I wanted to cry, to scream, to moan and beg.

I wanted to give in to him, but something held me back.

I couldn't give in to him.

If I admitted what I wanted, what I felt, it would be all over. There would be no going back.

He slipped his hand between my legs and the counter and started flicking my clit. His thrusts became harder, his cock swelled even more.

"Admit it," he whispered in my ear, his voice tight with desire. "Admit that you want to be mine. Mine to keep, mine to play with and mine to protect. Admit that I was the first man to fuck this pretty little face, this tight little cunt, and this perfect little ass. Tell me I was the first man, and that you want me to be the last."

His words made my head swim, and I couldn't help the soft moans that escaped my lips as he pushed harder and harder, that pressure growing in my core faster and faster, as his fingers applied more pressure to my clit.

"Say it," he demanded.

"Yes," I gasped.

"Not good enough."

"Yes," I said louder. "I want you to be the last man to ever touch me. I want to be yours, and nobody else's. Take me back to the hotel, keep me there, I don't care, I just—"

My words cut off with a cry of ecstasy as I came hard.

A few thrusts later he was following me over the edge into bliss.

It took me a few moments to recover. When I did, he pulled away from me to gently wipe his come from my body with the shirt I'd been wearing.

His fingers brushed over my skin as he checked me over. I could almost fool myself into thinking he was doing it out of genuine concern for me, as if there was something more hidden beneath the dominance.

But I knew the truth.

This wasn't care. It was control.

My freedom was an illusion, a cruel joke, and the moment I stepped into this apartment I had walked straight back into his trap.

By the time we got back to the penthouse, there was no pretense left.

No more illusions of escape, no more thoughts of running.

He didn't even bother putting the hood or handcuffs on me.

He knew the truth as well as I did.

As we rode the elevator up, he kept his arm around me, holding me close—not just possessively, although that was undeniable, but with what might have been protectiveness, so I couldn't disappear into danger again.

He was proving in no uncertain terms that there was no life for me beyond him.

Worst of all, some dark, treacherous part of me wondered if I ever truly had a life beyond him to begin with. And did I even want one anymore?

CHAPTER 22

ALINA

*P*ale oranges and pinks danced across the city as I watched the sun set on my sixth day in this prison. The city outside these glass walls looked peaceful, but that was an illusion—it was a gleaming cesspool of greed and malevolence, just like the gilded cage I now occupied.

Anyone looking at me would see some semblance of a Cinderella story. A poor girl plucked from squalor and dropped into a lavish penthouse with everything she could want. For the first time in years, I was clean, warm, and fed. My clothes—what little Pavel allowed me to wear—were soft silk and lace instead of threadbare Goodwill finds.

But decadence meant nothing without freedom.

Every door was locked. I had access only to the bedroom, its en suite, and occasionally the dining and living rooms—if Pavel felt generous and no visitors were expected. The moment his brothers arrived, I was shuffled back to the bedroom with threats of handcuffs and the hood.

I had even tried picking a lock once, only to meet the judgmental scowl of a massive armed guard who growled at me in Russian. His meaning was clear: I was far safer in my tower.

Pavel had transformed me from Cinderella into Rapunzel, locked away and forced to watch the world through glass.

The days blended together in monotonous routine. I'd wake to Pavel's hands on my body, his mouth between my thighs, or his fingers tangled in my hair, guiding me toward his hard shaft. He'd leave after breakfast and return at night. The splatters of blood on his clothes serving as silent reminders of the monster beneath the expensive suits.

I started counting sunsets to stay sane.

More than once, I wondered if I'd stumbled into the fantasy life some girls at the club dreamed about—being a kept woman, free from bills and responsibilities, ravaged by a well-endowed, rich, and powerful man obsessed with pleasure.

If I closed my eyes and forgot about the guards outside, about wearing only sheer Agent Provocateur pieces, maybe I could understand the appeal. In their dreams, those women could leave their towers. They chose their captors. They had friends, social engagements, freedom disguised as luxury.

For a moment, I gave in to the illusion. Maybe it was self-preservation, Stockholm syndrome taking root, or daytime television finally killing my last brain cell. I began seeing this situation from the perspective of some kind of twisted version of a 1950s housewife—taking care of my jailer, waiting for him to come home where I'd be useful again.

Was it so different from being a cleaning lady? Either way, despite the hints of deeper emotions I thought I'd glimpsed in him last week, he basically saw me as an appliance. At least this way, I was left in a sex-induced haze, endorphins flooding my brain instead of my back aching and my hands raw from bleach.

The illusion shattered each night when Pavel returned, knuckles bloodied, violence clinging to him like expensive cologne.

Tonight was no different.

I said nothing as he entered, shedding his jacket and kicking off his shoes. The metallic scent of blood made my stomach clench.

"Get on your knees," he commanded, pointing to a spot on the carpet.

Heat flooded my cheeks as I obeyed. Pavel didn't look at me, focused instead on his phone as he disappeared into the bathroom. He emerged moments later, shirt unbuttoned, belt undone but still hanging from the loops of his pants. His muscled abs were covered in tattoos I'd long since memorized but had not gotten the courage to ask the meaning behind.

It wasn't fair that someone so evil could be devastatingly beautiful.

He settled into his chair, attention still on his screen, and snapped his fingers, pointing between his legs. The silent command was clear: crawl to him like the pet he'd made me.

I hated him for treating me like a dog. I hated my body more for aching with need every time I saw him.

Swallowing my humiliation, I crawled forward and settled on my heels while he finished whatever held his attention.

"We need to discuss something, my pet," he said, finally setting down his phone. "I'll talk and you'll listen, without interruption. You're going to take my cock in your mouth and suck it like the obedient girl you're learning to be."

He unzipped his fly with deliberate slowness.

"If you can manage that without interrupting, I'll let you ride me until your body gives out. If not..." His eyes glittered dangerously. "You get the belt, then I fuck your ass until I'm satisfied. Understood?"

I nodded, my traitorous body already responding, my mouth watering in anticipation.

"Get to work, sweet thing."

I reached out, stroking his impressive length until he guided my head toward his lap. The moment my lips wrapped around him, he hummed in approval, and I closed my eyes, surrendering to the familiar ritual.

But it wasn't enough for him tonight.

His hands gripped my head as he pulled back and stood, holding me in place while he thrust deep.

"Fuck yes," he growled. "Take it all."

Humiliation flooded through me as I realized he was simply using my face, fucking my mouth like I was nothing more than a toy. Yet something dark inside me purred at being the source of his pleasure, at being chosen for this intimate violation.

He pulled out just enough to come on my face, his seed spilling across my lips. His thumb brushed over my lips before he pushed it inside my mouth. He watched expectantly, not releasing me until I'd sucked his thumb clean as well.

"Such an obedient girl," he murmured. "It makes everything I did for you worthwhile."

My heart stopped. "What you did for me?"

"Your father will never hurt you again. You're no longer responsible for his debt."

I drew my head back, the words hitting me like a physical blow. "I don't understand." I stared at him, not daring to believe what I'd heard.

"It's been handled." He pulled me onto his lap, one hand splaying possessively across my lower back while the other tilted my chin up to meet his gaze. "You're free of him."

Was it possible? Could I trust what he was telling me? Or was this just another game to keep me compliant?

"You're shaking," he observed, and I realized he was right.

His grip tightened around my waist, supporting me.

His thumb traced along my bottom lip, still swollen from his use. "Your life depends on understanding that you belong to me now. Completely. No debts, no obligations to anyone else."

His voice was quieter now. "He'll never hurt you again. Never demand anything from you. You're mine now, babygirl. Only mine."

Only his.

I noticed him catch himself, his jaw tightening as he fought against his own softening.

He muttered something in Russian that sounded like a curse at himself.

My mind reeled.

Free of my father's debt. I'd wanted that so desperately, needed it more than air.

But how? Had Pavel paid them off?

Only his.

Was I only his because he'd now bought and paid for me?

Did I now owe him?

Then I looked down at Pavel's bloodied knuckles where his hands now rested on the arms of the chair, a reminder of all the nights he'd returned home with blood splattered on his clothes.

Was one of those nights...? No. Oh god.

A sinking suspicion settled in my stomach.

My voice came out as barely a whisper, thick with dread. "What did you do to him?"

CHAPTER 23

ALINA

*H*is gaze narrowed. "What I had to."

"Why?"

"Because you are under my protection. Period." The way he said it, like it was just a fact of life, made my body hum with something I didn't dare give a name.

"Is he dead?" I asked.

"Yes." There was no hesitation, no pause.

He just told me the truth, and I didn't know how to feel about that.

I sat back for a moment, waiting for grief, shock, sadness—anything—to overwhelm me.

I felt nothing. Maybe I'd grieved the father I'd needed years ago, when he first chose gambling over his family. The man Pavel killed was a stranger who happened to share my blood.

Pavel watched my face carefully, and I caught something that might have been concern cross his features before his expression hardened again.

"Your father put you in danger. "His hand lifted and

smoothed comforting circles on my lower back. "Your grandmother is safe because you're mine. That's how this works—I protect what belongs to me." His voice softened slightly. "I've had her moved to a better place. She deserves proper care."

"Medicaid pays—"

"Medicaid paid for a shithole. I've had her moved," he rasped, pulling the slip away from my breast, his knuckles grazing my skin. "She's an old woman who raised you. She shouldn't suffer because of your father's mistakes."

The unexpected, fierce certainty in his voice made something clench in my chest.

Pavel had found my weak spot.

He found the one thing that would ensure I submitted to his rules.

I ground my hips down on his still hard cock. I was already wetter than I'd care to admit.

I teased his cock with my cunt, rocking back and forth, sliding my folds along his shaft while he sucked and licked my breasts.

Pavel grabbed my hips and turned me around so my back was to him, my legs tucked on either side of his thighs. He flipped up my slip to bare my ass to him as he leaned me forward and notched his cock at my entrance.

I stared in the mirror, studying the woman I had become.

My lips were swollen, a little bruised. My slip was hanging off my shoulders, baring my breasts and my spit-slicked hard nipples to the cold air, and my eyes looked glassy.

I watched in horrified fascination as the flush on my

cheeks traveled down my chest to the tops of my breasts as they bounced.

It was somehow both embarrassing and so incredibly hot, watching myself take all of him.

His hands sneaked around my body, his fingers going to my clit, drawing tight little circles, making my thighs tremble as I rode him harder.

Pavel growled something in Russian and my back arched.

This was who I was now.

And I hated it.

I hated him.

I especially hated myself for fitting so well into this new role.

* * *

THE NEXT DAY brought an unexpected change to our routine.

He came back early.

I was lying on the bed, staring at the wall while the TV showed reruns of *Judge Judy*.

I didn't move when he came in, not wanting to acknowledge my captor. At least, not until he threw a paper shopping bag on the bed next to me.

"Put these on. We leave in five minutes."

"What?"

"I'm not going to say it again." He left the room and, confused, I looked into the bag to find clothes—real clothes. A simple but well-made dress, underwear, a bra, and shoes.

The heels were high, and it would be impossible to run in them, but they were shoes.

I slipped off the teddy I was wearing and slid the new clothes on. The fabrics were buttery soft, silky and thick.

Everything fit perfectly.

Why was he giving me real clothes?

Should I be grateful or afraid? I didn't know. There was never any way to tell what kind of mood he would be in, what would happen when he came back each night.

Some nights were all about rough, kinky sex that left me satisfied but sore. More than once, I had a fresh set of lines whipped into my ass before he took me there.

Other nights he was kind; he would cuddle me, we would have a nice dinner, and he'd talk with me like I was his girlfriend, not a prisoner.

It messed with my head.

What was this? What was I to him?

The only constant was I was always naked, or practically naked.

Now I had clothes that were fairly modest and more expensive than anything I had ever bought.

The contradiction left me unsettled, but I did as I was told and got dressed.

Pavel didn't say a word as we left the hotel room and rode the elevator down to street level, where a car was waiting for us. Without being asked, once we were settled he reached over and adjusted the air conditioning, his eyes flicking to me briefly as if checking my comfort.

"You need to behave," he said. "I'm taking you to see your grandmother." His fingers drummed against the steering wheel. "There are people who would use her to get to me now. The only way to keep both of you safe is if you're officially mine."

"What do you mean, officially?"

"Married," he said simply. "It's not a romantic gesture, Alina. It's protection. For my family's business interests, for you, for her."

Wait. What?

He said married.

Like married, married?

That word ran over and over in my mind as I tried to understand what had just happened.

Married.

He drove us across town, and it wasn't until we hit the highway that I worked up the courage to ask a question.

"Marriage... that's really necessary?"

"Yes," he said, his knuckles white on the steering wheel. "My family needs some assurance on where you stand. And while my enemies won't touch my wife, they will torture and kill my captive." His eyes flicked to me. "Which would you prefer to be?"

The cold logic of it settled in my stomach like a stone.

Pondering all the ramifications of marrying into his family, I wasn't paying much attention to where we were until Pavel pulled the car into a parking lot, in front of what looked like a large house. He held my hand as we walked through the doors like we were any normal couple there to visit a relative.

The facility, however, was breathtaking.

The main lobby and adjacent rooms had a homey and casual atmosphere, while there were more staff than I had ever seen at any of the nursing homes that Medicaid paid for.

There were actual doctors walking while talking to family members. A full nursing staff, and it smelled like someone was cooking a feast.

In a rare moment outside of my gilded cage, I walked into my grandmother's cage.

Pavel signed us in then led me down a hallway, where I could hear my grandmother's bell-like laughter before I saw her.

She was in a spacious room, sitting in a full-body massage chair watching episodes of *Murder, She Wrote*.

"Oh, Alina, darling," she said when I walked through the door. It took her a moment, but she stood and walked over to me, giving me a hug.

She held me tight, with more strength and energy in her body than I had seen in well over a year. Her eyes were clear, her smile bright, and I had to push back tears of joy because I actually recognized the woman my grandmother was, not the shell Alzheimer's was creating.

"Grandma, how are you?"

"I'm fine, dear, just fine. Your new beau has me set up in this wonderful place. Tell me, why did you not introduce us sooner?" She leaned in and stage-whispered, "I like this one. He's such a sweet boy."

I looked back at Pavel, who gave me a smug smirk.

"Grandma, I don't think anyone has called him a boy in many, many years."

Pavel chuckled as my grandmother dissolved into a fit of giggles.

He let me sit and visit with her for some time.

He even played a hand of gin rummy with her, and I was surprised to see genuine amusement flicker across his face as she filled him in on the facility gossip.

He patiently listened to all her reports about which one of the nurses was cheating on her fiancé with a doctor, and who had a crush on the handyman. When my grandmother made a particularly sharp observation about one of the other residents, Pavel actually laughed—a real laugh that transformed his entire face for a moment.

He was kind to her, sweet.

I watched him adjust her blanket when she shivered, saw the way he made sure her water glass stayed full. Small, caring gestures.

For a moment, I almost forgot how much of a monster he really was.

Or at least I would have if he hadn't kept his gaze on me, the intent behind it clear. But even that gaze felt different now. Determined, rather than threatening.

If I wanted her here, if I wanted her happy, I needed to behave.

My freedom paid for her comfort and care.

The second I fucked up, her life was over.

When the nurse came to let us know that visiting hours had ended over an hour ago, Pavel glanced at me first and, seeing I wasn't ready to leave, shot that man a look that turned even my blood cold. The nurse backed away murmuring we could stay as long as we wanted.

But then my grandmother yawned, and we said our goodbyes and she made me promise to come visit again soon and to bring the nice man with me.

She had already forgotten his name.

It was clear she was being taken much better care of here, but the disease was still ever-present.

"Thank you," I said quietly as we walked back to the car. "For taking care of her."

Pavel's hand found the small of my back, the touch surprisingly gentle. "She matters to you. That makes her matter to me."

The simple statement shouldn't have affected me the way it did.

"The marriage thing... is it really the only way?"

"In my world, yes." His voice was matter-of-fact. "Do not forget, as far as my family is concerned you are a liability."

Oh yes. How could I forget? The only reason I was in this predicament was because I'd witnessed him commit a cold-blooded murder.

It seemed like a lifetime ago. Like it happened to someone else. Like it was nothing more than the hazy memory of a horror movie I'd once watched.

My voice was barely above a whisper since I didn't want anyone to overhear. "You can't still think I'd tell anyone…about what I…what I saw?"

His gaze was almost tender as he playfully pulled on one of my curls as if I'd said something cute instead of alluded to murder. "No. I don't."

I frowned. "Then why—"

"Because as my wife you would be untouchable. As my prisoner you are not only a liability, but you're also a target for my enemies." He opened the car door for me. "And that's unacceptable."

CHAPTER 24

PAVEL

I stood over the bed staring down at her sleeping form.

My knuckles brushed over her sleep-warmed cheek, pushing back a wayward curl to expose her neck.

So small. So innocent. So...vulnerable.

So...mine.

Or at least she would be, very soon.

Wife.

Over these last few weeks, the word had grown on me.

Returning home each night to her sweet body had become as necessary to me as air.

It wasn't love.

Love was not an emotion I was capable of.

But it was damn close.

Close enough to build a life.

My gaze ran over her body as the silk sheets hugged each delicate curve, lingering over her stomach.

What if she were already pregnant?

The idea of a beautiful baby with her eyes and smile filled me with a strange warmth. Again.

Not love…but close.

Last night had been different.

I'd come home after a particularly brutal day.

All I wanted to do was shower the blood off me and fuck her into submission. Fuck her until I forgot about anything else but the feel of her body accepting mine.

And yet…

She'd surprised me.

"Could we... could we watch a movie tonight?" she'd asked hesitantly after changing back into her sheer slip. "Something normal?"

Normal. Such a foreign concept in my world.

"What did you have in mind?"

"*The Princess Bride*. It's..." She'd searched for words. "It's my favorite. It's super funny. Although you probably won't understand half the references."

Something about her tentative request had intrigued me. "Very well."

Twenty minutes later, we were settled on the couch with a bowl of popcorn between us. I'd changed into gray sweatpants and a T-shirt—casual clothes I rarely wore, feeling oddly exposed without my armor of expensive suits.

She'd disappeared into the kitchen and returned with a bag of colorful candies, dumping them into the popcorn bowl.

"What unholy thing did you just do?" I teased, watching her mix the contents.

"M&Ms and popcorn." She shrugged, a slight blush

coloring her cheeks. "Sweet and salty. Don't knock it until you try it."

"It's against nature."

"It's not!" She grabbed a handful and held it out to me. "Try it."

I eyed the mixture skeptically before taking a piece. The combination was... unexpected. Not terrible, but strange. "Americans have no taste."

"Says the man who puts caviar on everything," she shot back, then immediately froze as if expecting punishment for her sass.

Instead, I found myself smiling. "Touché."

"Inconceivable!" some fool on the screen shouted, and Alina actually laughed—a real sound of joy that did something dangerous to my chest.

Her laughter was dangerous. It was like a drug. I found myself wanting more.

"What does that word mean, exactly?" I asked, genuinely confused by the varying contexts the word was being used in.

"It means unbelievable, impossible. But he uses it wrong—that's the joke. Inigo keeps pointing it out."

I watched her face as she explained, animated in a way I rarely saw. When the character finally said, "You keep using that word. I do not think it means what you think it means," I found myself chuckling.

"American humor is... strange," I observed, reaching for more of her bizarre popcorn mixture. The M&Ms had grown on me.

"You're getting popcorn crumbs on the couch," she giggled as she brushed the fabric.

There was no fear or hesitation in her voice. Just...normalcy.

For the next hour, we sat together like any couple might.

She explained cultural references, laughed at my confusion over American customs, and gradually relaxed against my side.

I found myself studying her profile more than the screen, fascinated by this glimpse of who she might have been in another life.

"The grandfather reading to the sick boy," I said during a quiet moment. "It reminds me of my babushka."

She turned to look at me, surprised by the personal revelation. "She read to you?"

"Russian fairy tales. Always with a moral about being careful what you wish for." I paused, remembering weathered hands and kind eyes. "She would have liked you."

Something shifted in Alina's expression—softness, maybe even tenderness. "My grandmother really does like you, you know. She keeps asking the nurses about 'that nice young man.'"

The moment the words left her lips, I saw the realization hit her.

The spell began to crack as reality intruded—the reminder of why her grandmother liked me, what I was holding over her head, the cage I'd built around both of them.

Her body started to tense, to pull away, and I couldn't have that.

Not tonight.

Before she could retreat into herself, I cupped her face and kissed her.

Soft, slow, nothing like the demanding kisses I usually claimed.

This was...gentle.

Coaxing rather than taking.

When I pulled back, her eyes were wide but no longer guarded.

"Let's keep watching your silly American movie," I murmured, tucking her under my arm and pulling her against my side.

She settled against me with a small sigh, her head finding the hollow of my shoulder as if it belonged there.

As the movie continued, her breathing slowed, her body growing heavier against mine.

By the time the credits rolled, she was fast asleep, her face peaceful in a way I rarely saw when she was awake.

One small hand rested against my chest, fingers curled into my shirt as if anchoring herself to me even in sleep.

I should have woken her.

Should have sent her to bed and maintained the careful distance that kept our arrangement simple and clean.

Instead, I found myself memorizing the weight of her against me, the soft whisper of her breath against my neck, the way her hair caught the light from the television screen.

Carefully, I slid one arm beneath her knees and the other around her back, lifting her sleeping form against my chest. She stirred slightly, nuzzling closer to my warmth, and something possessive unfurled in my chest.

Mine.

I carried her to our bedroom, moving slowly to avoid waking her.

In the low light filtering through the windows, she looked angelic—porcelain skin and dark lashes against flushed cheeks, lips slightly parted in sleep.

I laid her gently on the bed, her body sinking into the cool silk sheets.

She made a small sound of protest when I pulled away, and I found myself pausing, watching the way she unconsciously reached for me even in sleep.

Quickly, I stripped out of my clothes and slid into bed behind her.

The moment my arm came around her waist, she pressed back against me with a contented sigh, her body fitting perfectly against mine as if we'd been sleeping together for years instead of weeks.

This morning, taking her in, sound asleep in the circle of my arms, I understood something fundamental had changed.

She wasn't just my captive anymore, or even just my future wife.

She was becoming my home.

And that terrified me more than any enemy I'd ever faced.

CHAPTER 25

ALINA

*T*he emerald-cut diamond slipped down my finger again as I raised my hand to smooth the intricate beadwork on my sleeve.

The massive stone caught the afternoon light streaming through the penthouse windows, sending rainbow fractals dancing across the mirrors surrounding us.

"Stop fidgeting with that ring," Yelena scolded, pins between her teeth as she adjusted the hem of what might have been the most beautiful wedding dress I'd ever seen. "You've lost weight. Again."

I had.

The ring that fit perfectly two weeks ago now hung loose on my finger, sliding around no matter how I positioned my hand.

No matter how Pavel coaxed or demanded, food turned to ash in my mouth.

My stomach stayed knotted with anxiety, rejecting

everything but the smallest sips of water and occasional bites of plain bread.

"It's stunning," I whispered, staring at my reflection in the three-way mirror.

And it was—layers upon layers of silk and French lace that whispered sophistication rather than screaming wealth. The bodice hugged my torso perfectly, the sweetheart neckline both modest and alluring.

Tiny seed pearls and crystals had been hand-sewn into intricate patterns that caught the light with every breath I took. The skirt flowed like water, creating an ethereal silhouette that made me look like something from a fairy tale.

Everything I would have chosen...if I'd had a choice.

But that was the problem, wasn't it?

None of this was my choice.

I was standing in a penthouse with a breathtaking view of the river and the city's monuments—while trying on a custom haute couture wedding gown for a wedding I never agreed to.

The penthouse had been transformed into a bridal salon for the afternoon.

Dress forms displayed various undergarment options, jewelry boxes overflowed with sparkling accessories, and champagne glasses sat mostly untouched on silver trays.

It was surreal, like playing dress-up for the most important day of my life while feeling completely disconnected from the reality of it.

"Of course it's stunning. I don't do mediocre." Yelena stepped back to admire her work, her narrowed eyes critical as they swept over every detail. "Though Pavel giving me only two weeks to create a masterpiece was completely unreasonable. Do you know how many hours of hand-beading this required?"

She gestured to the intricate patterns covering the bodice and trailing down the skirt like constellation maps. I could only imagine the painstaking work that had gone into each tiny detail.

Around us, the other wives murmured approval— Marina with her warm smile and gentle hands as she adjusted the delicate cap sleeves, Samara holding up different jewelry options against my skin, Viktoria quietly observing with understanding in her eyes, and Nadia offering encouraging nods.

All married to men just as dangerous as Pavel, yet they glowed with happiness that seemed impossible given their circumstances.

From what I could tell, none of the others had a family member at the mercy of these monsters, so why were these women with killers?

How could they love such treacherous men so completely?

"The veil is next," Marina said, lifting a cascade of silk tulle adorned with the same intricate beadwork as the dress. "Yelena recreated Pavel's grandmother's veil from some old family photos and added beading to match your dress."

Family heirlooms, custom gowns, elaborate cere-monies—why was Pavel insisting on all these traditional elements?

He didn't love me.

We weren't dating.

This was to ensure my silence about the brutal murder I saw him commit.

Nothing more.

He wasn't my lover.

I was an enemy he was keeping close. Under control.

The contradiction of it all gnawed at me.

Why make this big show about a lie?

Why not just have a courthouse wedding?

Why do any of this?

Yet, at the same time, he had placed my grandmother in the best facility.

The staff had impeccable standards and were not overworked; my grandmother got the attention she needed. Pavel had her placed in the best room, ensuring she received the highest level of care.

"You know," Marina said quietly as Viktoria carefully positioned the veil, "I was terrified too. Right up until I walked down that aisle. I kept thinking about running, about fighting, about anything except saying those vows."

Nadia laughed. "Strictly speaking you didn't exactly *walk* down the aisle."

Yelena poked her head from around me to glare at Marina. "I still haven't forgiven you for how you ruined that beautiful veil I made by tearing it off your damn head in the middle of the ceremony."

Samara handed her more pins. "Be nice. The veil would have gotten in the way when she slapped Kostya."

My eyes widened as I stared at Marina in the mirror's reflection.

I couldn't imagine her slapping Pavel's brother Kostya, who was every bit as big and scary as Pavel. How did she even reach him to slap him? He was so much taller than her.

I couldn't resist asking even as my cheeks warmed. "Did he..." I hesitated. I didn't want to use the word *punish*. Even the word brought illicit images of Pavel forcing me to bend over a table as he strapped me with his belt like a misbehaving child. "Did he...get mad?"

Nadia bumped Marina's shoulder with her own then winked. "I think he was way more pissed off when she ditched him and returned to Chicago in the middle of their honeymoon."

Marina winked back. "He got my point, didn't he? At least I didn't try screaming the rafters down in the church like Viktoria."

I blinked and turned in my dress, which earned me a pinch from Yelena. "Eyes forward."

Viktoria passed out the champagne flutes. "Artem wouldn't know what to do with himself if I quietly did what I was told."

They all laughed.

What. The. Fuck.

It was like I'd stumbled into some parallel universe.

These women were joking about provoking their incredibly violent and terrifying husbands.

Even the idea of disobeying Pavel made me want to break out in hives.

"I wasn't even given a warning about my wedding," Samara added with a laugh that seemed genuine despite the horrifying circumstances. "Gregor just announced we were getting married after he practically kidnapped me onto his private plane. The officiant was waiting for us when we landed."

"At least you weren't carried down the aisle in an old pair of jeans and a T-shirt like a sack of potatoes while he threatened the priest," Viktoria chimed in, her eyes dancing with mischief.

Samara gestured with her champagne flute as she laughed. "That poor priest's face every time you kept answering NEVER to all his vow questions."

The sound grated against my nerves, highlighting just how alone I felt in my terror.

Jesus Christ. It just kept getting worse and worse.

"How?" The question burst out before I could stop it, raw and desperate. "How are you all so happy? They're killers. Monsters. They took your choices away, forced you into marriage, and you're laughing about it like it's some romantic comedy."

The laughter faded, replaced by understanding smiles that somehow left me feeling even more isolated.

"Because," Viktoria said gently, her voice carrying the weight of experience, "they're not just killers. They're complicated. Possessive, yes. Controlling, absolutely. Dangerous in ways that should terrify us. But devoted in ways that..."

"That what?" I pressed, genuinely desperate to understand how they'd made peace with their situations.

"That make you feel like the most precious thing in their world," Marina finished softly. "Like they would tear apart anyone who even thought about hurting you. Like you're not just wanted, but needed."

I wanted to scoff, to point out the insanity of Stockholm syndrome masquerading as love.

But Pavel's face flashed in my mind—the way he'd sat patiently with my grandmother, listening to her stories and laughing at her jokes.

The gentle hands that washed me after claiming my body so thoroughly I forgot my own name.

The way he'd held me during that movie, stroking my hair until I fell asleep feeling safer than I had in years.

How could the same man who threatened my grandmother's safety also ensure she received the best care available?

How could hands capable of violence be so tender when they touched me?

"He's holding my grandmother hostage," I said flatly, needing to voice the ugly truth that separated my situation from their romantic narratives.

"Artem threatened me," Viktoria replied without missing a beat. "Multiple times. Very creatively."

"Gregor bought me from my parents," Samara added matter-of-factly. "Literally purchased me like livestock."

"Marina was stalked for months," Nadia contributed quietly.

"But here we are," Marina said, spreading her arms to encompass our surreal bridal fitting. "Not just surviving but thriving. Loved, protected, cherished in ways we never thought possible."

Here they were indeed—radiant, protected, loved by men who would burn the world down for them.

But at what cost?

What had they given up to achieve this happiness?

ZOE BLAKE

"I don't understand how you made that transition," I admitted. "From terror to...this."

"Time," Viktoria said simply. "And honesty. With them, but mostly with ourselves about what we actually wanted versus what we thought we should want."

"What do you mean?"

"I mean," she continued, her voice gentle but firm, "when was the last time you felt truly safe? Not just physically, but emotionally? When did you last have someone anticipate your needs, care for your wellbeing, make your happiness their priority?"

The question hit harder than I expected.

The honest answer was never.

My entire adult life had been about survival, about shouldering responsibilities that weren't mine, about making everyone else's needs more important than my own.

I looked at the women around me, now deep in conversation about something happening at the compound.

They were all glowing, radiant with happiness.

They didn't know the specifics of my story.

I didn't know what I was allowed to tell them.

They told me a little of theirs and it seemed like they were in...similar situations.

But now they were happy, in love and flourishing under the protection and support of the most dangerous men in the world.

Pavel mentioned me going back to school.

Would he let me do that?

Would I be allowed to create the future I wanted, as long as I stayed by his side?

It seemed too good to be true.

I was lost in thought when the air shifted.

"Ladies."

The temperature in the room plummeted.

Pavel's voice cut through our conversation, and even these fearless women straightened slightly.

The easy camaraderie of moments before shifted into something more formal, more careful.

"Time for you to leave."

I met his eyes in the mirror, my breath catching at the intensity I found there.

Something dangerous flickered in those dark depths— not anger, exactly, but something that made my pulse spike with equal parts fear and unwanted anticipation.

He filled the doorway like a storm cloud, his expensive suit doing nothing to civilize the predatory energy that seemed to radiate from him.

The other women exchanged glances, a silent communication passing between them that spoke of experience with their own dangerous husbands.

Yelena helped me out of my dress and into a robe before packing the dress up along with her tools, while everyone else gathered their things with practiced efficiency, no questions asked, no protests offered.

Yelena pressed a quick kiss to my cheek, her voice barely above a whisper. "The dress will be ready first thing tomorrow morning. Try to get some rest tonight."

Marina squeezed my hand. "Everything will be fine. Trust me."

Samara and Viktoria offered encouraging smiles, while Nadia simply nodded her understanding.

Then they were gone, leaving me alone with Pavel, who had walked in and caught me in a wedding dress that suddenly seemed more like a costume for a play I'd never auditioned for.

The silence stretched between us, heavy with unspoken tension.

I remained frozen in place, afraid to move, afraid to breathe too loudly. In the mirrors surrounding us, I could see him studying me from every angle.

"Did they have to go?" I asked finally, lifting a champagne flute I hadn't touched all afternoon.

The crystal felt impossibly delicate in my trembling hand as the bubbles tickled my nose, sending another wave of nausea through my already unsettled stomach. "We were having fun."

It was a lie, and we both knew it.

I'd been too anxious to truly enjoy anything, too caught up in my own spiraling thoughts to engage properly with the women who'd tried so hard to include me.

"Yes." His gaze never left mine in the mirror, dark and unreadable. "You and I need to talk."

Oh god.

Nothing good ever followed those words.

Not in my experience with Pavel, and certainly not when delivered in that particular tone—calm on the surface but with undercurrents that made my skin prickle with warning.

CHAPTER 26

PAVEL

I was going to catch shit from my family for kicking out the wives, especially when they were having fun.

Damien was going to be particularly pissed at me for rushing his wife.

The glare she gave me promised her husband's anger as she carefully peeled Alina from the couture wedding dress that I wasn't supposed to see.

Yeah, all of them were going to get shit from their wives and they would all happily pass that down to me.

Still, Damien and the others would have been far more pissed if I allowed them to stay, given my condition.

Not only could I not protect them, but I also didn't want them freaking out over the amount of blood that was seeping into my shirt under my jacket.

There was only so long I could keep it hidden.

They had all seen their own husbands bleed, hell, a few of them were responsible for that blood.

I knew they weren't weak or squeamish.

None of them would faint at the sight.

But they knew I'd been on a mission with their husbands.

If they spotted my condition, then they would have worried about what might have happened to their men.

Kostya had explained once or twice that an annoyed wife was a pain in the ass, but far better that than a freaked-out wife.

A sentiment I didn't understand, but which Artem had wholeheartedly agreed with.

The moment the women left, I turned to Alina. "I ordered food. Wait for the guards to knock with the room service."

She nodded as she swapped the robe for the T-shirt and yoga pants I had given her for the girls' visit. I would have complained, but those pants hugged her ass in a way that made gods weep and reminded me of the first time I laid eyes on her.

And I had more pressing matters to attend to.

I headed to the bathroom, carefully pulling off my suit jacket.

The shirt underneath was soaked with blood. It was already sticking to the wound and drying around the edges. Taking it off was going to hurt like a bitch.

A sharp gasp at the door made me turn.

Alina stood there, her eyes wide and the color draining from her face.

Something close to concern flashed across her face.

It must have been the blood loss.

There was no way she was worried about me.

In time, maybe.

But for now, she didn't see me as a lover but rather as a jailor.

If that was what it took to protect her, then I would be her monster.

"Babygirl, you shouldn't see this. Go back to the other room. I'll be out in a moment, and we'll have dinner," I said, turning back to the mirror.

She didn't move, her gaze locked onto the blood.

"You're hurt."

"It's just a scratch."

It wasn't.

The bullet had only grazed me, but it cut deeper than I had originally thought.

Nothing vital was hit, but I was bleeding a lot, and I would be left with a brutal scar that would mar the tattoos I had covering my side.

The annoyance at the ruined art was almost as bad as the pain itself. That piece had taken forever. It was slow and excruciating. Not only the tattooing itself, but the itching afterward was brutal. Now it was ruined.

Coming home to my fiancée covered in blood was not how I wanted the night before our wedding to go.

I had intended a quiet night where we talked, and I told her what our lives together would look like. I would give her the rules she was expected to live by and the new freedoms she would have as my wife.

The gunfight had been...unexpected.

The Colombians were proving to be more of a threat than Damien had led me to believe.

They should have barely had enough men or fire-power to be anything other than an inconvenience.

After they kidnapped Yelena, Damien had all but wiped them out.

The ones who terrorized Alina should have been barely more than low-level street thugs.

Last time any of us had dealt with them, they weren't even on our radar. They ran some poker rooms and Solovyov had tried to steal a gun shipment from us using their muscle.

That firefight resulted in a bonfire that I thought wiped most of them out.

It didn't.

Either they had funding I was unaware of, or something else changed.

They were different now—better organized, better funded.

Something about their power structure had been altered, but I couldn't put my finger on it.

Their sudden discipline, their influx of cash—it was a serious problem that had me considering calling Roman in again, despite how pissed Gregor had been when he learned I used him to kill Solovyov.

Satan himself would love to get his hands dirty, and it had been too long since I had seen my favorite unhinged cousin.

Gregor and Artem weren't going to like it.

They loved Roman like the rest of us did, but there was something in him that we had all grown out of in our teenage years.

We all had a darkness to us.

We were unafraid of death or pain, and we took what we wanted.

Roman was in a league of his own.

Blood spill was a sport to him, a game to be played with either a surgeon's precision or reckless abandon.

He had this wildness to him, this untamable core that made him...unpredictable.

Both Artem and Gregor could appreciate Roman's skill and passion for his work, but that wild unpredictability made him a liability.

They would get over it...eventually. I had no issues pissing off my cousin and brother if it meant getting rid of the Columbian threat and keeping my girl safe.

Besides, after the way Roman took care of Solovyov, I owed him a drink.

The immediate crisis, however, was the wound bleeding through my shirt. I needed to focus on that first.

Alina ignored my command and stepped into the bathroom.

I watched her reflection, frozen, not wanting to spook her as she reached for the buttons on my shirt.

She hesitated, her hand floating in the air between them as her rich brown eyes met mine in the mirror.

I didn't stop her.

When I didn't move, she pressed further and started working on the buttons of my shirt.

It was the first time she had touched me willingly.

The first time she initiated any kind of contact.

Fitting, I thought darkly, that both of our hands were soaked in blood.

Still, every time her fingers brushed my skin, I savored the contact.

She peeled the shirt from my shoulders.

I clenched my teeth to stifle the yelp ripping up my throat as she pulled the soaked fabric from my wound.

She hissed when she saw the wound, and I closed my eyes, waiting to hear the disgust or the reprimanding tone from her.

I braced myself for even worse.

What if she mocked my pain? What if she said I deserved it?

I had earned the injury by protecting her.

Avenging the life those assholes allowed her father to steal from her.

I could tell her that, but to what end?

The only thing that would've come of that would be to make her aware of a threat that would be taken care of long before she had to face it.

An annoyed wife was far better than a freaked-out one.

"I don't want you to see this. Leave. Now." I tried to keep my voice strong, but the blood loss was making the room spin and I felt cold and tired.

"Where is the first aid kit?" she asked, ignoring my demand. I'd enjoy punishing her for that... later.

I gestured with a nod of my chin, growing more impressed by the second at her calm demeanor. Brows furrowed with determination, head slightly tilted as she focused, and not once did she look away squeamishly.

She ordered me to sit on the edge of the tub.

I had to hold back a grin at her cute, authoritative tone.

I'd play along for now and remind her who I was tomorrow.

Digging into the cabinet, she dragged out the large paramedic bag. In my world, a basic first aid kit with gauze and Band-Aids didn't cut it.

I had everything I needed to avoid hospitals—drugs, suture kits, and proper surgical supplies.

Anything that required IV medications or blood, I'd have to call Mikhail to come patch me up.

This shouldn't need a field medic, just a steady hand with a needle and thread.

She bit her lip as she washed her hands while surveying the supplies and the wound. "I suppose I'd be wasting my breath telling you to go to a hospital."

I raised an eyebrow. "What do you think?"

"I think there is a large gash in your side, and most of your blood is pooling on the floor."

"Hospitals ask questions I am not prepared to answer. You don't have to be here, I can—"

"Well, it's going to need stitches." She talked over me with a resigned sigh. "I'll prepare what's needed."

She tore open the suture packet with her teeth.

Under normal circumstances, that shouldn't have been sexy.

But fuck, it was.

My little kitten was a bit of a savage.

I knew she had a primal side, but I had been sure it only came out when she was backed into a corner, or she was pinned under me.

This was new, and I'd have to find a way to bring it out of her that didn't require a bullet. Maybe a shallow stabbing would suffice?

Alina worked methodically, gloved hands preparing

my wound, cleaning it, and removing any stray debris with the tweezers.

Her touch was surprisingly gentle, a lot better than Kostya's heavy-handed butterfingers.

"Do you want something for the pain?" she asked, eyeing a bottle of morphine.

"No, I want to stay clearheaded."

She met my gaze in the mirror and nodded. Then she touched the wound, and a flash of pain blinded me for a second as I sucked a breath in through my teeth.

"Maybe just an aspirin," I said and reached for the bottle.

"No, aspirin will thin your blood and make it harder to clot. You already lost too much."

"Careful, someone might think you care."

She met my eyes in the mirror again and raised her eyebrow at me.

"Someone has to pay for my grandmother's fancy new place."

Why was her attitude so fucking hot?

"Ready?"

This time, I gave her a nod and braced myself.

She slowly and precisely began stitching my flesh closed. Her small hands were so delicate, so dainty that I barely felt the stitch or even the pull of the thread through my skin.

The pressure of the fingers splayed on my back, the soft whoosh of her breath against my skin, were far more noticeable than the bite of the needle.

My skin was oversensitive, but not for the needle. For her.

"Where did you learn how to do this?" I couldn't imagine where she would have picked up this particular skill set.

She sighed, her eyes closing for a moment before she reopened them and focused on my back.

"My grandmother. When her dementia got really bad, she started falling. There wasn't any money for frequent emergency room trips, so I watched hundreds of YouTube videos and learned how to care for her myself."

Fuck.

I had not expected that.

I thought she was going to tell me she thought about being pre-med or binge-watched some medical drama. Hell, I almost expected a little hint of her fire with a quip about me keeping her locked away so she'd been practicing on the guards.

I didn't expect heart-wrenching honesty.

She really was an incredible woman.

Too bad she hated my guts.

Not for the first time, I wished we had met under different circumstances. One where I could take my time, woo her with affection, attention, and then teach her to love the chase as much as I did.

Or anything where I had the luxury of time.

When she was finished, she tied off the sutures.

"I need to clean up," I said as she reached for a bandage.

Her hand stopped just over the bandage, hovering there for a moment, and I stared at it, wishing she would lay it back on my skin.

Instead, she pulled her hand away and nodded.

"When you are done, I will bandage the stitches."

Then she was gone.

I quickly washed at the sink and followed her out of the door, needing to know where she was.

When I joined her in the dining room, she already had dinner set up.

The shift from the bathroom's intimacy to the dining room's formality was jarring. Here, with proper place settings and polite distance between us, the moment we'd shared seemed almost like a dream.

The mood felt strange—tense, yet... intimate.

I opened my mouth maybe a dozen times to say something as she picked at her pasta.

I just didn't know what to say. How did I start a genuine conversation that wouldn't remind her what I was, and what led her here?

How did I show her I may be a monster, but there was more to me than blood, knives, and bleeding wounds?

Tomorrow, we'd be married.

Alina would be my wife, and I didn't know how to speak to her.

I should tell her that these past few weeks had been some of the best of my life.

That coming home to her was the highlight of my day, every day. I should tell her I'd begun craving her company, and I'd do anything in my power to make her happy.

I should've said something to show her I may be a monster, but I was her monster.

That I had become obsessed with earning one of her elusive smiles.

That the idea of her carrying my child, of capturing

even a piece of what my brothers and cousins had, filled me with something unfamiliar.

Hope.

It was strange and uncomfortable at first, but I had grown accustomed to it, and now I was afraid I'd miss it if it disappeared.

The hope was for us.

Hope for our future.

Hope wasn't something a Russian mafia enforcer like me ever allowed myself.

It was a luxury I refused to afford.

Hope was a fleeting thing.

It was addictive, and I wasn't sure I'd survive the withdrawal.

CHAPTER 27

ALINA

"*E*verything is ready, and we are almost good to go. Alina, are you ready?" Samara's smile was bright and happy and everything I wished I was feeling.

This was not supposed to be how I felt on my wedding day.

It wasn't supposed to be happening like this.

"I–" I opened my suddenly parched mouth and tried to say something, anything.

The words wouldn't come.

Yelena peeked out of the wooden door into the sanctuary of the church.

I could hear people laughing, talking in a mix of English and Russian, but it all morphed together. It seemed to get louder and louder the longer she held the door open.

I was hidden away with Samara, Yelena, and my soon-to-be sisters-in-law in a side room where all the brides took a moment to gather themselves before walking down the aisle and pledging their life to the man they loved more than anything.

That was not why I was here.

I was here to pledge my life to a man that I didn't love, who didn't love me.

A man that I barely knew and who was holding me captive.

The same man who had come back to our hotel room last night with a long gash in his side that I had to stitch up before we sat in silence and ate, both of us thinking about the commitment we were to make today.

No, I pushed those thoughts away.

I had to do this.

This wasn't a choice.

My grandmother's life depended on it.

Pavel wasn't all bad.

Maybe if I could focus on the positive, I could calm down enough to take a full breath and get through this in one piece.

Just one full breath and I could compose myself and act like the bride everyone expected.

All I had to do was think of the good things Pavel had done.

He put my grandmother in a state-of-the-art facility that couldn't have been cheap. She adored it there and adored Pavel. He also used her life to keep me behaving.

He took care of my father's debt, but he also killed my father.

I wasn't sure if that went in the positive or negative column.

The sex was—nope. I couldn't go there.

The penthouse he kept me prisoner in was a lovely cage.

My chest squeezed harder.

This wasn't working.

" I–" I tried to say something again, but I couldn't take a full breath.

The small room felt suffocating, the scent of old wood and candle wax mixing with my panic. The wooden walls of the room felt like they were getting closer and closer, and it was getting harder and harder to breathe.

I couldn't do this.

My lungs fought for air that seemed too thin, too sparse. I wasn't getting the oxygen I needed, anyway.

My hands were clenched by my sides to keep them from ripping at the delicate lace over my chest and around my throat. The pearls that one of the girls handed me—a wedding gift from Pavel—felt like a noose.

The girls saw something was wrong, and they hovered nearby trying to soothe me, rubbing my back and my arms, cooing sweet words, telling me it was natural to be nervous.

Everything was going to be fine. I was marrying a good man.

That last one almost made me laugh, and it just made everything worse.

Despite their gentle touches and soothing words, the panic only intensified.

"Just breathe," Nadia said, like it was the simplest thing in the world. "Breathe in, hold it for a few seconds and then breathe out."

I tried to mimic what she was doing, but I just couldn't.

Marina, looking a little frightened, bolted from the room and a moment later she came back with Pavel in tow.

He had been waiting with his guests, taking their congratulations and well wishes while waiting for the lavish ceremony to start.

Why was he doing this?

Why not just drag me to a courthouse?

I just didn't understand.

Why did he have to pretend this was real, that we were in love and ready to ride off into the sunset together?

What did he gain from this?

Was it just another way to show me I had no choices?

Lying to a judge and signing a piece of paper was one thing, but I didn't think I could put on this performance in front of so many people.

How was I supposed to lie to God?

I couldn't do this.

The walls moved in faster, pressing into me.

An icy chill ran up my back, tightening around my throat as my entire body erupted in a cold sweat.

Pavel took one look at the dress and growled. "Everybody out. Now."

The women left without saying a word.

With fewer people surrounding me it should have been easier to breathe, but instead Pavel's large body and commanding presence sucked in all the air.

A look I had never seen on Pavel's face before crossed his stern features.

If I didn't know better, I would have said it was something close to anxiousness.

That couldn't have been it. Maybe I was misreading, and it was annoyance.

He closed the door behind him, and the second we were alone, I couldn't take it anymore.

I collapsed on my hands and my knees and started clawing at the bodice of the dress, gasping for air.

I couldn't breathe.

The room was spinning and no matter what I did, I felt like the air was being choked out of me.

Pavel didn't hesitate.

His arms wrapped around my waist, lifting me. He then sat me on the nearest table before he pulled out a knife from his back pocket and, in one swift motion, sliced through the dress.

He first cut the delicate lace around my throat, slicing the pearls too, and letting the precious beads fly across the floor. Then he sliced the side of the bodice so it was no longer squeezing my ribs.

The pressure eased and air rushed back into my lungs, and the panic shifted.

I could breathe, but tears started pouring down my face, ruining my once perfect makeup.

"I'm so sorry, I can't do this," I sobbed. " I can't do this. Please don't make me. I just can't."

I could hear the hysteria in my voice, but I couldn't make it stop.

The room was still spinning, and it felt like I was spiraling into a mess of chaotic fear and desperation.

"*Moy kotyonochek*," he murmured. "Please, talk to me."

His voice was soft and pleading, and it just made the tears come faster. "Please, I can't do this. There are too many people. They will know it's a lie. Please."

I expected him to insist in his usual gruff way.

He could have told me to get a grip, to control myself, or my grandmother would pay dearly for my disrespect.

He could have blamed me for the pearls now scattered all over the floor.

There were a thousand things I would have expected.

Pavel's lips pressed onto mine wasn't one of them.

The shock of it stalled my panic just for a moment. My heartbeat slowed, only a fraction, and the icy chill turned into something warm.

His kiss was soft at first and soothed something deep inside me.

But when he pulled away, the familiar panic began creeping back, my breathing turning shallow again.

"Please." My body trembled as my fingers wrapped around the sharp edge of the counter so hard they ached.

He pried my fingers from the counter's edge and put them against his chest as he pressed his forehead to mine.

"You need strength, *moy kotyonochek?* Take mine." He kissed me again, this time deeper.

As he pressed his tongue into my mouth, he held my hands to his chest, forcing me to feel his strength, his power, and letting me borrow from it.

Something shifted inside me as I felt his steady heartbeat beneath my palms, his unwavering presence anchoring me. The adrenaline still raced through my veins, but with a new purpose.

I wrapped my fingers around his lapels and held him closer to me as I melted into his kiss.

His hands moved down my arms to my sides, his fingers just gracing the skin that had been exposed when he cut the dress.

The kiss turned hot, desperate, and I needed more.

So did he.

His hands moved down to my thighs.

Finding the slit in the skirt, he pushed it aside.

My hands moved down his chest, over the buttons of his shirt, to the smooth, cold metal belt buckle.

It took me a moment to get it undone, but once I did, I slipped my hands in his pants and wrapped my fingers around the hard steel of his cock.

He sucked in a breath between his teeth.

"*Moy kotyonochek*," he groaned before sliding my panties to the side to expose my wet cunt. "Hold on to me, let me center you."

He took his cock out of my hands and lined it up with my entrance.

I spread my legs wider for him, silently begging him to fuck me. I knew that if he was inside me, if he was taking me, then I wouldn't think of anything else.

While he was taking and giving me so much pleasure, the rest of the world would fade into nothing.

That was what I needed.

He was what I needed.

"Tell me you want me, tell me you want me to take you in the back of this church," he purred into my ear.

"No," I panted. "I need you."

He pushed inside of me with one long, hard thrust and I tipped my head back, loving every second of the delicious stretch.

Once he was seated deep inside me, he stilled.

Looking deep into his eyes, I felt... complete.

He leaned down and kissed me with more gentleness than I thought he was capable of.

He touched me like he worshiped me as he pushed in and out of me slowly, like he needed to feel every inch of me, like I needed to feel him.

This wasn't the brutal, animalistic sex we usually had.

It was so much more.

He was using his body, his mouth, his cock to center me. He grounded me to him, and I was helpless to do anything but give in to him.

My body already responded to him with heat and need, and this felt deeper.

When he sealed his lips to mine again with a silent demand to give in to him, I did just that. I came with a muffled cry, and he followed me right over the abyss.

He didn't pull away.

He stayed with me, his arms around me, his cock inside me, linking us together as he kissed me while we both came down.

Then he cradled my face in his hands while looking deep into my eyes.

"Lust may not be love, but it's something, babygirl. You have no one in your corner. No one to care for you. No one to protect you. The people who should have protected you betrayed you. Now there is no one to shelter you from all the bullshit life throws at us. Let me be that man for you."

A fresh wave of tears tracked down my face.

"Let me be the man who will burn the world to the ground to keep you safe."

I took in a deep, shuddering breath then I whispered back to him, telling him my deepest fear.

"But we don't love each other. You're only marrying me to keep me from talking to the police. What happens when you tire of me? What happens when you find someone better? Who will protect me then?"

He exhaled, pressing a slow kiss to my forehead as he pulled me close, stroking my hair. Soothing me in a way I didn't know another person could.

"Trust me. That's not the only reason and I will never tire of you."

He didn't explain further.

Instead, he kissed me again while pulling out of me, then after tucking himself away, turned to storm to the door and open it just a crack, making sure no one could see me while I got myself together again.

"Tell all the guests to leave. Family only," he barked to someone outside.

I heard a muffled, "You got it, boss."

My panic flared again as I looked down at my destroyed wedding dress.

He had cut the delicate Italian lace.

The corset bodice was sliced and the slit in the leg was ripped clear up to my hip.

"You don't have to kill me," I muttered when Pavel returned to my side.

"Alina, you are going to be my wife, I—"

"No, that's not what I mean." I gave him what I hoped looked like a reassuring smile. "Yelena will kill me for you when she sees what we've done to her beautiful dress."

Pavel shrugged out of his suit jacket and draped it over my shoulders.

I loved that I was now warm and surrounded by his spicy scent.

"I'll block the first bullet," he said with a grin before scooping me into his arms and carrying me down the aisle.

The church felt different now—more intimate with only family present.

Candlelight flickered off the stained-glass windows, casting colored shadows across the wooden pews. His brothers and cousins sat on either side of the aisle.

Family.

It was strange to think there was literally no one here at my wedding for me.

No one except Pavel.

I had a pang of regret that my grandmother wasn't here.

To his credit, Pavel had asked me if I wanted her here.

I'd said no.

At the time I told him I was worried about her dementia and disrupting the routine which was so important to keeping her calm and stable.

The real truth was I didn't want her witnessing this.

No one said anything about him carrying me to the altar or the state of my makeup.

There was no judgment on any of their faces, and as we stood in front of the priest, I was starting to relax when, just as the ceremony was about to begin, a horrified voice cut through the church.

"What the fuck happened to my dress?"

CHAPTER 28

ALINA

*M*rs. Pavel Ivanova.

I was Mrs. Ivanova.

Married.

I was married.

Married!

The words repeated over and over in my head, and they still didn't sound real.

Two weeks in, and I still couldn't believe it.

Probably because, in many ways, nothing had changed.

I was still being held as a prisoner in the penthouse, only able to have access to the computer and talk to Grandma when Pavel was here and he allowed it.

He had never told me no unless he was heading out the door, but still.

The desire to see her, to hug her and let her gush over the pearls that Pavel had someone collect and restring, gnawed at me constantly.

I was still under guard and not allowed to leave, or go

into the office, or do anything that required contact with the outside world.

He saw I was going stir-crazy, and he would whisper in my ear that as soon as he knew he could trust me, I would have more freedom.

What did that even look like?

A kid's e-reader that didn't have a web browser but which he could download approved books on?

Would he take me out and walk me twice a day like a dog?

It was frustrating, and I was losing hope that it would ever be different.

Then a week ago he started letting me have visitors.

Fortunately, the second they were given the green light, Yelena, Nadia, Samara, Viktoria, and Marina visited often.

And they brought something even better.

Work. A purpose I could focus on.

They enjoyed keeping me busy with the financial documents and legal paperwork for their gallery. I considered it a win.

It was almost enough to feel like a job. It gave me something to pour my energy into. My days were consumed with optimizing their businesses, setting up better accounting software, formalizing payroll, and negotiating better vendor agreements.

Marina was working on adding a small coffee shop and café to the gallery, something simple where artists could hang to get inspired, or people could chat over coffee while they decided which pieces would look best in their home or office.

That gave me plenty to work on—permits, food vendor licenses, and even a local roaster, tea house and bakery to supply the signature food and drink.

We were even looking at setting up a few appointments to try the coffee before Marina would decide who to go with.

Not that I'd be allowed to go with them.

No one brought up how I wasn't allowed to leave.

No one said a thing about my having to use Viktoria's computer and not having one of my own to work on. Not even a single eye was batted when I said I couldn't work on this when they weren't there.

It was like they understood and respected the boundaries that Pavel had set.

Which was both a relief and grated on my nerves.

How was this normal for them?

There was so much I had to look up, so much I had to research, and it would have been far easier to do if I were alone. But the girls were understanding and excited about the work I was doing for them.

I started small by tackling SEO enhancements, growing their online presence, and the results were already paying off.

The girls reported increased traffic and booming sales at the gallery. Their social media pages had a lot more traffic, too, and they had become a bit of an Instagrammable destination.

Not that I could see for myself.

I burned with jealousy every time Samara gushed over the light that came in through the massive windows, and

Marina talked about people watching with the most fascinating, eclectic clientele.

Everything from seasoned collectors looking for the next big thing, to young, hungry entrepreneurs and frat bros turned finance bros looking to seem cultured to the ladies. Her favorites, though, were the young couples who were starting together and didn't know shit about art.

They didn't know who was up-and-coming and what would keep its value. But they knew what they liked. They knew what made them feel.

Honestly, the frat bros sounded more entertaining as they overpaid for art just because Nadia batted her eyes.

But the longing to experience it myself grew stronger each day. To see it for myself. To people-watch and sip cappuccinos with the girls and to enjoy the sunlight on my face.

Actual sunlight that hadn't been filtered through UV glass.

Pavel still refused to let me go in person.

He had offered to take me several times, but I had always refused.

The thought of going on my own, of hanging with just the girls, consumed my thoughts.

If I had any hope of carving out a sliver of normalcy in this forced marriage, he had to trust me.

That night, over dinner, I chatted about the gallery.

Pavel listened.

More than that, he asked questions.

Not about the art, but about what I was doing for them.

How the new accounting software worked, what SEO

meant and why it was important. I guessed having his business easily searchable was the last thing he wanted.

He even asked about the start of the café idea. It was still in the information-gathering phase, but he seemed invested.

Still, his curiosity appeared to be genuine.

So did the pride he had in my work.

Instead of brushing it off as unimportant—optimizing a website for the pet project of his cousins' and brothers' wives—he treated it like I was contributing in some significant way. When my throat got tight at the realization, I knew then how desperately I wanted his approval. I craved it.

The most I thought I could hope for was that he was pleased with me and would give me more freedom. I didn't know how to deal with him being proud of me.

A lump formed in my throat, and I tried to push it down with a deep breath.

It was… almost normal.

That night when he sat next to me on the sofa and went to turn something on the TV, I took the remote from him and tossed it on the floor.

For the first time I kissed him first. I crawled on top of him and stripped his shirt off, running my fingers over his bare chest.

Something came over me, and I needed to show him how much I liked the way he made me feel.

The need to prove I could be good, that I could give myself to this marriage, to him, overwhelmed me.

And I just wanted him. The craving for his rough, tattooed hands on me, his mouth licking and sucking my body, and the satisfaction I knew only he could provide took over.

I kissed my way down his chest, the nerves leaving my body as he laced his fingers in my hair. This time, he didn't push me down.

He let me take my time exploring his body with my fingers and my tongue.

Every time his abs flexed under my touch and his breath hitched, or a low growling moan left his lips, I got bolder.

His approval, his arousal, fueled my own.

I took him in my mouth, and he let out another moan that made my heart pound and gave me the confidence to do whatever I wanted to him.

He was at my mercy...at least for about five minutes, when his control snapped and he threw me back on the sofa cushions, burying his face between my thighs until he made me scream his name. Twice.

The way he touched me, the way he kissed me as he pushed inside me, felt like more than it had. It felt intimate, like we were building something more than him just pulling pleasure from my body as he chased his own end.

He was chasing something else, trying to tell me something, and I found myself desperate to understand it.

After we caught our breath, he picked me up and carried me into the bathroom and started our own little post-sex ritual.

He went to the tub and filled it with steaming water and while he was getting the temperature right, I would study the maze of patterns and images in his tattoos. He was covered, and there was always something new to explore.

That night, my eyes went to the tattoo on his right side, covering his ribs. The ones I had to stitch over the night before our wedding. I had tried to line up the ink as best as possible, and I think I did a pretty good job. The skin was still raised and a little red, but the image was clear.

Chains. They were broken, links shattered.

I didn't ask about his tattoos. Ever.

They seemed like something deeply personal.

And as Samara had explained earlier when she was talking about a painting, art had different meanings to different people, evoked different responses in them. An image may make one person feel one way, and someone else feel another.

The broken chains on his ribs made me think of where we could be. If only he would trust me enough to break his iron-like grip on my life. Trust me enough to know I wouldn't betray him.

Why couldn't he trust that I wouldn't run?

"Which scent did you want?" he asked, pulling me from my thoughts.

A smile graced my lips.

He always asked which of the expensive bubbling bath oils I preferred for the night.

For such a large, terrifying, tattooed mafia enforcer, Pavel loved his bubble baths, and I loved the way it felt to relax against his skin in the warm water.

"Amber and vanilla," I answered. That scent was the perfect mix of feminine and masculine.

More often than not, it would lure me into a waking sleep where I could pretend that this was real.

That he loved me and I loved him.

It was the only time I let myself succumb to the fantasy.

This time I couldn't give in to it. I laid my head on his shoulder; my heart pounded too hard as I chewed on my bottom lip. Could I ask him? Would he let me?

"I can practically hear your mind working overtime. What's wrong?" Pavel asked, placing a kiss on my shoulder.

"Nothing," I said, mostly meaning it.

"Tell me." This time, the kiss was followed by a nip.

With a deep breath, I shored up my courage and asked him again.

"Let me go to the gallery. Alone. Please. I want to go work at the gallery, see the paintings and people watch. If you went with me, I would feel like I had to rush because you have so much that keeps you busy."

"Alina," he said with a warning tone.

"Look, I won't go to the police. I would never go to the police. I'm not fighting this, I'm not fighting you, I'm accepting this marriage, but part of that is being part of your family and bonding with the other wives. Please, I want—"

He cut me off with a sweet kiss.

"Okay," he said, wrapping his arms around me and pulling me against his chest.

"Okay?" I wasn't sure I heard him right.

I had meant what I said.

Nothing could make me run to the police.

It felt like this was changing, like we were changing.

And maybe... just maybe...

This wasn't love.

Not yet.

But it was something. The realization should have terrified me. Instead, a warm flutter of hope settled in my chest.

Despite everything—despite the lack of choice, the captivity, the way this all began—something real was growing between us. I just needed him to trust me, to give me some freedom.

Pavel was quiet for a long moment before he spoke again.

"Next week," he said. "You can go."

My breath caught.

"But with a guard."

I hesitated for only a second before nodding.

It was a compromise.

He was showing me some trust.

It was a baby step, and I'd take it.

CHAPTER 29

ALINA

"Seems about right," I sighed as I gazed out the penthouse window.

I knew he was going to go a little overboard, but this seemed extreme, even for Pavel.

Below, the street was swarming with an armored motorcade, a small army of scary-looking men in full SWAT gear standing guard.

In the center was a massive black Range Rover that looked more like a tank than a car meant to drive on city streets.

I'd even bet the Range Rover was bulletproof.

With a resigned sigh, I considered my options.

I knew Pavel didn't play around, but when I agreed to have a guard with me, I was thinking I would have one, maybe two armed men with me.

Ones who worked with or for Pavel, but clearly in his mind that wasn't enough.

Since the hotel was in Washington DC, where the rich and powerful—politicians, dignitaries, international leaders—stayed, the presence of an elite security team wouldn't raise any eyebrows.

For most of the people here, the interruptions of security slowing down traffic was just another inconvenience on any given Tuesday.

I swore more people took the Metro not because they liked public transit or hated finding a parking spot, but solely so they could avoid the inconvenient bullshit of security motorcades.

There might have been a few people slowing down trying to get a peek at who they could be guarding, wanting to get a photo of some celebrity if they were lucky, or a politician and their side piece they could sell to a tabloid if they were really lucky.

No one would realize the real reason they were there was to take me to a gallery owned by my husband's family.

But that was because no one knew the truth about this city and who really ran a lot of it.

The Russian mafia owned this entire building.

After overhearing a few of Pavel's conversations, I was pretty sure they owned most of the block, and half a dozen buildings throughout the city, and even more in industrial areas in Virginia and Maryland.

There was a part of me that wondered if they also used it to get blackmail on the politicians and businessmen who stayed here.

If not, it seemed like a wasted opportunity.

Though considering Pavel didn't waste the opportunity to put me in the care of a small army, I'd bet very few opportunities passed by the Ivanov men.

I knew the Russian mob was connected, but the elite security force outside was overkill.

It would have been overkill if it was for the president.

Royalty traveled to third world countries with fewer guns.

I was just going down the street.

And they were there just for little, unimportant, unassuming me.

I didn't know if I should've felt claustrophobic, embarrassed, or oddly touched.

He must've spent a fortune on this, all to keep me safe.

Or to keep me under lock and key, I wasn't sure which.

No wonder Pavel had said he needed a week to arrange for a guard.

He hadn't just sent a bodyguard—he had mobilized a small private army.

I considered refusing.

It was well within my rights to throw a fit and demand a more reasonable entourage. Not that he would care. Not that it would make any difference at all.

These weren't the terms I had agreed to. I had agreed to a guard, not a full-blown military escort, and I had half a mind to confront him about it.

But then I reconsidered.

There were too many things I didn't know. I didn't know why Pavel came home a few weeks ago and tried to bleed out in the bathroom.

I didn't know where he went every day and what he did.

He loved talking about how I spent my day but wouldn't say a word about his.

When I stitched him up, I noticed a lot more scars, some very old, barely more than a slight discoloration.

Others were fresher, still in various stages of healing.

Some were tiny little scratches, others considerably larger and more than a few were puckered like they were slashes, or grazes—actual gunshot wounds.

His tattoos camouflaged them from a distance, but up close, I saw every single one of them, and they scared me.

Maybe it wasn't safe.

People could be after him, and willing to use me to get to him or his brothers.

But if that was the case, why weren't the other women locked down?

Maybe Pavel just didn't trust me yet, and going overboard was his way of compromising.

It was going to take time. It was going to take baby steps.

I had to keep reminding myself that this was a step in the right direction.

He was letting me out of the penthouse without him.

That was progress.

For the moment, I was going to have to just take the win.

Pavel entered the room, a cocky smirk pulling at the corners of his mouth. "Your chariot awaits."

I smirked right back. "We'll talk about our very different definitions of a guard when I get back."

"One hour," he reminded me.

"Pavel," I whined.

One hour was not enough time.

I didn't even know if that entire motorcade could get to the gallery in a single hour.

It looked like a damn parade.

I might have gotten there faster if I walked.

"One hour," he said again, gripping my chin with two knuckles and tilting it up so I met his eyes. Something I couldn't quite read flashed across his eyes and he let out a resigned sigh. "One hour starting when you arrive. The driver will send me a message when you get there and that is when the timer will start."

I nodded, giving him a bright smile and before I even realized what I was doing, I pushed up on my tiptoes, leaned in, and kissed him goodbye on the cheek.

Time stopped.

It was such a small, simple gesture, nothing compared to the intense, kinky-as-fuck sex we had regularly, and yet —somehow—it meant more.

It wasn't some carnal need that was fueled by hormones or chemistry.

The kiss was affection.

Pure, simple affection.

It was a sign of care and tenderness.

One that slipped out like it was a habit.

Pavel's fingers brushed my lips. "Hurry back to me, *moy kotyonochek*."

My heart fluttered, and a calm warmth slid over my body.

When did that nickname become so endearing to me?

Unable to speak, afraid I might change my mind and spend the next hour in my husband's bed, I turned and rushed out.

The gallery visit started perfectly, but something felt off not long after I arrived.

The sun was shining and the second I stepped out of the car, Nadia pulled me into a tight hug, and I hugged her back.

And I laughed. Really laughed.

I could breathe fresh air. I felt the sun on my face, and it was incredible.

The girls were thrilled to show me their progress; the business was thriving under their work, and I could see the positive effects of my guidance.

God, that felt good.

I had spent so long filling drinks and emptying garbage cans just to survive, that I forgot what it felt like to do something that had a direct impact.

Something that wasn't just supporting other people's work or self-destructive habits.

I felt normal for the first time in almost three years.

It was the first time since those men showed up that I didn't have a sword hanging over my head.

I wasn't waiting for the other shoe to drop.

I could just live.

I could just be me without the crippling debt pulling me down. There was no gnawing hunger in the pit of my stomach, no worrying how I was going to make rent, or if someone was going to lunge at me. I was smiling, laughing, sharing in the excitement of women who I barely knew but who treated me like family.

As my grandmother would have said, I was finally acting my age.

But as we toured the gallery, I couldn't shake the

feeling we were being watched. More than once, I caught glimpses of unmarked cars lingering across the street, their occupants too interested in our building. When I mentioned it to Marina, she brushed it off as normal city surveillance, but the knot in my stomach only tightened and the unease persisted.

Pavel's guards kept checking their phones, their expressions growing grimmer with each message.

Something was happening, and they weren't telling me what.

When the guard, a man in a black-on-black tactical suit came into the gallery and tapped his watch, I knew the fun was over, but I wasn't sad.

This was a good first step.

I would get back to the penthouse and Pavel would see that I was in one piece, and I could start talking to him about letting me have my own computer, or tablet. Just something basic where I could continue the work the girls needed me to do.

I wanted to be productive; surely Pavel could understand that, and we could make some arrangement.

The second I stepped out of the building, ready to head to the Range Rover and back to the penthouse where I had every intention of showing my husband how grateful I was for his trust, the peace I was feeling shattered.

Red and blue lights started flashing, sirens blared, and people froze in the middle of the sidewalk.

Police.

They were everywhere.

The street was suddenly swarming with officers, their

presence suffocating as they moved like a single unit closer and closer.

Step by step, they were caging me in.

Pavel's guards reacted instantly.

I was pulled against one's back, the others circling me, forming a wall of muscle, guns, and anger.

The tension escalated in seconds. One of Pavel's men drew his weapon, and immediately three police officers had their guns trained on him.

"Put down your weapon," one of the cops yelled.

That was it. I would never be let out of the penthouse again.

One of the men yelled something back in Russian.

"Not bloody likely," one of the others translated. "You have your weapon drawn on our charge."

The sound of safeties clicking off echoed around us. This was about to become a massacre.

If I didn't do something fast, it was going to end poorly.

Then, if I survived, I'd never be allowed out of the bedroom.

Hell, this might push Pavel so far back he'd make me wear that hood again.

People screamed around us.

Someone actually yelled that Russia was invading.

As the pedestrians scrambled for cover, I peeked out between two of the men's shoulders.

I could see more than a few people were hiding behind planters and turned-over tables, holding up their phones to record.

TikTok was going to love this.

A man in a bulletproof vest, gun drawn and held with two hands straight out, stepped forward.

"Alina Russo. We need you to come with us."

My stomach dropped.

This couldn't get any worse.

How did they know my name?

What could they possibly want with me?

The fear of disappointing Pavel warred with my terror of innocent people getting caught in any crossfire. Children were crying somewhere behind the overturned café tables. This had to stop.

Without thinking, I heard myself say, "My name is Alina Ivanova."

I placed my hand on the guard's shoulder and pushed silently, demanding he step aside just enough I could see.

I gave him Pavel's last name.

That meant I represented him, and I was not going to address a cop while cowering behind a guard.

The cop barely reacted. He just nodded. "Fine. Alina Ivanova, you need to come with us."

"Why? Am I being arrested?"

"No, ma'am, we just would like a word at the station."

"She's not going anywhere," one of the guards growled, lifting his gun.

The lead officer's finger moved to his trigger. "Stand down or we will open fire."

Fuck.

This was about to turn into a bloodbath.

I needed to end this now, or Pavel was never letting me out of the penthouse again.

"If you don't cooperate, I have the authority to arrest you and every one of your guards."

Jesus, this was going from bad to fucked very quickly.

I needed to find the best option in this incredibly tense situation.

If I resisted, innocent people would get hurt, a few cops and a few of Pavel's men would die.

If I went with them, my husband would think the worst.

Then who knew where I would end up?

But the choice was made for me when I heard a child's terrified sobbing nearby. I couldn't let this escalate further.

"Please call my husband," I whispered. "Tell him where I am."

The guard in front of me stiffened. "Ma'am, I can't let you—"

Before I could second-guess myself, I broke free of my guards' protective circle.

I lifted my hands to show I was unarmed.

"Please put your weapons down. I'll cooperate."

"That's a wise choice," the cop sneered with so much malice I wondered if it was. There was nothing but disdain and disgust in his eyes.

He grabbed my arm and twisted it behind my back, forcing me into the back of the car.

It was a stupid move.

There were so many cameras, I couldn't wait to see what Pavel did to this man for laying his hands on me.

As I was forced into the back of the police car, the girls ran outside.

Their shocked faces, and Viktoria pressing her phone to her ear, were the last things I saw before the car pulled away.

In the car, the radio crackled to life. "All units, be advised—the Ivanov family has been notified. Expect immediate retaliation. Request backup at the station."

The officer driving glanced at me in the rearview mirror, and for the first time, there was fear in his eyes.

"Lady, I hope you know what you've gotten yourself into," he muttered.

My stomach twisted.

Fear, nerves, apprehension?

I didn't know, maybe all three.

What the hell was Pavel going to say when he found out that after weeks of begging for a little freedom, he had finally let me outside without him...

And I ended up in police custody.

The radio crackled again: "Detective Morrison, you need to know—we just intercepted communications. The Russians are mobilizing. ETA fifteen minutes to the station."

Fifteen minutes.

Pavel was coming, and he wouldn't be coming alone.

CHAPTER 30

ALINA

I had no phone. No money. No identification.

For all I knew, these police officers could be taking me to some black site off the grid where I'd be swallowed whole, out of reach of the law.

FML.

No.

Stop it.

I was letting my love of true crime podcasts get away from me.

The hard plastic seats of the squad car dug into my tailbone as I strained to listen for any more news about Pavel over the police radio.

I leaned forward and tried to get the attention of the two officers. "Where are you taking me?"

The one in the passenger seat turned his head and said something to the driver in Spanish.

They both laughed.

A sick feeling settled in the pit of my stomach.

Something didn't feel right about all this.

I concentrated on the passing buildings and each turn the car made, just in case.

Fuck, why hadn't I asked Pavel if he had my phone and wallet?

With a start, I realized it was because I hadn't needed to.

I fell back into my seat as it settled over me.

Somehow, my life had shifted from constantly pinching pennies and considering the buying of brand name bread a "luxury" to one where I hadn't needed my own money...for weeks. Everything I needed had been taken care of by Pavel.

Clothes, food, shelter.

My grandmother.

It was strange to go from being forced to grab naps on the bus between two jobs to spending my days sleeping in, wearing beautiful clothes, working on dream projects like the boutique art gallery with my new friends...

Friends! I had friends now. Real friends. Not coworkers who were forced to scratch through a miserable slog together like army veterans bonded over a shared horrific experience.

If it weren't for the other wives, I might have spiraled over how pathetic it was that I could completely ditch my phone for weeks without worrying about missing a single phone call or text.

I'd been so in my head over the circumstances around how I'd met Pavel and the way he had snatched control over my life that I hadn't really taken the time to truly appreciate the ways he'd made my life better.

All those mornings I was spiteful and irritated when he told me I should just rest and relax (a four-letter word) and wait for his return when I asked what I was supposed to do all day. I chafed at his dominance and my quiet submission without realizing how badly I needed someone to take care of me for once.

I caught my reflection in the rearview mirror and started.

If I looked past the fear...I looked...healthy.

Gone was the sallow tinge to my skin that came from countless days without sunlight or fresh air. My cheeks had filled in. There were no more dark circles under my eyes. Even my hair had taken on the lustrous sheen that only came from eating a nutritious diet and getting decent sleep instead of scarfing expired gas station sandwiches washed down with cheap wine.

Without my noticing it and defying all common sense, my tattooed, violent mafia enforcer husband had somehow forced a happy, balanced life on me.

Sucking in a deep breath, I raised my chin. I was no longer an alley cat eking out a meager existence in the shadows.

I was Mrs. Pavel Motherfucking Ivanova.

Owning the power in my new persona, my gaze narrowed. "I hope you assholes are prepared for the shitstorm my husband is going to unleash on you when he finds out what you've done."

The men exchanged a look before the one in the passenger seat banged the caged wall separating us. "Shut the fuck up, whore."

Whore.

Even the dancers who worked at the Velvet Dream were never called whores by the police. I should know, I'd witnessed enough of them getting pulled in for questioning. And had been sent by Lou on more than one occasion to bail them out in time for the dinner rush.

Something was definitely not right about this.

I forced the panic down.

All of this...whatever this was...would be over soon.

There wasn't a doubt in my mind that Pavel would tear the city apart until he found me.

He may not love me...

I swallowed past the pain that thought caused. Unpacking that emotion was for another day, perhaps one where I wasn't shoved in the back of a police car.

So he may not love me...but he was possessive of me, of that I was certain.

I was his little kitten. His *kotyonochek*.

He would rescue me.

He would.

If for no other reason than I was his wife now. His wife. And although I was new to all this, I at least knew from the other girls that being his wife meant something in his world.

The squad car pulled past the entrance to the police station and circled around to the back.

The unease in my gut intensified.

When the car door swung open, a part of me wanted to resist but I knew that would only piss them off further.

The moment I exited the car, they yanked my arms forward and slapped handcuffs on me.

"Hey! Am I being arrested?"

The man jerked me forward and pressed his face so close his nose almost touched mine. "I'm not going to tell you again to keep your fucking mouth shut."

I turned my head to the side and prayed Pavel was already on his way.

They dragged me through a scarred metal door to the side of the loading dock. On the other side was a dingy hallway with a flickering fluorescent light. We passed several doors before I was shoved into a small room with only a single table and two metal folding chairs.

They slammed the door shut behind me.

I turned and shouted as I fisted my hands together and banged on the door. "Hey! Hey! Let me out of here!"

No answer. I tried the doorknob. Locked.

The room was small with putty-colored walls, a suspicious brown splash stain on the far wall. I wrinkled my nose at the sour, musky scent.

Not knowing what else to do, I sat and waited.

It only took a few minutes for the door to swing open.

I sprang up. "I demand to know what this is all about!"

Without saying a word, the burly man in the cheap suit who entered hauled off and slapped me so hard, my body slammed against the wall. The handcuffs rattled as I raised my arms to cup my cheek.

"Shut up, whore."

Seriously, what the fuck was with all these men calling me a whore?

Before I could say anything further, he grabbed me by the hair and dragged me across the room and tossed me into the other chair as if I were a dirty rag doll.

Tears I refused to shed pricked my eyes.

He lowered his bulk into the chair across from me. The metal creaked and groaned. "You're going to tell me everything you know about the murder of Brutus Slinsky."

I blinked. "Who?"

He leaned forward and slapped me a second time. With my cheek already hot and bruised, I couldn't resist crying out.

He pointed his fat finger at me. "Every time you don't answer you're going to get hit. And if you keep being a bitch, I'm going to toss you into the men's holding cell. Maybe a few hours of getting gangraped by the scum of the earth will change your tune."

The horror of my situation washed over me in waves.

I wasn't stupid.

There was no point in asking for a lawyer or demanding a phone call. There was a reason why these animals had hauled me in the back way. Why I hadn't been brought to the front desk for processing. Whatever this was, it was definitely off the books. Which only increased the danger I was in.

Brutus Slinksy? That must be the man Pavel murdered.

My lips thinned as my gaze narrowed. I spoke with the confidence of a woman who knew her man, her protector, was this very moment on his way to rescue her. I raised my voice in case anyone was listening or could hear me on the other side of the door. "My name is Mrs. Pavel Ivanova. Call my husband! I want my husband! "

With that, I hauled up a disgusting loogie to the back of my throat and spit right in his face.

"You fucking cunt."

He slapped me again.

Then reached for his belt. "Time to teach you a lesson."

CHAPTER 31

PAVEL

I thought I knew the limits of my rage. I thought I understood how hot the fires in my soul could burn and how cold my blood could run.

Then my phone rang in the middle of a meeting with Artem and Gregor, and everything I thought I knew about fury shattered into a thousand pieces.

"Boss—" The voice was breathless, panicked. Kirill. One of my most trusted men. The man I'd personally assigned to shadow my wife.

I held up a hand, silencing Artem mid-sentence as he outlined our expansion into the docks. Gregor's eyes snapped to mine, reading the shift in the room like the predator he was.

"Where is she?" Three words. Ice-cold delivery. But inside, my blood was already turning to liquid fire.

"Police station on Hayes Street. Boss, there were twelve of them, maybe more. They were ready for us, armed and—"

"You let them take her." Not a question. A death sentence.

"We tried to stop them. There was almost a shootout in the middle of the street, but she—she ordered us to stand down. Your wife took control and—"

I was already moving, chair scraping against marble as I stood. My brother and Gregor were on their feet a heartbeat later, reading my body language like a battle plan.

"Since when do my men take orders from anyone but me?" My voice was deadly quiet, but the rage underneath was a living thing, clawing at my chest.

"She's strong, boss. Stronger than we expected. She saw the situation was about to go to hell and she prevented a bloodbath. But they have her, and I don't know why, and I—"

"Shut up." I cut him off, my free hand already reaching for the gun holstered under my jacket. "Get back to the penthouse. Now."

I ended the call and looked at Artem and Gregor. Artem's jaw was tight, Gregor's hand already moving toward his own weapon.

"*Los Infideles?*" Artem asked.

"Don't know. Don't care." I was stripping off my jacket, removing the shoulder holster. Going into a police station armed like this would be stupid. The ankle piece would have to do. "Someone took my wife."

The words tasted like acid in my mouth. My wife. The woman who'd become my entire fucking world without me even realizing it was happening.

Gregor was already pulling out his phone. "I'll call Kostya, get him down there with the legal team."

"No time." I was moving toward the door, my brother and Gregor flanking me like we were going to war. Because we were. "I want her back. Now."

The elevator ride to the garage felt like an eternity. My hands were shaking—not from fear, but from the effort it was taking not to put my fist through the metal walls.

"Pavel." Artem's voice was calm, measured. The voice he used when I was about to do something spectacularly violent and stupid. "We need to think this through."

"No." I stepped out as the doors opened, heading straight for the Range Rover. "We need to get my wife back before I burn that entire fucking precinct to the ground."

Gregor slid into the driver's seat without being asked. He knew better than to let me behind the wheel right now. Artem climbed into the passenger seat, already dialing numbers.

"Kostya? Yeah, it's Artem. Hayes Street precinct. Now. Bring everything you've got."

The entire ride to the station, I thought about what they could be doing to her, why they would have her. We had no issues with the local police. To the best of my knowledge, there were no open investigations.

Even if there were, my family was well above their fucking pay grade.

If this was about the US government taking issue with what we'd been doing, the FBI would have brought in Gregor or Artem. Not my fucking wife.

Did they think they could get her to turn on me?

The thought made my vision go red. If some rookie cop thought he could use her to make a name for himself, I was going to teach him exactly what happened to people who touched what was mine.

The second the Range Rover pulled up to the police station I got out, not even waiting for the car to come to a complete stop. I marched in, right past the receptionist and into the bullpen, where a dozen officers stopped and stared.

"Where is my wife?" I said. I didn't yell. There was no need to. Everyone there knew who the fuck I was and what I was doing there.

Two men in suits approached me, detectives, most likely.

"Mr. Ivanov–"

I didn't stop to listen to them. I pushed right past them and went to the corner office where a portly man with a pockmarked face was sitting behind the large desk.

"Where the fuck is my wife?" Anger and promises of violence were laced into every syllable.

He looked up, ready to yell at the interruption until he recognized me. The blood drained from his face as I stalked into his office. His jowls trembled with fear.

"Bring me to my wife, or I'll start with your fingers and work my way up until there's nothing left of you but screams and regret. Then I'll do the same to every cop in this building while your families watch."

He nodded, his eyes wide.

Shaking, he stood and led me through the bullpen and down a long, bland hallway with doors on either side.

"She's in here, just answering a few questions for

Detective Cortez. I was just about to come down and check to see if she needed anything, water or—"

He took a ring of keys from his belt and started fumbling with them.

"Is she?" I asked.

"Is she what?" He stopped and looked up at me.

"Is she answering any of your questions?"

"No, actually. The only thing she has said was to call you. She has been very uncooperative."

With no patience for his fumbling, I took a step back and kicked the door in.

Alina sat in the small, sterile interrogation room. She was pale and trembling, her wrists bound in metal cuffs, red where the metal bit into her delicate flesh.

Anger flared in me.

Then when I met her eyes, and she turned her head to the side to show the red handprint across her face, I fucking lost it.

I walked over to Alina and tilted her chin up so I could see the impression on her face more clearly. It wasn't a crisp single handprint—there were several that over-lapped. Someone had dared to strike her multiple times.

"Pavel, I didn't say anything." She turned her head to look me in the eye, pleading for me to believe her.

"You need to teach your bitch some fucking manners," the detective sneered.

In a glance, I took in the man's stance...and his hands on his belt buckle.

A howl of rage was torn from me as I pulled my hand back and slammed my fist into his face, the crack of his jawbone beneath my knuckles satisfying.

He spun and collapsed on the floor, out cold.

Fucking pussy.

He went down with one little hit. I wanted to hit him again, over and over, like he had struck my wife.

But at this moment, Alina was my only concern.

There would be plenty of time to work my rage out as I slowly tortured him to death later.

Kicking him over, I reached into his pocket for his keys.

Alina flinched at the sudden violence.

A whimper left her lips, and her eyes were glassy with unshed tears.

She wasn't sobbing, but her lips trembled, and when I reached for her cuffs, her breath hitched.

"Please, Pavel," she whispered. "It wasn't me. I didn't betray you. I would never–"

Finding the small handcuff key, I nodded. "I know, kitten. I'm so sorry this happened, but I am so proud of you for the way you handled it. You did everything right."

The cuffs fell away with a sharp click, and the moment her wrists were free, I grabbed her face in my hands and crashed my lips against hers.

I needed her lips against mine; I needed to taste her and know that she was back in my arms where she belonged.

That I had her now, and she was safe.

She kissed me back, her kiss just as desperate.

Her hands grabbed the lapels of my jacket as she pulled me close, pressing her body against mine in a way that was possessive, hard, claiming.

She needed this contact, the reassurance, as badly as I did.

"I know, baby," I murmured against her mouth. "I have you now. These assholes are going to pay for laying a finger on you. I am going to make every single one of them wish they were never born. They will be a warning to anyone who thinks about touching you again."

"Because I am yours," she said before kissing me again.

Fuck, that felt good to hear.

She was mine; she was always going to be mine.

Body and soul.

She was the woman I was going to come home to every night, the one who would make life worth living. I had always lived to further the interests of my family. It was my passion, my meaning behind life. Now it was her.

Everything was for her.

It was strange, how certain I'd been—how, from the moment I learned the police had taken her, I knew it hadn't been her doing.

I knew she wasn't going to betray me.

There was no logical reason for that certainty. I was aware that our relationship was built on force, manipulation, and control.

But still, when it came to Alina—I trusted her. Completely. Even though I had forgotten that I controlled her grandmother's fate.

That was a terrifying revelation. Leverage was how I knew who to trust and who not to. Leverage and blood.

But Alina was different. I didn't need the leverage, but just the same, I trusted her.

A knock at the door had me breaking the kiss and

turning to the now open door behind me, ready to lash out with the fury still simmering beneath the surface.

Artem entered and looked down at the detective still unconscious on the floor. He grabbed his sleeve and ripped it up to show the *Los Infideles* tattoos on the inside of his forearms.

Definitely not a cop.

"Take that piece of garbage out of here," I said to Artem without looking away from Alina.

The unconscious detective was dragged from the room by two of Artem's men who had materialized in the doorway.

None of the other cops moved to stop them.

They knew better. Everyone in this building understood exactly what was going to happen to Detective Cortez once we got what we needed from him.

He'd wake up in one of our warehouses, and by the time I was done with him, he'd beg me to let him die. But first, I had to get my wife to safety.

Kostya stepped around the drag marks on the floor like they were nothing more than spilled coffee.

"We need to talk," Artem said.

I looked around this little room that wasn't supposed to be used for interrogations. There were no cameras, no window with two-way mirrors. This was a room meant for lawyers and their clients to have privileged conversations.

That asshole brought her in here, knowing there would be no evidence of what happened.

My blood started boiling again as I thought of all the things that could have happened to her.

Alina's hand rested on my shoulder and that calmed me enough to think clearly and face Artem.

"Why the fuck did they take her?"

Kostya shot a look at Alina.

"She can stay," I said, not wanting her out of my reach, let alone out of my sight.

"Of course, but first we need to document the marks on her face for our records. The police didn't orchestrate this. *Los Infideles* were behind it all. They bribed and blackmailed to get a few of their men police badges and access."

"How?" I asked.

"They have a new leader. A ghost in the underworld. We don't have the specifics yet, or why Alina was a target. But we know they have money, power, and a lot of influence. We think it might be related to whoever had been funding Solovyov."

"Fuck."

First, I was going to take my wife home. I was going to fuck her until we both felt better, then I was going to get to work.

I meant what I had said.

I was going to burn their world to the fucking ground and hang their corpses from the fucking rafters as a message to everyone else in our little world, including this ghost.

This was what happened when you fucking dared to touch my wife.

CHAPTER 32

PAVEL

I carried Alina out of the precinct, glaring at anyone who dared to come near us.

No one was getting near her again. Not now. Not ever.

Especially as I could feel the strength leaving her body as she relaxed into my hold. She had held strong for so long, and now it was time for me to be strong for her.

I settled her into the passenger seat of the Range Rover, clicking the seat belt for her before I closed and locked the door.

Three of my men were waiting—the one who came and got me, and the two that followed her to the police station to make sure that was where they took her.

I was man enough to recognize that they did everything they could to handle the situation as best as possible. Any other outcome could have been far worse.

But that didn't mean I was letting them off the hook.

"I'm taking the car," I said, holding out my hand for the keys.

They were instantly handed over.

"The three of you fucked up. You allowed someone to lay hands on my wife. There's still an opening at the office building cleaning crew. You three will work there as janitors until I can stand the sight of you."

"Yes, boss," they said in unison. Relief washed over their faces.

They were getting off light and they fucking knew it. I should've been taking hands, leaving bullet holes. Alina's safety was the highest priority. But so was her well-being, and I had to get her away from here and back to our penthouse.

Artem waved his hand, telling me to wait, and I replied with a middle finger as I climbed into the driver's seat.

There was no way I was trusting anyone else to drive her.

The ride was silent. When we got back to the hotel, I picked her up out of the seat, holding her to my chest as I brought her into the penthouse.

Her small body curled against my chest, shuddering. She was too frail, too thin, and I had let them get to her.

Alina didn't fight me, she didn't protest. She simply let me carry her, hold her.

That was the part that gutted me.

My strong, defiant little kitten was silent.

She had been quiet before, but even in that silence there was a tension, an air of hostility and defiance.

Alina wasn't the kind of girl who could have her spirit broken, or so I thought.

God knew I relished her fight, her never-fading spirit. The only time she had ever not fought was when she gave in to pleasure seconds before coming. That was the sweetest victory each time.

Now she was quiet, but there was no fight in the air, no anger or resentment. There was no victory in this, only failure.

She was shaken, exhausted, and too raw to pretend otherwise. Those men just took her; they plucked her off the street and interrogated her.

There was no way for me to know what they said. I knew he had hit her in the face, but what else?

Had he touched her? I didn't think so. I got there as fast as I could, but that didn't mean he didn't threaten to.

What had she seen? What had she gone through before I showed up?

I had failed her. Profoundly failed her.

It was my job to make sure nothing like that ever happened. Yet it did. I had men surrounding her, and it still happened.

I could've lost her.

If they didn't want to talk to her, if they just wanted her dead, then they could've—

The thought sank deep, twisting like a knife in my gut.

She was my wife, and I had let my dark, twisted, fucked-up world get too close. I had allowed my enemies to touch what was mine.

That would never happen again. I couldn't allow it to happen again.

Not even if it cost me my life. I didn't give a fuck if I had to claw my way back from hell itself. I would protect her.

I took her straight to the bedroom and sat on the edge of the bed with her still in my arms.

The plan was to tuck her into the bed and let her sleep, recover, but I couldn't stand the idea of leaving her, or even having her out of my arms. Not yet.

With one arm braced around her waist, my other hand stroked the back of her head, my fingers weaving through her soft hair. I could say I was trying to soothe her, but really, it was for me.

I had to know she was there. I was the one who craved the constant reassurance that she was fine, that nothing else could happen to her, that she was protected in my arms.

She wasn't the only one who had been shaken. Every time I closed my eyes, I saw all those guns pointed at her in the video. I saw the red handprint on her face and the lines around her delicate wrists.

Every time I closed my eyes, I was reminded how close I came to losing her.

"You're protected now, *moy kotyonochek*," I murmured into her silky hair that smelled of the vanilla shampoo the hotel stocked. "I've got you. No one can get to you here. No one can touch you. You are secure. I'm here."

She didn't answer, but her hands fisted my shirt, holding onto me as if I were the only solid thing in a world spinning out of her control. She clung to me like I was her lifeline, and that was exactly what I wanted to be.

It was what I had to be, because if I was her anchor, then she was mine.

I craved control of the situation. Be the one she came

to when she was scared, the one who sheltered her from the storm.

It was a dangerous realization.

She was mine. Not just owned—not just claimed.

She was mine in a way no one else had ever been. In a way that I didn't know was even possible. She was mine in a way that made me understand the foolish things Artem and Kostya had done.

I understood why Kostya chased Marina from Russia to New York, then Chicago, and back again. I understood why Artem faced down an army by himself to keep Viktoria protected.

I'd do the same, and so much more for Alina.

The way my heart ached and my soul burned made me understand how Gregor's priorities had changed and why the world worked the way it did.

I loved money; I craved power, and I had always lost myself in the beauty of violence. But none of it mattered anymore.

All of it paled when compared to this woman, who was quivering in my arms.

There was nothing I wouldn't do for her. Nothing I wouldn't gladly give up just to see her smile, to hold her body against mine.

I used to scoff at men who thought like this, but I had been a fool because I didn't understand what this was. What it meant.

I was in love with her.

Not just because she had a hot body or was a natural submissive. It wasn't because of the glimpses of fire sparking in her eyes when she fought me.

It was because she was made for me, and I for her. She was the other half of me, and I could not live without her by my side.

The realization hit me like a sledgehammer to the chest.

She was my everything, and I had let her be taken from me.

I had to show her I was sorry. I had to prove I was capable of taking care of her, of being the man she deserved.

Slowly, carefully, I peeled her out of her ruined clothes. They smelled like cop coffee and the enemy. I was going to have them burned.

I went to the closet intending to grab one of her shirts and yoga pants, but I grabbed one of my T-shirts instead. It was an older one that had softened with age.

I slid it over her head, and she still said nothing as she slid her arms into the sleeves before wrapping her arms around her waist.

The T-shirt was far too big. It practically swallowed her whole. It was almost enough to hide the way her body shook.

I picked her up again, letting her curl against my chest as I sat down on the bed.

She let me. There was no fighting, no struggling, not even a grunt of protest. She just laid her head on my chest and trembled.

She was quiet. Too quiet. Too vulnerable.

Alina was always so fucking strong, and now she needed me. She needed me to be her refuge, to make her feel sheltered and cared for.

That was what I intended to do.

So I took care of her. I took care of her in a way I knew no one else had. Not for a very long time.

With a press of my lips to her forehead, I left her on the bed and moved to the bathroom to draw a warm bath, filling the tub with the rose-scented bubbles she often preferred.

When I brought her in, she didn't fight me. There was no fire in her eyes, no acknowledgement of what was happening. Not even as I stripped her and rolled up my sleeves before I gently lowered her into the water.

I wanted to go in with her, but this wasn't about my comfort. It was about hers.

Keeping my touch gentle, I washed her. My firm hands massaged the bodywash into her shoulders while I tried to release the tension she was holding onto, and then I carefully washed her long hair, taking time to massage the luxurious lather into her scalp until she melted into the bathtub.

I even took my time combing the conditioner through her curls, gently detangling her locks. Showing her how I felt.

I wanted to tell her. I wanted to say the words, but why would she believe me?

How could I say I loved her when I had taken her, locked her away, and then let her be taken from me?

I wrapped her in a thick robe, lifted her into my arms, and carried her back to bed.

She collapsed onto the comforter, still not saying a word as she stared into space.

I brought her hot tea, coaxing her to take small sips.

She did as I asked but said nothing. It was like she was there, but not. Like she had escaped into her own mind.

I wanted her here with me, but what I wanted wasn't important. She had to process what had happened, and all I could do was hope that she would let me in when she was ready.

The sun set, casting long shadows across our room as we lay in bed together. I would have stayed there all night if she needed me to, but then her stomach growled.

Without a word, I sent a text down to room service, ordering comfort food.

Tomato soup with grilled cheese and extra crusty bread. It was my go-to meal when life was a bit too much. The thick, rich soup always seemed to warm me from the inside out, and I hoped it would do the same for her.

When it was delivered, she was still lifeless, just staring at the wall. At least the shaking had stopped.

I brought the food into the bedroom, setting it up on the bedside table, then settled her into my lap.

"Babygirl, I know you're hungry. Can you eat a few bites for me?"

She nodded, her body going limp against mine.

I tore a piece of the sandwich and dipped it into the soup, then brought it to her lips.

Alina resisted at first. But I just pressed my lips to her temple and murmured, "Eat for me, babygirl. I have to take care of you. Please let me."

She opened her mouth obediently and chewed, then swallowed. With every bite, she seemed a little more present, a little more alive.

Each small act of care changed me. It made me realize

how delicate she was, how far I had pushed her, and how much she meant to me.

She was mine.

Yet my world had broken her. I hadn't broken her, and not for lack of trying. I had pushed her to new limits, but all it took was one outing to go terribly wrong, and she shattered in my arms.

She was so strong; she fought me tooth and nail, even when I made it impossible. Even before me, she had dealt with her father's debts and the assholes that came with that, even going as far as giving up her entire life to pay his debt and support her grandmother, and she barely frayed.

This woman was made of steel, and yet, I let them take her and break her.

After she had eaten half a sandwich and a bowl of the soup, I was satisfied and let her rest. Alina curled into me, her cheek resting against my chest, her fingers tracing small circles on my shirt.

I didn't think she realized what she was doing.

She didn't realize how deeply it affected me. Just having her touch me, willingly touch me of her own accord, was so deeply soothing.

"I knew you wouldn't betray me," I murmured, breaking the silence.

She tensed in my arms, and for a moment, I was afraid she was going to disappear into her head again. "You were so angry."

"I wasn't angry at you, baby. I was angry that anyone dared to put their hands on you. They had no right. I was... afraid they had taken you from me."

She swallowed hard, fingers tightening in my shirt. "I was scared."

I closed my eyes, pressing a slow, deliberate kiss to her hair. "I won't let it happen again. You will be protected, sheltered. I swear it."

She tilted her head, gazing up at me remnants of that fear swimming in her dark eyes.

"You promise?"

I cupped her face, my thumb stroking her cheek. "I swear to you with everything that I am."

She hesitated, then whispered, "Then I'll hold you to it, Pavel."

My chest ached.

She trusted me. She believed me.

Anyone who tried to take her from me again would beg for death before I was done with them.

CHAPTER 33

PAVEL

$\mathcal{W}$e had an unseen enemy.

That much was certain.

Someone had been lurking in the shadows and stalking our organization for some time now.

But they fucked up...big.

They made the mistake of going after my wife.

For that, they would die. Painfully.

One thing was clear, *Los Infideles* had a new, very well-funded leader, with intimate knowledge of our business.

A war was coming.

Usually the prospect of blood and violence would set my pulse racing.

Although I didn't seek it out, I didn't exactly shy away from violence. In my world, it was a necessary tool of business. Every now and then you needed to remind both your enemies and your allies why you were to be feared, and your authority never questioned.

This would give us the opportunity to reassert the dominance of the Ivanov bratva. Especially with my brothers now in the country to reinforce Gregor, Damien and Mikhail's already extensive and influential syndicate.

A new era for the Ivanovs was coming.

And yet...all I could think about...all I wanted to do... was get back to Alina.

The last thing I wanted to do this morning was leave my bed. I could have stayed there forever, just savoring her warmth cuddled up against my body while the soft cadence of her breathing surrounded me.

It had been a few weeks since those fake cops had tried to use her to get to me.

The bruise on her cheek had faded but the memory of the traumatizing event hadn't.

It still was a battle within me to leave her side each day.

Never again would I allow her to be put in danger.

Hopefully the message of that pussy "detective's" badly mutilated body found in a ditch right outside the precinct had sent a very clear message.

Don't. Fuck. With. Us.

It would only be a matter of time before we learned the hidden leader's identity.

Then we would strike.

Gregor had reluctantly agreed to bring in Roman for just that reason.

I'd gone with him and Damien to inspect the new dock warehouses we had purchased to receive arms under the radar.

We were headed back to the city and I was already anticipating all the decadent things I had planned for my new wife when I spotted a JoAnn Fabrics coming up on the right.

I leaned forward from the back seat and tapped Damien, who was driving, on the shoulder. "Do me a favor and pull in there."

Damien raised an eyebrow as he realized where I was pointing. "Are you serious?"

"Just do it."

Gregor turned to stare at me from the passenger seat. "I'm sorry, are we cutting into your craft time?"

I threw off my seat belt as our Range Rover pulled into the parking lot. "Fuck off."

Alina and I were visiting her grandmother at the end of the week, and I wanted to bring her some yarn and a few other supplies. Her grandmother was a sweet woman. Neither of them deserved the bullshit her father put them through.

I was more than happy to be the one to step in and spoil them both rotten.

Like my brothers, my life had a new focus beyond blood and money.

And it felt good.

A rush of cool air hit us as the metal doors slid open.

The store was brightly lit with an aggressive number of fake flowers at the entrance.

All eyes turned to stare as three towering, tattooed Russians invaded the pastel paradise of suburban crafting.

Several women grabbed their young children and pulled them out of our path as we walked deeper into the store.

After passing wedding favors, fabrics, and something

that looked like an entire aisle dedicated to something called scrapbooking, I found the yarn.

Damien shook his head. "Fuck. Who knew there were so many colors of fucking yarn."

I smacked his chest and gestured to the horrified women scurrying out of the aisle. "Watch your fucking language around the women. Have some respect."

Gregor picked up a bundle of pink yarn. "What is this for?"

I placed my hands on my hips as I surveyed the yarn options. "Alina's grandmother."

He smirked. "No, I figured that. What is she making—a scarf, a hat, a sweater?"

I gestured with my hands. "What are those blankets with all the squares?"

Damien chimed in. "Afghan."

I pointed to him. "Yes! Afghan. She's making an afghan for one of the nurses who takes care of her."

Selecting an eye-catching teal yarn, I held it up for their inspection. "What do you think about this one?"

Gregor shook his head. "That's acrylic."

My brow furrowed as I looked at the yarn in my hand and back at him. "So?"

"You only use acrylic for the baby shit." He gestured to the store manager who was hovering at the end of the aisle staring at us. "Back me up on this."

The woman's eyes widened as her mouth dropped open. After trying to form a response, she shook her head and ran off.

Gregor frowned. "Trust me. I'm right."

Damien nodded. "He is. You want to use the good

stuff," he offered as he picked up a soft gray yarn. "This is wool. It's better."

I snatched the yarn from his hand and stared at the lion on the label. "How do you two know so much about this?"

Gregor shrugged, his massive frame dwarfing the display. "I'm a dad. You learn this shit fast."

Damien pointed to his chest. "When you're married to a designer you learn to pay attention to this crap if you want to get laid."

I nodded sagely as I grabbed a few yarn packages. "How many do you think we need?"

Damien held up his cellphone. "We could call Boris in Chicago. He knits."

"Oh, good idea."

Gregor shook his head. "Just get them all. She can always make matching armchair covers with anything leftover."

Damien intervened. "Wait. You can't just get all gray."

"Why not?"

"The blanket will be boring if it's all one color."

I tapped my temple then pointed at him. "Good point. The scarf Alina is knitting for me has at least four colors."

Gregor gave me a knowing look.

I raised an eyebrow. "What?"

He lifted one shoulder. "Nothing. I just remember a couple of cocky assholes arriving in America a few months ago spewing bullshit about how me and my crew had gotten soft and lost our edge and now..." He swept his arms wide. "We're in a fucking JoAnn Fabrics."

He wasn't wrong.

It was startling how dramatically my brothers' and my lives had been changed since arriving in America. It was hard to believe that all three of us were happily married to three amazingly beautiful, intelligent, and strong women.

Gregor had every right to take every derogatory thing we'd said about his domestic bliss and shove it right up our asses.

But that didn't mean I had to admit it to him.

I flipped him the bird. "You don't need to tell me you all were a terrible influence."

He slapped me on the shoulder. "You're welcome."

Damien held up one of the gray skeins against a pale purple yarn. "What do you think of the heather gray with the lavender?"

I nodded. "I think that works. How much do we need?"

"How big is the blanket?"

"Don't know."

"We should just buy it all just in case."

"Good idea," I said as I turned to search for a cart.

Walking to the end of the aisle I spied an empty cart next to a woman looking at wooden birdhouses. "Are you using this?"

The woman backed away as she stammered while hugging her purse to her chest. "Um...n-no...take it."

Ignoring her reaction, I smiled. "Thank you."

Rolling the metal cart back to the yarn aisle, we piled all the available gray and purple yarn into it.

As we headed back toward the cashiers, we passed the paint aisle.

Gregor turned. "Is that buy one get one free on canvases? I should get a few for Samara."

Damien pointed to a few aisles down. "While you're doing that, I'm going to grab Yelena some sketch pads and pencils, she mentioned at breakfast she was running low."

As Gregor headed down the paint canvas aisle, he tossed over his shoulder, "We should call Mikhail and ask if Nadia needs anything."

I pulled out my cellphone. "On it."

An hour later, we rolled three cartloads up to the cashier. As the employee checked us out, another woman in line cleared her throat.

We all turned.

She blinked and backed up a step. After visibly swallowing, she pointed at our cart. "That is a chunky yarn. You'll...you'll want to make sure you have 7 or 8mm needles for it. The regular ones will be too small."

We all exchanged a look.

I shrugged. "I have no idea what needles she has."

The older woman pointed over her shoulder. "I could help you pick some out."

After giving her a wink, I stretched my arm out. "Lead the way."

With bright red cheeks, the woman giggled as she led me back to the yarn aisle. As we walked more women joined us.

"Does she have a pattern? I can select a few that I've done and liked."

"You only have two colors, three really would be better."

"I'd recommend at least one crochet hook just in case."

It was amusing to be surrounded by so many women who under any other circumstance would have crossed the street at my approach…and with good reason. "That would be very helpful, thank you."

An employee whose head barely reached Damien's elbow piped up. "I noticed you only have two sketchbooks in your cart. They were buy two get one free."

"No kidding? Thanks!" He headed off back down the aisle to get another notebook.

After some time and a whole gaggle of women to help, we returned to the cashier.

After ringing up all our items, the cashier asked, "Do you have any coupons?"

My brow furrowed. "Coupons?"

Half the women around us reached into their purses, pulled out their coupons and waved them in our direction.

"Take mine."

"No take mine."

"I have a twenty percent off your whole order discount!"

"You can use my employee discount."

We exchanged an amused look between us.

After years in the shadows, being mothered by craft store ladies while buying yarn to make my girl happy wasn't the worst way to spend an afternoon. Domestic bliss had its perks.

CHAPTER 34

PAVEL

"Spit it out, my little kitten," I said, reaching over the center console to run my hand over Alina's thigh. "I can practically hear you overthinking."

It had been a little over a month since the incident with the cops, and things had settled into a routine of sorts.

Honest-to-God, domestic fucking bliss.

And I loved it.

Alina was still not allowed to go anywhere without an armed guard or me by her side. But now, it was less about my questions of trust and more about her safety. I knew she wasn't going to run away or go to the cops.

Even if she wanted to—which I was fairly sure she didn't—she knew how treacherous it was. She was perfectly content not putting herself in harm's way.

And after witnessing both of my brothers pull out their hair in frustration as their wives ran straight into danger, I could appreciate Alina's newfound survival instincts.

It also helped that I had loosened the reins a lot. I'd given her a top-of-the-line laptop and phone so she could contact the other wives and her grandmother whenever she wished.

And I was even content to accompany her. The afghan her grandmother was knitting with the yarn I bought was coming along nicely. But my real reward was seeing the way her face lit up when I returned home with the bags of supplies.

Most women would demand diamonds, furs, cars.

Not my babygirl.

She was over-the-moon thrilled with a few bags of yarn.

I truly was the luckiest fucking man on earth.

The moon peeked through the trees, casting flickers of light on the dark pavement as I drove us to the compound in Virginia.

Alina and I had spent a few hours with her grandmother, and now we were headed to a family dinner with Artem, Viktoria, Kostya, and Marina.

I thought the change of scenery would make Alina happy, but she was sitting in the passenger seat, playing with the hem of her dress, distracted.

The moonlight reflected through the windshield, giving her skin the most beautiful ethereal glow.

The car had been quiet—but not the comfortable silence I'd grown used to. Something was off.

She shifted beside me, her fingers still toying with the hem of her dress.

"Come on, kitten, tell me what's wrong. I can't fix it if you don't tell me. You're not worried about having dinner with my brothers, are you? I know they can be a pain in the ass, but they aren't that bad if you're drunk."

My joke fell flat.

I wasn't sure she even heard it. And then it didn't matter whether she did or not.

She blurted out, "I think I'm pregnant!"

I blinked, stunned, the words slamming into my chest like bullets.

Pregnant.

My foot left the gas for the brake as I pulled over to the shoulder, cutting across the lane with a hard jerk of the wheel. The city had already fallen away behind us— we were on a stretch of highway flanked by dark forest, the compound still miles ahead.

The engine idled low, headlights catching on the guardrail as I shifted into Park and turned to her.

Trying to process what she just said, for several long seconds, I couldn't speak. I could only stare at her— absorbing that she was not just the woman I loved, but the mother of my child.

She started rambling, her voice rushed and cracking:

"I already love this baby more than my own life and if you don't want her, that's fine, I'll raise her on my own like my grandmother raised me and I don't need you even though with every pulse of blood in my veins all I want is to be by your side until my dying breath and—"

I cut her off with a kiss so hard it made her gasp.

"Open your eyes, sweetheart," I whispered as I cupped her cheek. "I want you to stare right into my eyes so you know I'm telling you the truth when I say that I think you are the strongest, kindest, most beautiful woman I have ever known. I love you more than a crude brute like me could ever possibly express."

My mind raced with worry.

What if she didn't want to hear it?

What if she didn't feel the same way?

It didn't matter. She needed to know, and I needed to tell her.

The words left my lips before I could stop them.

And they were true.

I loved her.

The only reason I hadn't already said them—roared them from the rooftops until the entire world knew how protected she was—was because I didn't want to scare her.

Alina gasped softly. A single tear ran down her cheek.

I leaned in and kissed it away.

She blinked as more tears welled. "Really? You love me? Truly?"

"Of course, I love you. You're my sweet little kitten."

She swallowed, looking almost afraid to ask. "And the baby?"

My hand splayed over her stomach. "I didn't think you could make me any happier than I already was... but damn, woman... you still surprise me." I kissed her cheek and whispered into her ear. "I couldn't be happier about the baby."

A wobbly, slightly watery smile practically beaming from her beautiful face, she peppered my cheeks in kisses, saying, "I love you too, Pavel, so much, and I can't wait for us to meet our chi—"

Blinding white light exploded through the windshield, turning the world into a glaring nightmare.

Another set of headlights blazed to life behind us, filling the rearview mirror and effectively blinding us.

My chest tightened.

This wasn't random.

This was a coordinated attack.

"Get down!" I roared, throwing the Range Rover into Drive.

The engine screamed as I floored the accelerator, but we were boxed in, with nowhere to run. Trees and guardrails on both sides, death closing in from the front and back.

In the driver's side mirror, I caught the silhouette of assault rifles being raised.

"Pavel!" Alina's terrified scream cut through the chaos.

The first shots shattered our rear window.

They weren't trying to capture us.

They were here to kill my wife and my unborn child.

Over my dead fucking body.

Metal shrieked against metal as we collided with the barrier.

The other car didn't stop—it pushed harder, grinding against us until our Range Rover flipped over the railing.

Glass erupted in a thousand deadly fragments as we tumbled off the elevated road into the dense forest below.

The world became a chaos of spinning metal, shattering glass, exploding airbags, and the sickening crunch of trees splintering against our car.

Then nothing but cold, horrifying darkness.

CHAPTER 35

ALINA

*B*lood. Smoke. Silence.

Unfamiliar voices drifted through the haze —flowing, melodic words I couldn't understand. Italian, maybe Spanish.

The sharp ringing in my ears made it hard to focus, competing with the insistent dinging from the dashboard.

Every breath brought the acrid taste of blood, gasoline, and burnt rubber, burning my lungs and making me cough.

Each movement sent lightning bolts of agony through my skull.

Sirens wailed in the distance, but I couldn't tell how far away they were—or even if they were for us. The sound warped and twisted as I fought to open my eyes and take stock of the wreckage.

What the hell had just happened?

My vision swam as I reached toward the driver's side, desperate to touch my husband. I needed to know Pavel was okay.

My hand found his shoulder, then his neck, feeling for his pulse. Strong and steady.

He was alive.

I was alive.

Every inch of me hurt, but I was breathing. My hand went to my stomach. Glass littered everything, but the only blood came from shallow scrapes and cuts.

I took another breath, my lungs protesting the smoke as I turned to look at Pavel.

He was unconscious, his head slumped to the side with a bleeding cut on his forehead.

The driver's side door hung wide open, twisted metal gaping like a wound.

When had that happened?

Brushing at the deflating airbags to get them out of my way so I could take a better look at where we'd landed and how we might get out of this situation, I stifled a scream when I realized what I was seeing.

A figure in a tailored black coat stood over the wreckage, his gaze methodically scanning the destruction.

Ice shot through my veins as his eyes found mine.

"Help," I tried to call out, praying he worked for Pavel's family—or was a first responder.

He said nothing. Just pointed.

Three more men materialized at the opening of the destroyed door, their hands already reaching for Pavel.

"No," I croaked. "What are you doing?"

They ignored my protest completely. I grabbed Pavel's shirt with desperate fingers, but they yanked him away, the fabric ripping in my grip.

They hauled his unconscious body up the small

embankment to the road above, then vanished into the night like ghosts.

Shouts echoed in the darkness. Engines roared to life.

Then silence.

Who were these people?

Where had they taken my husband?

Tears blurred my vision as I choked on the smoke pouring from the engine and filling the cabin.

The world tilted dangerously, and my eyelids grew heavy.

Maybe if I just closed them for a moment, I'd wake up back in our bed—warm, safe, and whole.

No. I couldn't. I had to stay alert. I had to get out of this car.

For my baby.

For our baby.

The screech of tires on the pavement above jolted me back to reality.

This wasn't a dream.

This was war.

Someone had forced us off the road and grabbed my husband.

New headlights cut through the darkness above.

I tried to call out, to beg them to go after Pavel, but no sound came.

My throat was raw from smoke and terror.

A massive figure came charging toward the wreckage, his face a mask of barely contained violence.

CHAPTER 36

ALINA

"Who are you?" I asked, pressing myself back into the seat.

He looked dangerous—bigger and darker than the Ivanovs I knew, but there was something familiar in the sharp angles of his face.

"I'm Roman, Pavel's cousin."

His eyes were dark, almost black, but his voice carried that same commanding authority I recognized from Pavel's family.

Those dark eyes swept over the crushed car—then over me.

Cold calculation.

Like he was assessing whether I could still be saved.

Finally, they locked onto mine.

"Where did they take him?"

Despite his intimidating size and the aura of violence that clung to him like a second skin, something about his protective urgency made me trust him.

I pointed toward where they'd disappeared.

"Do you know who they were?"

I shook my head before a sob escaped my lips. "You have to get him back. He's going to be a father. I need him back. I can't do this without him."

Roman's jaw tightened, a muscle ticking as he bit out a curse.

He moved around to my side of the car and tore the door completely off its hinges.

I flinched as metal screeched and gave way. He'd torn the door clean off—like it was nothing.

His hands framed my face, grip firm but surprisingly gentle as he tilted my chin, examining the damage.

There was something lethal in his stillness, like a predator deciding whether to strike.

"Are you hurt?" he asked, his voice deceptively quiet. This was probably as close to gentle as a man like him could manage.

I swallowed hard, unsure how to answer when my entire world had just been ripped apart.

"Pavel—"

"I know." His expression turned murderous. "I'm going after him. But first, I need to make sure you're okay. I'm not rescuing him just to have him put a bullet in my head for abandoning you."

"I'm fine," I said, struggling to sit up and fumbling with my seat belt.

He gave me a curt nod before straightening and drawing a gun from his coat, checking the chamber with the fluid precision of a man who lived by violence.

When those dark eyes found mine again, my own desperation was reflected there.

"You're his now. That makes you family. And no one fucking touches what belongs to the Ivanovs."

I stood by the wreckage, one hand clutching torn pieces of Pavel's shirt, the other pressed protectively over my stomach.

Please, God. Bring him back to me. To us.

TO BE CONTINUED...

Captive Prize, Ivanov Crime Family, Book Seven

ABOUT ZOE BLAKE

Zoe Blake is the USA Today Bestselling Author of the romantic suspense saga The Cavalieri Billionaire Legacy inspired by her own heritage as well as her obsession with jewelry, travel, and the salacious gossip of history's most infamous families.

She delights in writing Dark Romance books filled with overly possessive billionaires, taboo scenes, and unexpected twists. She usually spends her ill-gotten gains on martinis, travels, and red lipstick. Since she can barely boil water, she's lucky enough to be married to a sexy Chef.

ALSO BY ZOE BLAKE

IVANOV CRIME FAMILY TRILOGY

A Dark Mafia Romance

Savage Vow

Gregor & Samara's story

I took her innocence as payment.

She was far too young and naïve to be betrothed to a monster like me.

I would bring only pain and darkness into her sheltered world.

That's why she ran.

I should've just let her go…

She never asked to marry into a powerful Russian mafia family.

None of this was her choice.

Unfortunately for her, I don't care.

I own her… and after three years of searching… I've found her.

My runaway bride was about to learn disobedience has consequences… punishing ones.

Having her in my arms and under my control had become an obsession.

Nothing was going to keep me from claiming her before the eyes of God and man.

She's finally mine… and I'm never letting her go.

Vicious Oath

Damien & Yelena's story

When I give an order, I expect it to be obeyed.

She's too smart for her own good, and it's going to get her killed.

Against my better judgement, I put her under the protection of my powerful Russian mafia family.

So imagine my anger when the little minx ran.

For three long years I've been on her trail, always one step behind.

Finding and claiming her had become an obsession.

It was getting harder to rein in my driving need to possess her… to own her.

But now the chase is over.

I've found her.

Soon she will be mine.

And I plan to make it official, even if I have to drag her kicking and screaming to the altar.

This time… there will be no escape from me.

Betrayed Honor

Mikhail & Nadia's story

Her innocence was going to get her killed.

That was if I didn't get to her first.

She's the protected little sister of the powerful Ivanov Russian mafia family - the very definition of forbidden.

It's always been my job, as their Head of Security, to watch over her but never to touch.

That ends today.

She disobeyed me and put herself in danger.

It was time to take her in hand.

I'm the only one who can save her and I will fight anyone who tries to stop me, including her brothers.

Honor and loyalty be damned.

She's mine now.

Fierce Pursuit

Konstantine & Marina's story

I'm the only one standing between her and those who want her dead.

I was married to her sister—a woman who died in the crossfire of my Russian mafia world.

To her, I'm nothing but a monster with blood-stained hands.

She doesn't see they're the same hands keeping her alive.

She's fled from me repeatedly, each escape bringing her closer to the enemies hunting us both.

The hatred burning in her eyes only matches the forbidden heat igniting between us.

The rival bratva won't stop until she's eliminated.

My solution? Make her mine—a marriage placing her untouchably under my protection.

She fights me at every turn, fierce and beautiful in her rage, blaming me for her sister's death and her shattered life—she can never learn the truth.

As danger closes in, I'm torn between my vow to protect her and the desperate hunger that consumes me whenever she's near.

When an ambush leaves her bleeding in my arms, everything changes.

This marriage isn't negotiable anymore.

She'll wear my ring and bear my name.

She'll be mine, even if I have to break her to keep her.

Twisted Proposal

Artem & Viktoria's story

I'm not the hero in this story—I'm the monster who claimed what wasn't his to take.

I was supposed to sell her to the highest bidder, a marriage that would seal alliances and strengthen her family's power.

But seeing her bloodied and defiant changed everything.

Her father and brothers thought they could use her as a pawn.

They didn't realize I was playing a different game entirely.

I destroyed them all, leaving her seemingly free—only to chain her to me instead.

She thinks she can escape, build a normal life away from the violence she was born into.

She doesn't understand that what I protect, I possess completely.

And now, she's mine.

The problem?

She fights me with every breath, refusing to be anyone's property…especially mine.

Her fierce defiance only makes me want her more.

What she doesn't know is that her freedom required blood payment, and that debt is coming due.

As enemies close in, threatening what's mine, my decision is final.

She will be my wife.

She will wear my mark.

She will surrender to me completely.

Even if I have to break her first.

Sinister Promise

Pavel & Alina's story

The only thing more dangerous than what she witnessed…is me.

She was supposed to be a problem—one I would deal with, forget, erase.

Instead, she became my obsession.

A hotel maid drowning in her father's debts, working among killers and Bratva bosses, believing silence would keep her safe.

Then she saw something she shouldn't.

She should have run. Should have screamed. Should have begged.

Instead, she held my gaze, defiant and unbroken.

Now, I can't let her go.

The only way to keep her alive is to make her mine—a marriage that will satisfy Bratva law and place her firmly under my control.

What I offer isn't protection…it's possession.

She fights me with every breath, her body betraying her with each trembling response to my touch.

Her eyes promise escape while her pulse races beneath my fingers.

She swears she'll never belong to me, not understanding that her resistance only fuels my determination.

Every whispered threat. Every stolen kiss. Every brutal promise draws her deeper into my world.

Because I don't just want to own her.

I want to break her. Then claim her completely.

And I always get what I want.

Captive Prize

Roman & Zoya's story

She stole what belongs to me. Now I'll take everything from her.

A problem I need to fix. A war I need to win. A woman I can't afford to desire.

Her fatal mistake? Taking an Ivanov.

My cousin is missing, his pregnant wife left for dead.

The guilt is a noose around my neck, tightening with every second he's gone.

I was never fully Ivanov—half Russian, half Cuban, never enough.

But this time, I'll prove myself.

I'll infiltrate Los Infidels. Find Pavel. And kidnap the fierce mafia princess responsible.

She fights me with every breath—clawing, cursing, daring me to shatter her completely.

The real problem?

I don't just want to break her. I want to possess her.

Hate bleeds into hunger. Revenge twists into obsession.

Suddenly, our war isn't about family loyalty, it's about dominance.

She won't bow.

I refuse to yield.

One of us must fall.

And I never lose.

RUTHLESS OBSESSION SERIES

A Dark Mafia Romance

Sweet Cruelty

Dimitri & Emma's story

It was an innocent mistake.

She knocked on the wrong door.

Mine.

If I were a better man, I would've just let her go.

But I'm not.

I'm a cruel bastard.

I ruthlessly claimed her virtue for my own.

It should have been enough.

But it wasn't.

I needed more.

Craved it.

She became my obsession.

Her sweetness and purity taunted my dark soul.

The need to possess her nearly drove me mad.

A Russian arms dealer had no business pursuing a naive librarian student.

She didn't belong in my world.

I would bring her only pain.

But it was too late...

She was mine and I was keeping her.

Sweet Depravity

Vaska & Mary's story

The moment she opened those gorgeous red lips to tell me no, she was mine.

I was a powerful Russian arms dealer and she was an innocent schoolteacher.

If she had a choice, she'd run as far away from me as possible.

Unfortunately for her, I wasn't giving her one.

I wasn't just going to take her; I was going to take over her entire world.

Where she lived.

What she ate.

Where she worked.

All would be under my control.

Call it obsession.

Call it depravity.

I don't give a damn... as long as you call her mine.

Sweet Savagery

Ivan & Dylan's Story

I was a savage bent on claiming her as punishment for her family's mistakes.

As a powerful Russian Arms dealer, no one steals from me and gets away with it.

She was an innocent pawn in a dangerous game.

She had no idea the package her uncle sent her from Russia contained my stolen money.

If I were a good man, I would let her return the money and leave.

If I were a gentleman, I might even let her keep some of it just for frightening her.

As I stared down at the beautiful living doll stretched out before me like a virgin sacrifice,

I thanked God for every sin and misdeed that had blackened my cold heart.

I was not a good man.

I sure as hell wasn't a gentleman… and I had no intention of letting her go.

She was mine now.

And no one takes what's mine.

Sweet Brutality

Maxim & Carinna's story

The more she fights me, the more I want her.

It's that beautiful, sassy mouth of hers.

It makes me want to push her to her knees and dominate her, like the brutal savage I am.

As a Russian Arms dealer, I should not be ruthlessly pursuing an innocent college student like her, but that would not stop me.

A twist of fate may have brought us together, but it is my twisted obsession that will hold her captive as my own treasured possession.

She is mine now.

I dare you to try and take her from me.

Sweet Ferocity

Luka & Katie's Story

I was a mafia mercenary only hired to find her, but now I'm going to keep her.

She is a Russian mafia princess, kidnapped to be used as a pawn in a dangerous territory war.

Saving her was my job. Keeping her safe had become my obsession.

Every move she makes, I am in the shadows, watching.

I was like a feral animal: cruel, violent, and selfishly out for my own needs. Until her.

Now, I will make her mine by any means necessary.

I am her protector, but no one is going to protect her from me.

Sweet Intensity

Anton & Brynn's story

She couldn't have known the danger she faced when she dared to steal from me.

She was too young for a man my age, barely in her twenties.

Far too pure and untouched.

Unfortunately for her, that wasn't going to stop me.

The moment I laid eyes on her, I claimed her.

Determined to make her mine ... by any means necessary.

I owned Chicago's most elite gambling club, a front for my role as a Russian Mafia crime boss.

And she was a fragile little bird, who had just flown straight into my open jaws.

Naïve and sweet, she was a temptation I couldn't resist biting.

My intense drive to dominate and control her had become an obsession.

I would ruthlessly use my superior strength and wealth to take over her life.

The harder she resisted, the more feral and savage I would become.

She needed to understand ... she was mine now.

Mine.

Sweet Severity

Macarius & Phoebe's story

Had she crashed into any other man's car, she could have walked away—but she hit mine.

Upon seeing the bruises on her wrist, I struggled to contain my rage.

Despite her objections, I refused to allow her to leave.

Whoever hurt this innocent beauty would pay dearly.

As a Russian Mafia crime boss who owns Chicago's most elite

gambling club, I have very creative and painful methods of exacting revenge.

She seems too young and naive to be out on her own in such a dangerous world.

Needing a nanny, I decided to claim her for the role.

She might resist my severe, domineering discipline, but I won't give her a choice in the matter.

She needs a protector, and I'd be damned if it were anyone but me.

Resisting the urge to claim her will test all my restraint.

It's a battle I'm bound to lose.

With each day, my obsession and jealousy intensify.

It's only a matter of time before my control snaps … and I make her mine.

Mine.

Sweet Animosity

Varlaam & Vivian's Story

I never asked for an assistant, and if I had, I sure as hell wouldn't have chosen her.

With her sharp tongue and lack of discipline, what she needs is a firm hand, not a job.

The more she tests my limits, the more tempted I am to bend her over my knee.

As a Russian Mafia boss and owner of Chicago's most elite gambling club, I can't afford distractions from her antics.

Or her secrets.

For I suspect, my innocent new assistant is hiding something.

And I know just how to get to the truth.

It's high time she understands who holds the power in our relationship.

To ensure I get what I desire, I'll keep her close, controlling her every move.

Except I am no longer after information—I want her mind, body and soul.

She underestimated the stakes of our dangerous game and now owes a heavy price.

As payment I will take her freedom.

She's mine now.

Mine.

CAVALIERI BILLIONAIRE LEGACY

A Dark Enemies to Lovers Romance

Scandals of the Father

Cavalieri Billionaire Legacy, Book One

Being attracted to her wasn't wrong… but acting on it would be.

As the patriarch of the powerful and wealthy Cavalieri family, my choices came with consequences for everyone around me.

The roots of my ancestral, billionaire-dollar winery stretch deep into the rich, Italian soil, as does our legacy for ruthlessness and scandal.

It wasn't the fact she was half my age that made her off limits.

Nothing was off limits for me.

A wounded bird, caught in a trap not of her own making, she posed no risk to me.

My obsessive desire to possess her was the real problem.

For both of us.

But now that I've seen her, tasted her lips, I can't let her go.

Whether she likes it or not, she needs my protection.

I'm doing this for her own good, yet, she fights me at every turn.

Refusing the luxury I offer, desperately trying to escape my grasp.

I need to teach her to obey before the dark rumors of my past reach her.

Ruin her.

She cannot find out what I've done, not before I make her mine.

Sins of the Son

Cavalieri Billionaire Legacy, Book Two

She's hated me for years… now it's past time to give her a reason to.

When you are a son, and one of the heirs, to the legacy of the Cavalieri name, you need to be more vicious than your enemies.

And sometimes, the lines get blurred.

Years ago, they tried to use her as a pawn in a revenge scheme against me.

Even though I cared about her, I let them treat her as if she were nothing.

I was too arrogant and self-involved to protect her then.

But I'm here now. Ready to risk my life tracking down every single one of them.

They'll pay for what they've done as surely as I'll pay for my sins against her.

Too bad it won't be enough for her to let go of her hatred of me,

To get her to stop fighting me.

Because whether she likes it or not, I have the power, wealth, and connections to keep her by my side

And every intention of ruthlessly using all three to make her mine.

Secrets of the Brother

Cavalieri Billionaire Legacy, Book Three

We were not meant to be together... then a dark twist of fate stepped in, and we're the ones who will pay for it.

As the eldest son and heir of the Cavalieri name, I inherit a great deal more than a billion dollar empire.

I receive a legacy of secrets, lies, and scandal.

After enduring a childhood filled with malicious rumors about my father, I have fallen prey to his very same sin.

I married a woman I didn't love out of a false sense of family honor.

Now she has died under mysterious circumstances.

And I am left to play the widowed groom.

For no one can know the truth about my wife...

Especially her sister.

The only way to protect her from danger is to keep her close, and yet, her very nearness tortures me.

She is my sister in name only, but I have no right to desire her.

Not after what I have done.

It's too much to hope she would understand that it was all for her.

It's always been about her.

Only her.

I am, after all, my father's son.

And there is nothing on this earth more ruthless than a Cavalieri man in love.

Seduction of the Patriarch

Cavalieri Billionaire Legacy, Book Four

With a single gunshot, she brings the violent secrets of my buried past into the present.

She may not have pulled the trigger, but she still has blood on her hands.

And I know some very creative ways to make her pay for it.

I am as ruthless as my Cavalieri ancestors who forged our powerful family legacy.

But no fortune is built without spilling blood.

I earn a reputation as a dangerous man to cross and make enemies along the way.

So to protect those I love, I hand over the mantle of patriarch to my brother and move to northern Italy.

For years, I stay in the shadows…

Then a vindictive mafia syndicate attacks my family.

Now nothing will prevent me from seeking vengeance on those responsible.

And I don't give a damn who I hurt in the process including her.

Whether it takes seduction, punishment, or both, I intend to manipulate her as a means to an end.

Yet, the more my little kitten shows her claws, the more I want to make her purr.

My plan is to coerce her into helping me topple the mafia syndicate, and then retreat into the shadows.

But if she keeps fighting me... I might just have to take her with me.

Scorn of the Betrothed

Cavalieri Billionaire Legacy, Book Five

A union forged in vengeance, bound by hate, and... beneath it all...a twisted game of power.

The true legacy of the Cavalieri family, my birthright, ties me to a woman I despise:

the daughter of the mafia boss who nearly ended my family.

Making her both my enemy...and my future wife.

The hatred is mutual; she has no desire for me to be her groom.

A prisoner to her families' ambitions, she's desperate for a way out.

My duty is to guard her, to ensure she doesn't escape her gilded cage.

But every moment spent with her, every spark of anger, adds fuel to the growing fire of desire between us.

We're trapped in a volatile duel of passion and fury.

Yet, the more I try to tame her, the more she fights me,

Our impending marriage becomes a dangerous game.

Now, as the wedding draws near, my suspicions grow.

My bride is not who she claims.

Made in United States
Cleveland, OH
20 June 2025

17853215R00213